THEIR SPIRIT UNBROKEN

RYAN KIRK

WATERSTONE
MEDIA

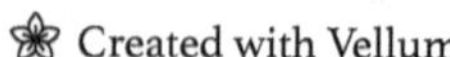 Created with Vellum

For Randy
You've taught me more than you know

PROLOGUE

A cool breeze blew from the north, causing the torches to flicker in the fading sunlight of early evening. The breeze, a welcome companion through the summer months, now carried a hint of a bite, causing Bo to shiver. He wished the torches provided him as much heat as they did light.

Da, standing guard next to him, noticed him shiver. His friend, much larger than him, laughed. Bo welcomed the sound. Da's laughter was deep and honest and reminded Bo that the world contained great joys. Little bothered Da, including the cold.

"Already cold?" Da chided. "Autumn hasn't even started yet. You're in for a long winter, friend."

Bo grumbled good-naturedly. "You might never feel cold, but the rest of us do." Back in the barracks, Da's indifference to cold bordered on legendary. Once, during training, another guard had dumped a bucket of snow on Da while he slept. He didn't even wake up.

The two guards stepped back from the edge of the wall and continued their patrol of the palace grounds.

The only sound Bo heard was their heavy boots against

the well-worn stone of the palace walls. Off in the distance, Jihan was quiet, preparing for the Harvest Festival. Bo and Da maintained the silence of two men who were used to spending long hours together at a time. Conversation occurred in fits and starts, neither of them compelled to fill the silences with empty words.

Da spoke when they reached a corner. "I'm eager for the festival this year."

Bo broke his gaze from the lawn below the palace walls to glance at his partner. "More than usual?"

Da nodded, a gesture that revealed his true meaning.

Bo smiled, returning his attention to the quiet grounds below. "You found someone."

"Jealous?"

"Grateful. Perhaps now you'll stop eyeing my sister every time she visits."

Da laughed again. "You shouldn't get your hopes up."

Bo joined in his friend's laughter, his own quieter and more restrained. He'd never been as free with his emotions as his companion.

They approached the main gates, twin pillars towering over the rest of the wall.

"I'm glad," Bo admitted. "Who is it?"

"No one you know. The daughter of a silk merchant. She's kind."

Bo grinned as he heard the feeling in his friend's voice. A good match, though he would have expected no less from Da. Despite being one of the youngest in their guard unit, Da possessed a wisdom far greater than his years. Other guards often came to him for advice. More than once, Bo had marveled at Da's choice to become a guard. His heart seemed too soft. His competence, likability, and judgment guaranteed him a quick rise through the ranks, though. His friend would order him around soon enough, Bo suspected.

He almost asked Da about his plans for the festival, but an unusual sight drew his attention to the road below.

Their patrol had taken them to the top of the main gate, and the two of them looked down the road leading from the palace to the city of Jihan. The road was made of stone, wide enough for six carts, and lined with two rows of trees that ended five hundred paces from the gates.

The gates were closed, as they usually were these days. Traffic still passed through small doors, heavily guarded by other men in Bo and Da's unit. He hated that duty, much preferring to walk the walls. This late at night, few visitors walked the road that led to the palace.

Bo fixed his gaze on a man wearing the white robes of a monk, walking with a steady pace up the road. He shook his head and fought the urge to spit.

Da, alert as always, shook his head. "Your hatred is unbecoming, friend."

"They make my skin crawl. Do you know why he is here?"

"An audience with the princess." Da always paid more attention to the events happening inside the palace.

Bo almost did spit then. "Why?"

Da shrugged. It wasn't their place to know.

As the monk approached the gate, he looked up and saw Bo and Da staring. Bo swore he saw anger in the monk's eyes, but he was sure Da would suggest he only saw a reflection of his own emotions.

Da was too understanding, by far.

The monks carried too much guilt, were responsible for too much suffering. Jihan itself had been the victim of a battle between monks thirty years ago. Ten years ago, a monastery far to the west had tried to wrest control of the land from the local lord, a rebellion that had decimated the lord's army.

Bo hated their mysterious powers, hated the way too many monks lorded that power over others.

He was far from alone.

But he also knew he would find no support from Da. His friend remained hopelessly optimistic, even as the empire spiraled into chaos. Bo believed that war was coming. Da called him a pessimistic fool.

The monk passed below them without incident. Bo and Da continued their rounds. Three circuits of the wall would complete their duty for the night.

Da told Bo of his plans for the Harvest Festival, laying out in exquisite detail how he planned to win the merchant's daughter's heart. Bo laughed in disbelief. "You'll be broke," he observed.

Here, the wall they walked came close to the walls of the palace itself. Their unit wasn't elite enough to have duty inside the palace, but Bo knew they were close to areas reserved for the use of the princess. He idly wondered how her audience with the monk was going. He wondered how close she was at that very moment.

He was still wondering when the walls of the palace exploded outward.

Bo had no warning. One moment, he was walking the defensive walls of the palace with a man he had known for years.

The next was filled with stone, blood, and chaos.

Rock and wood rained around him, and a wave of pressure picked Bo bodily up and slammed him against a merlon.

For a moment, his world went dark.

When he came to, dust settled around him.

He noticed the silence first. For a long moment, the world seemed frozen, the illusion only shattered by soft sounds of his own leather armor complaining as he brought himself to sitting.

The eerie quiet lasted only a moment. Then he heard shouts off in the distance, the whole palace coming to life in response to the disaster.

Bo looked down at his hands, saw them grimy and gray. They shook as he looked at them, as though they possessed a life of their own.

He moved his legs.

Somehow, he had survived. He felt something wet trickle around his eye. One shaking hand reached up, then came away smeared with blood.

Da.

Bo shot to his feet and studied the surrounding area for the first time. Twenty paces beyond the wall he stood on, the palace was no longer whole. A jagged circle of open air ruined the elegant lines of the building. Bo realized he was looking into the princess's rooms.

Da.

Bo blinked dust out of his eyes. He stumbled forward, searching.

Da had been walking a pace ahead of him, but Bo saw no clue to his friend's current whereabouts.

Bo's stomach churned and his breathing became fast and shallow.

Where was Da?

He had been right here.

Bo spun around, looking behind him, wondering if he'd gotten turned around. Still no sign of Da.

Bo continued, stepping gingerly, avoiding the broken rubble that littered the walkway.

How much time had passed?

Sounds were coming closer. Voices, concerned and loud. He couldn't make out specific words, but he understood their tone.

Friends.

His mouth was dry, his pace increasing as he walked back and forth, searching for Da. His eyes roved everywhere, saw movement inside the palace, but he ignored it.

Then, sudden movement. Bo tore his attention away from the wall to the palace. The princess stood there, her dress in tatters, but her head held high and defiant. Bo had never stood this close to her.

He didn't care. Da was missing.

His gaze returned to the walls, saw a patch of red fabric among the gray dust.

Bo dashed forward. He scrambled toward the pile of stone, grasping and pulling at the rock. Quickly, he uncovered a corpse in the shape of his friend.

"No!" he shouted, his voice hoarse, his throat coated with the same dust that covered the body.

He grasped more stones, threw them away, uncovered the man's face.

Da.

He was barely recognizable. A stone had caved in part of his forehead. Da's eyes were wide, frozen in surprise for forever.

"No, no, no, no, no," Bo moaned.

The guilty stone hadn't escaped far. Covered in blood, it rested next to the fatal wound it had caused.

They'd been one pace apart, at most.

On his knees, Bo curled over, resting his head against his friend's chest, hoping to hear that strong heart he had so often relied on.

But the heart had gone silent.

Da was gone.

1

———

Bai walked the evening streets of Windown, basking in the busyness of the night market. The Harvest Festival was still days away, but merchants and customers alike prepared for the holiday. The spirit was in the air. Smiles came easily to vendors as wares flew off their tables, and laughter split the air as men drank too much together.

Having grown up in a small town, Bai adored the energy of larger cities. Windown was far from the largest city in the empire, but it was at least four times the size of Galan, the town she grew up in. In Galan the streets would be quiet by this time of night, even as the holiday approached.

She also enjoyed the larger cities for a more selfish reason. They fed into her own power. The energy of so many people flowed around her, creating a life-giving river that she drank deeply from. She opened herself to those currents of energy, reveling in the tingle of power running through her limbs, right down to her fingers and toes.

Hien, walking beside Bai, didn't seem nearly as pleased. The woman had a solid ten years on Bai, the first hints of gray darkening her otherwise night-black hair. Those stray hairs were the only reliable sign of the woman's age. Hien could outrun most men with half her years. She moved with a grace that came from decades of martial experience.

Hien's eyes roamed back and forth across the street, searching for danger.

Bai grinned at the other woman. She believed they were in no real danger here.

Hien had gotten word a few weeks ago, through means Bai still didn't completely understand. A woman had attracted violent attention in a brothel in Windown. She would risk her life to escape. Hien asked Bai to accompany her, and Bai agreed, having nothing more pressing.

They had arrived in Windown this morning. Tonight they planned to scout the area and tomorrow they would help the woman escape. They'd done this more times than Bai could count, the years piling on opportunities.

Hien treated every street corner as a potential ambush, every passerby a possible enemy.

Sometimes, the situation warranted such caution. They'd made enough enemies in their lives that some paranoia was reasonable. But they had just arrived in town and possessed no known enemies here. Windown hosted a small monastery, but Bai was reasonably certain she'd never crossed paths with any monks from here.

Reminding Hien would do no good. The woman woke up in a state of heightened awareness and didn't relax even in her dreams.

Bai would be tempted to poke fun at her, but Hien's abilities had saved her life more than once.

Bai stopped at a small food stall, drawn in by the scent of fresh noodles. She turned to Hien. "Want a bowl?"

Hien gave a quick nod as she scanned the market.

Bai ordered two bowls of noodles and stared with

delight as the chef prepared them. The smells made her mouth water with anticipation. They'd only eaten dried meat and some rice for the past few days.

They sat down at an outdoor table. Hien ate at her noodles slowly while Bai attacked hers like a foe that needed vanquishing.

Bai finished well before Hien and took in the sights. From their table she saw the corner of the brothel, tucked into a quiet corner of the market. It was a two-story building, surrounded by a few others.

The market was riddled with ways in and out, so they didn't need to worry about getting trapped immediately after their rescue. The most likely areas of concern were the roads out of town. The two primary roads would be closely guarded if an alarm was raised. Fortunately, no walls protected Windown, so it would be easy enough to escape if events went poorly.

She hoped that wouldn't be the case. Easy would be ideal.

When Hien finished her noodles the two women turned their attention to the task at hand. Tomorrow morning Hien would meet with the woman and finalize their plan, but tonight they needed to scout their options. If Hien had taught Bai one lesson well over the past decade, it was that preparation often meant the difference between success and failure. When Bai had first discovered her abilities, she enjoyed running head first into problems. Hien demonstrated a better way.

They made a large circle around the brothel. They worked in silence. Later, they would compare their observations. Bai noticed places where a person could hide, where an ambush might conceivably be set. She looked for alleys and paths that ended in a wall or other obstruction.

After they completed their rounds they found a dark corner. Hien stood guard while Bai opened herself up to more energy, filling her legs with borrowed strength. At a nod from Hien, Bai leaped to the rooftop two stories above.

She landed as lightly as a feather, then tested the footing to make sure the roof was stable. Back in Kulat, she'd been running along the rooftops and fallen straight into a family's dining room. She hadn't been hurt, but her shame still lingered when she thought on that moment.

Convinced that the roof would easily support the two of them, she waved at Hien. The woman pulled out a rope from her pack and uncoiled it. She took a weighted end and tossed it into the air with practiced ease. Bai caught it and anchored herself as Hien pulled herself smoothly up the rope and onto the rooftop.

Despite Hien's fitness, she was breathing hard when she stood next to Bai. Bai gave the other woman a chance to catch her breath, then they walked together to the other side of the roof where they could look down on the brothel.

Bai paid attention to the windows. Several were open, letting in the cool night air. That boded well for a discreet entrance. If the women inside could open their windows freely, it gave her and Hien a way of getting in and out without being noticed.

She filled her legs with power and jumped across the gap between the buildings. Looking back, she saw Hien glaring at her. Jumping across had been a bit of a risk, but it allowed Bai to scout the rooftop here, too. Sometimes there were access points to the building on the roof. A quick study of the surroundings told her that wasn't the case here. Bai was about to leap back across when she felt a gathering of power nearby.

She frowned and focused her attention. She'd been so

interested in the brothel and its surroundings she hadn't paid enough attention to the streets. A small group of monks approached the market.

Curious, she walked over to the front edge of the brothel's roof and crouched down. She allowed most of the energy to drain from her body. If the monks sensed her, she would have a considerable problem.

Her eyes ran over the crowd below, but she didn't see any monks. Their white robes stuck out even in a crowd. But she still felt them, and they were getting closer.

There.

Her sight and sense agreed. A group of three young men approached the brothel. None of them wore the white robes of their station, but their gait gave them away. They were men who spent their entire lives training to fight. They could wear loose-fitting traveling clothes, but she wouldn't miss a monk in any disguise.

Once she picked them out, she knew they only had one destination in mind, their eyes fixed on a point straight ahead.

And she was squatting on top of it.

She hurried out of sight. Once she was as far away from them as possible, she summoned the power to leap across the rooftops and return to Hien.

Hien had seen the entire episode, but without being gifted, could only guess at what had happened. "Who are they?"

"Monks."

"In a brothel, without their robes?"

Bai nodded. There weren't any prohibitions about monks visiting brothels, even within the monasteries. So why hide who they were? It was true that public opinion had turned against the monks in the past several years, but that rarely put a damper on their activities. They were the strongest warriors in the empire, and why would the strong worry about the opinion of the masses?

Bai considered the problem. The appearance of the monks probably meant little. If they visited the brothel again tomorrow, it might be a problem. If she used her powers, any nearby monks would likely notice them.

But they still had plenty of options. Breaking the woman out of the brothel shouldn't prove too challenging.

As she and Hien worked their way back to the streets, Bai hoped she wasn't wrong.

2

Delun crested the small rise that hid Two Bridges from view. The mere sight of the town took a weight off his shoulders. How long had it been since he had last been back here? Two months? The days and weeks blurred in his memory.

Too long.

Delun stopped, taking a moment to inspect the landscape. He noticed the differences first. New houses were being built on the outskirts of town, and the streets looked more crowded than ever before.

Two Bridges, like most of the empire, was growing. For most, the last decade had been one of peace and prosperity. Despite the tensions that simmered underneath the surface there had been no major conflicts. Even the Kulat Rebellion had only destroyed the lives of a few hundred people, and most of those had been from the failed military response. People didn't care much about wars that didn't affect them personally.

He let his eyes travel to the mountain ridge high above.

Snow already settled on some peaks, and before long travel to the monastery would be difficult. But for now, the path looked open.

He wanted to shed the weight that burdened his heart. But he couldn't outrun memories as easily as enemies.

He'd just come from a small village, so small it wasn't even named. There had been rumors that the village intended to begin an armed rebellion against the monasteries.

The rumor had to have been someone's poor idea of a joke.

They had hated the monasteries well enough. Delun walked into the village wearing his white robes and immediately been attacked. But the village possessed less than a dozen able-bodied men. Now there were less than half that many. The fight was quick, but bloodier than Delun preferred.

He'd left, disgusted with the situation. They'd attacked so fast he'd had no choice in his response. He'd offered coin in recompense, but had been harshly turned down. Now the village would hate monks even more than they had before.

And that was how it went, one day at a time. Delun created a story that would travel from mouth to ear across the empire. Another story about the evil monks who sought only power and money.

People would never learn about the lives he saved, the criminals he imprisoned or killed. Those stories remained as secrets. But every time a monk erred, the whole empire knew.

Seeing the outline of the monastery high above gave him an unreasonable amount of hope. He had grown up here, and perhaps this was the one place where he still found peace. Thirty years ago, the monastery at Two Bridges had burned. Since then it had kept itself relatively aloof from the affairs of the empire, becoming a haven for some of the strongest and most talented monks the empire had ever known. He had trained there for years as a child before becoming a full-fledged monk. Its rooms would always provide him shelter.

But not if he didn't get moving. He startled with the sudden realization he'd been standing in place for several minutes. He strode forward, eagerly looking forward to a meal in town before completing the intense hike up the mountain.

Delun received more than his fair share of glares as he came into Two Bridges. He did his best to ignore them and put forward the monastery's best face. He returned the glares with smiles, but halfway through the growing town he lost his appetite. There was no joy in eating a meal where one's company wasn't desired. Some dried meat still rested in his pack, enough to sustain him to the ridge the monastery rested on.

Soon he was on the other side of the town, the anger at his back. His attitude improved slightly outside of town, but regret and sorrow weighed down his heart. He had dedicated almost his entire life to the monasteries. They weren't perfect. He understood that, better than most. Some of his work targeted other monks.

But the monasteries were the empire's best hope. The empire needed strong and wise leaders who had the ability to change the world. The monks could be those leaders if the empire gave them the chance.

To this day, Delun remembered having his own young life saved by a monk. That was the day he discovered exactly what he wanted from life.

He lived his dream day after day, but it wasn't what he

had imagined. For all the good he performed, the world turned further away from the monasteries.

Delun questioned whether he should even continue.

Some small part of him hoped that Taio, the abbot he had grown up with inside the walls of the monastery, would have some answers for him, some guidance that would show him the way. With every step he climbed up the mountain, he kept his eyes on the summit.

The path to the monastery was wide and well-traveled. For the first half of the ascent the trail wound its way up the mountain while surrounded by tall pine trees. Delun breathed in the fresh scent deeply, the smell reminding him he was close to home. After about a mile, he broke out of the trees and came to a small intersection. From here he looked out on the valley below. Two Bridges was just beneath him, the cleared ground around the edges of the town a sign of its expansion.

Delun rested for a moment, snacking on the last of his meat while he watched the valley below. From up here the world seemed quieter and more peaceful, a bit of distance making all the difference. Eventually he turned and continued his journey.

The trail remained wide and easy to navigate. The monastery above was over a hundred years old. While people didn't travel the path every day, enough made the journey to keep the trail wide and unbroken. Tall granite slabs rose to Delun's side.

It didn't take him too long to reach a small marker in the road. Monks had placed the marker about twenty-five years ago to commemorate a duel, a duel that changed the world. Delun stopped to examine the slab of rock, cut smoothly by a powerful attack. Another hole in the rock a few paces on was about as wide as Delun's thumb.

The Dragon's Fang attack.

This was the place where a rebel had ambushed a monk named Jian. Two masters of their age had fought here, but Jian had lost. The duel on this road led to the Battle of Jihan, which had led to the Rebellion of Kulat.

Delun's mind wandered as he traced the ripples of history. The same events probably would have come to pass anyway, but this fight had been the seed that started it all. Being as Delun had been discovered and saved during the Battle of Jihan, he supposed he could trace the path of his life back to this place as well.

All times were times of change, but this age was different. These changes would echo down the halls of history. Delun didn't know which direction the empire would take. He only hoped it was one that gave the monks the respect and authority they deserved.

With the sun racing toward the mountaintops, Delun figured he had better pick up his pace. He pushed hard to the end of the trail, resting only when he crested the last switchback that brought the monastery into view. A thick rock wall surrounded the monastery, a wall that had stood unbroken for over a hundred years. From the trail, a few of the taller buildings could be seen peeking over the wall. Delun's spirits lifted as he saw the only place that he considered home.

Monks let him through the gate with little fanfare. They sensed his power just as he sensed theirs. Beyond that, they all knew him.

As soon as he stepped into the courtyard, a thin smile broke out on his face. Taio, the abbot of this monastery, stood in the courtyard providing a few students with additional instruction. Taio saw him enter, gave him a welcoming nod, then returned to his students.

Delun stayed for a bit and watched. He'd been on the road for months, and although he knew Taio's teachings well, perhaps there was something for him to learn.

He was quickly disappointed. The students were younger, in ways beyond their age. Delun saw the problem as soon as they began. Taio was attempting to demonstrate the third single-handed attack, but the teachings flew over the students' heads. The third attack, both the one-handed and two-handed versions, was the first that required true focus of one's will. A natural gift and training made the first two signs relatively straightforward. But the third often separated competent monks from those still stuck on the basics. These boys didn't have the patience. They ran through the moves too quickly. They never achieved focus.

Taio ordered them to try a dozen times while Delun watched, but no one succeeded. The abbot, more patient than Delun remembered, tried again and again to slow them down, but the lesson never held. Finally, Taio ended the session, giving gentle words of encouragement to the young men as they returned to their daily tasks.

Taio came and sat on the stone next to Delun. He sighed.

Delun offered the rest of his water skin. Taio accepted it with a nod of thanks. "You're gentler than you used to be."

Taio grunted, his attitude clear. "They can't handle strict training. They complain and sulk the following day, stealing their own valuable practice time."

Delun frowned. He'd heard similar statements at other monasteries. Still, he was surprised to hear it here. Years ago, they had admitted only fully trained monks into this monastery. Delun knew they had relaxed the rule, but he hadn't expected to see such untrained recruits. "How are you?"

Taio handed back the water skin. "I've been better." The abbot studied Delun. "But I feel better than you look."

The two men sat in silence for a few minutes, watching the daily routine of the monastery as evening approached. Just being back here made him feel better. He felt comfortable surrounded by the sights, the smells, and the routines.

Taio finally stood up. "You should stay for a while."

Delun shook his head, wishing he could accept. "There are rumors of a plot in Jihan."

Taio took a step and stood directly in front of Delun. "There's always a plot in Jihan. And you look more ragged than I've ever seen you. You can't solve all the empire's problems on your own, and I doubt a week will matter."

"A week?"

"Until the Harvest Festival."

Delun blinked. Somewhere in the back of his mind he had known that the festival was approaching, but he'd never thought of it.

He stood up and stretched. A week wouldn't be too bad, and staying here had a tremendous appeal. His temptation was strong.

He rubbed at his temples. His duty was to the people of the empire, and that meant no rest for him. "I appreciate the offer."

Taio shook his head. "Fine, then. It's an order. You need sleep and rest."

Delun still could have left, but his will was weak. A rest sounded fantastic. He nodded.

Taio smiled. "I thought you would eventually see things my way. And maybe while you're here, you can train some of these young men how to fight."

Delun groaned inwardly. He'd only been here a few minutes, but he already knew that if he was forced to teach, he would be looking for a way out.

3

---

 ei looked up sharply from his teacup. Daiyu, his wife, raised an eyebrow at the motion, posing a silent question.

"There are two gifted coming up the mountain."

Daiyu grimaced. Lei knew she had been looking forward to some quiet time alone with him. The last few weeks had been busy, and they had intentionally set aside time to simply be with one another. The visitors, whoever they were, couldn't have chosen a worse time. Still, Daiyu knew well how duty interfered with pleasure. "I'll see you when you return. Don't be long."

Lei reached out and held her hand for a moment. The temptation to shun his responsibilities pulled at his heart. All he wanted to do was spend his afternoon here, alone with Daiyu.

The world had other plans.

He stood and grabbed his sword from the corner of the room. Neither of the powers hiking up the path were strong, but one of them felt unique. When he'd first noticed the second power, he'd thought it might be Bai. The similarity was striking, but it wasn't his old student.

Lei opened the door to his house just in time to see the young man who had been watching the pass today run up the stairs to his porch. The man stopped short. "There are two people coming up the path."

A range of replies occurred to Lei. The man had shirked his duties. Lei should have received warning far before he could sense them. He'd lecture the outlook later, but he didn't have the energy to do so now. He gave a short nod and stepped down the stairs.

Lei didn't hurry. Though the two visitors were close enough for him to sense, the last few switchbacks up to his village were steep. He had several minutes before they crested the ridge.

The outlook followed Lei as he walked through his village. It had grown in the past few years. Despite their attempts at secrecy, word of the village had slowly spread. Those who lived below, in Kulat and Galan, had softened their attitudes, making the decision easier for many.

People came here for varied reasons. Some sought a simpler life, others fled from enemies, still others ran from the empire. He and Daiyu welcomed anyone they judged would contribute to their small enclave.

Several people wandered about this afternoon. The air was brisk, but those who lived here tended towards hardy. Lei greeted friends and neighbors and accepted condolences as he could. One or two wanted to speak with him at length. He promised that he would, but that visitors were coming.

He reached the edge of the village before his guests appeared. When he saw the man leading the pair, he immediately relaxed. He hadn't seen the monk for years, but it was definitely Yang.

Yang was the abbot of the closest monastery, a full day's journey away in the city of Kulat. At one time, Yang had almost rebelled against the whole monastic system, but after the Massacre of Kulat, he had ended up as abbot.

Lei kept a close eye on events in the surrounding area. At least, he tried as much as a man who lived in self-imposed exile could. He'd heard little but good news since Yang had taken over, and the abbot had earned his trust several times over.

A young woman walked behind Yang. Her eyes were wary and her body tense. She was the one who felt almost like Bai.

The powers might have been similar, but the personalities were anything but. A single glance told Lei that the young woman in front of him was closed off, private, and ready for a fight. Although they'd just met, he saw a woman who'd had a turbulent life.

Lei gave Yang a short bow, which was returned slightly deeper. A small acknowledgment that although Yang was an abbot, Lei's strength was far greater.

They exchanged pleasantries and Lei led them back into the village. He trusted Yang, but the woman's silent presence left him on edge. Lei planned to lead them to the common room, but Yang asked if they could take the path to the clearing above. Lei, more curious than worried, agreed.

They climbed the path without a word, and Lei's memories of training Bai surfaced from the depths of his past. She probably hadn't known then, but he'd felt the importance of those grueling days.

Yang seemed to peer directly into his thoughts. "You feel it, too?"

Lei struggled to express the changes he had sensed for the past couple of months. Feelings, instincts, and rumors had gradually coalesced into something more, something he struggled to understand. "A circle is closing."

Yang nodded. "Well said. My father was a tailor, and I would say that the strands of fate are finally coming together. But we feel the same, I think."

They crested the steep path that led to the clearing. A small mountain lake rested ahead of them, crystal blue waters inviting and cold. Tall pines surrounded the clearing, in clumps that grew year after year as the small forest spread.

Yang breathed in deeply. "You still train here, don't you?"

It was half a comment, half an inquiry. Lei confessed that he did.

"I figured as much. You've created a new legend, you know, or perhaps your first. There are ever fewer people who know your past."

"For the best, I'd imagine."

"Who knows? But the past is unchangeable, even for you. Any monk within three miles of this place can feel you when you train, though."

Lei hadn't heard. Yang and Bai were the only gifted who visited his village, and neither had visited for over a year. For as interested in news as he was, though, his patience still wore thin. This had been time for him and Daiyu. "Why are you here, Yang?"

Many monks would have shown disgust at Lei's directness, but they had known each other for years. He spoke without preamble. "I want to convince you to join the monastery."

Lei frowned. "You know that I won't."

"Which is why I brought her." Yang gestured toward the girl, who immediately summoned an incredible amount of power. The girl sprinted, covering a dozen paces in less than a heartbeat. She leaped into the air, feet spinning in kicks almost too fast for Lei to track. She landed softly, and within a moment her power had completely vanished.

Lei attempted to keep the amazement off his face but failed. The powers were eerily similar to Bai's. Bai was capable of greater power, but Lei wasn't sure she had the same control this young woman did.

"Her name is Rong. She was the first one I found."

Lei tore his gaze away from the young woman to stare at the abbot. "The first?"

"There are over a dozen now. Men, women, even two children."

"All like her?"

Yang shook his head. "The power manifests differently in each."

Lei felt the world shift underneath his feet. Such variety? "How far have you searched?"

"No more than three days' journey away from Kulat."

"So many?"

Yang just nodded, giving Lei a chance to absorb the information.

The abbot might as well have appeared and claimed that humans could now fly. Lei had suspected change was in the air, but he had never imagined it would come so fast and be so widespread. "What about the other monasteries?"

"They cling to the past, as they always have. We are building something new in Kulat, Lei. I believe you need to be a part of it."

Lei wasn't sure what to say. He had guessed something

like this had been Yang's purpose, but he'd never imagined that he'd be tempted, especially after the news Daiyu had learned just a week ago. "I cannot," he said.

Yang didn't look surprised. "Don't you see, Lei? You were the harbinger of it all, the one who pierced the mysteries. Before you, no one had connected to the source. Now, many can. Then Bai came with gifts we had never seen before. Today there are more, with gifts no other abbot would even dare to recognize. The gift, our powers, are changing before our very eyes. And we are here to witness it, to guide it, even. I need your strength, but more than that, I need your wisdom."

Lei met Yang's gaze. "Daiyu is dying."

Yang didn't answer, but Lei saw the surprise in his eyes. "You're sure?"

Lei nodded. "The best healers have come in response to my summons. The growth is large and incurable."

"How long?"

Lei shrugged. "Months, maybe. Perhaps less."

Yang looked devastated. Lei knew he disappointed the abbot with the news, but not because Yang was close to Daiyu. The abbot respected Lei's wife, but his sorrow was more personal. Yang now knew that no matter what he said, Lei would not join him.

The abbot did not push further. He stepped up to Lei. "I am truly sorry, Lei. Just know that our doors in Kulat are always open. It would delight us to have you."

"For what it is worth, Yang, I appreciate all that you have done. If I am able, I will help how I can. Like you, I am fascinated by these developments."

Yang acknowledged the kindness, then turned down the mountain with Rong in tow. His visit had been short, but

Yang had never wasted time. Lei watched them go, wondering on Yang's words.

Although few people admitted it, the monasteries had given the empire peace and prosperity for decades. If the power the monasteries relied on was changing, Lei feared what would become of the empire.

4

_____

Bai sipped at her tea while watching the busy streets. She tapped her fingers against the side of the cup, glancing back and forth between the street and her companion. She didn't like this setup.

Hien had met with the woman this morning. The conversation had been quick and discreet. Two private guards, hired by the brothel, watched the woman as she moved through town. Hien had pulled the woman aside as Bai created a commotion behind the guards, drawing their attention for a few minutes.

Their final plan was as simple as they came. The woman would make an excuse to leave sometime this afternoon. She'd bring anything she could. Bai and Hien would take care of the guards and they would be out of Windown before anyone was the wiser.

Simple and easy. No different than a dozen times before.

Except for the monks.

They kept wandering the street outside the teahouse. Enough monks had passed by that Bai worried they'd noticed her. But the monks raised no alarm. They didn't even glance in her direction.

Across from her, Hien raised an eyebrow. "Could you stop?"

Bai forced her fingers to relax. She spread them out wide and laid them on the table.

"Your knee, too?"

She hadn't even realized. Obediently, she quit.

"Why are you nervous?"

"Another monk passed a minute ago."

Hien sighed. "If they haven't attacked, they haven't noticed you."

Most days Bai would have agreed. Today, something didn't sit well with her, but she had no detail, no fact she could use to prove her case. She tried to relax, turning her attention to Hien.

Though her friend's appearance wouldn't alarm a random passerby, Bai's trained eye picked up on details most missed. To a stranger, Hien looked like an older woman, hair starting to gray, skin beginning to wrinkle. If that stranger watched Hien for a few moments, they might admire the energy with which she moved, but little else.

Bai saw a warrior. Perhaps past her physical prime, but decades of experience made her more dangerous than ever. Small bulges sometimes appeared as Hien shifted in her seat, briefly revealing the wide array of weaponry the woman wore hidden under her loose-fitting clothes. Bai had known Hien for over ten years, and she'd never known the woman to carry less than five blades. It was a wonder she didn't stab herself every time she moved.

Her friend had a concerned look on her face. The question came out of the blue. "Will you return home with me, once this is over?"

Bai broke away from Hien's gaze and turned to the street. Hien had decided that after this rescue she would make the long journey across the empire back to Lei's village. It was the place they both called home, though neither spent much time there. She'd invited Bai to join her.

Bai didn't know. Seeing friendly faces always appealed to her, but Bai had little reason to return. Hien wanted her back in the area for another reason.

Rumors claimed that the monastery in Kulat had changed its direction. Both Bai and Hien listened to tales of strange warriors. Bai couldn't separate truth from the fantastic. Hien argued that Bai should return and seek others like her.

Bai had little desire. The last time she visited Kulat she had killed the previous abbot as he rebelled against the empire. Although she knew Yang, the current abbot, would welcome her, she saw few compelling reasons to return to a place that held only terrible memories.

The sight of a woman walking down the street saved her from further contemplation.

The woman they had been waiting for.

Bai didn't know her name. Hien had mentioned it several times, but she had promptly forgotten.

The woman had seen better days. She wore heavy makeup that made her look ready for the evening, but her sunken eyes and slouched shoulders told an entirely different story. A large man walked in front of her. He wasn't overtly menacing, but he cleared a path for both of them. A triad.

Hien was about to set a few coins on the table, but Bai was quicker. The older woman smiled. "I should be paying for you, for your help."

"For the pleasure of your company."

They left the teahouse and separated, their long experience guiding them. Hien took point. Bai was stronger and faster, but Hien had made first contact and would escort the woman away from the town to a safe location. Bai usually observed, only acting when the escapes went wrong.

Watching Hien work still inspired Bai. She almost vanished like a ghost in the crowds, and if Bai hadn't kept an eye on her, she would have been nearly impossible to track. The lone triad, so confident in his own superiority, would never see her coming.

Bai's prediction became a reality soon enough. A hood pulled over her head, Hien slipped through the crowd until she walked beside the triad, slightly behind him. He never saw her. Bai couldn't see the small dagger, but she saw the quick motion of Hien's arm, saw the triad stumble, suddenly supported and guided to the edge of the street by Hien.

The dagger was poisoned. Not to kill, but for sleep. The triad never saw Hien's face, and his stumble didn't attract attention. A drunk triad at this time of the afternoon barely merited a notice.

Then Hien made contact with the woman. As they spoke, Bai took point, scouting the area. The woman might never even know Bai had helped, but Bai acted as the eyes and ears that allowed Hien to focus more on the woman. Once outside of Windown, Hien would take the woman the rest of the way to the shelter alone. There would be little danger once they escaped the city limits.

Watching Hien comfort the woman made Bai think of their own first meeting. Hien had broken her out of a cell, helped her escape from a town that wanted her blood. Bai didn't know exactly what Hien was telling the woman, but she could imagine. She'd heard much the same so many years ago, even if the words were different.

It will be okay.

From anyone else, the words may have sounded trite and empty. But Hien inspired trust. Looking back on their escape from Galan, Bai couldn't believe Hien had managed to both calm her and guide her as well as she had.

The woman tonight was no different. Within moments she was following Hien, taking the first steps toward her new life.

Bai and Hien exchanged a quick glance. Hien gave a short nod, and Bai turned and led the way, alert for the first sign of trouble.

Everything seemed safe enough. Windown, like every town and city in the empire, was preparing for the Harvest Festival. Held every year to celebrate the conclusion of the harvest, it was one of the largest celebrations, bringing in people from all over the land. During the day, merchants bustled about, preparing for some of the most profitable days of the year. The activity provided plenty of cover for the three women.

Bai felt the energy of the city, like a beating heart underneath her feet.

She led the women toward the main road that led out of the city. Hien's rescue had gone so well, she didn't see any need to run through the back alleys. She took wide streets that led them out of town.

Bai was twenty paces ahead of Hien and the woman when she turned a corner and came face to face with a group of six men blocking the road.

Bai's first instinct was to label them triads, warriors sent to retrieve the woman, but a quick glance gave lie to that explanation. The men all had shaven heads, and even their resting stances were similar to one another. Now that they had her attention, she felt them, too. She'd been so focused on spotting guards from the brothel she'd forgotten completely about her first fear.

They didn't wear white robes, but their shared identity was obvious.

Monks.

Bai didn't panic. Even this close, they might not sense her. Only a trickle of energy flowed through her at the moment, and it would take a sensitive monk getting close to her to notice.

She changed direction, but saw the way the eyes of the men followed her.

She stopped and cursed.

They had cleared the area, meaning they likely had one outcome in mind.

A few moments later Hien came up behind her. Her stance was wary. No doubt she'd noticed Bai's shifting behavior. She'd left the woman ten paces behind. Hien looked at the group arrayed in front of them. She identified them quickly enough, even though she wasn't gifted.

"Monks."

Bai nodded. "They're for me. Go on."

Hien didn't move. "I can help."

Most people would run in fear of confronting a monk. Hien didn't, and Bai knew the woman's words weren't an empty boast.

"No. She needs you more."

Hien looked torn.

"I'll be fine. Go."

Without another word, Hien retrieved the woman. They walked away. The monks followed Hien and the other woman with their eyes, but did not pursue. Bai was grateful. Her assumption had been correct.

The monks advanced on her. She drew power into

herself. Her senses sharpened and her limbs filled with new energy. Inside Windown, surrounded by so much life, the energy she could draw from was vast.

Usually her talent surprised monks. But these expected it, because their advance never faltered. They knew who she was and what gifts she possessed. They responded by forming the signs of attacks and shields with their hands. Two of the six drew daggers.

Bai's eyes widened at that. Weapons weren't permitted for monks. For some, it made them too dangerous. The question was, were the monks able to channel their energy into the weapons, or did they intend to stab her?

She hoped it was the latter. She'd never fought against energy-infused weapons, but she'd seen firsthand the damage such attacks created.

The semicircle of monks advanced on her. Their eyes glittered with hate.

"For our fallen brothers!" The monk who shouted was one of the two that held a dagger. Bai pegged him as the leader.

The monks attacked together. Waves of invisible energy darted at her, her own gift warning her of the blows.

She stepped into them, feeling the attacks infuse every inch of her body with additional power. She sprinted forward, the shields the monks relied on for protection only slowing her for a moment. Bai drove her fist into one monk's stomach, then spun around and snapped a roundhouse kick at another's chin.

She controlled her strength. With the power she'd already absorbed, she easily could have killed both with her blows. Holding back, she merely left them unconscious.

Amid the remaining monks, she barely had time to react against the next wave of attacks. Two attacks felt familiar, but two techniques surprised her. Sharp crescents of energy snapped at her. Afraid for the first time in years, she leaped high over the attacks, landing softly on a roof above and behind her.

Despite her soft landing, the roof crumbled as soon as her weight settled. For a second, she wondered why. As the cracking sound from the walls below reached her ears, she understood.

The attacks from the daggers had cut through the whole house.

As stone and wood collapsed, Bai leaped from one rooftop to another. Thankfully, the second house remained firm under her feet.

The monks tracked her, hands focusing power as they prepared their next assault.

She couldn't allow them the opportunity, especially not the two with daggers. Families lived in these houses. She leaped down, drawing power into her fist as she punched at the two dagger-wielding monks. They were agile, though, giving up ground and avoiding her blows.

She pressed forward, letting more strength rush into her legs. The two monks couldn't backpedal quickly enough. She caught one with a kick across the shins, crashing him to the ground. Before he recovered, she snapped another kick at his head, causing his eyes to lose focus and his face to go slack.

In the time she took to disable the first weapon-wielding monk, the second gathered all his strength into his dagger. With rage burning in his eyes, he lashed out, a sharp wave of energy sending the dirt of the road underneath their feet flying.

She stood too close to dodge. Without thinking, she held out her left hand, as though she could stop the blow with a feeble gesture. She felt a sharp, fiery pain as the cut struck her hand, but her body absorbed the energy.

Bai clenched her hand into a fist. The attack had been terribly focused, filling her entire body with fire. She had encountered this before. Her body threatened to burst like an overfilled water skin.

She stepped forward. To her perception the action had been simple enough: a single step toward her assailant. But that single step carried her directly in front of him. Her control over her body faded as the energy coursed through her limbs.

Bai raised her right hand and made the symbol for the first attack, holding the attack right in the monk's face. Her ability to project energy like the monks was nearly useless. But she'd absorbed so much power even she couldn't fail.

She released the power from her hand, like pricking the water skin with a knife point. The strength rushed out of her, directly at the monk's head.

The result shocked her. The monk flew, his body landing at an unnatural angle against the ground. Without having to check, Bai was certain the monk was dead.

The final two monks, unarmed and terrified of suffering the same fate as their brothers, turned and ran.

Bai was about to chase them when she noticed the blood dripping from her left hand. She opened it and looked at her palm. A gash ran from her fourth finger down nearly to her wrist. Though not deep, it bled freely. As the excitement faded from her body, the pain worsened.

She looked up at the fleeing monks and decided they weren't worth her time. She had more pressing concerns.

The monks had figured out how to hurt her.

5

Delun stood on the wall of his monastery, staring out at the impressive vista below.

Though the harvest festival didn't begin until this evening, the season's first snows had already fallen on the monastery courtyard. The wall gave visitors an expansive view of the jagged mountains to the east and glimpses of the valley to the west.

Delun gazed at the snow-capped peaks, tall and mysterious. The mountains pulled at him, calling him with promises of brutal simplicity. Survive or die. Brave expeditions sometimes wandered into the range. They rarely returned, but when they did, it was with tales of hardship and failure.

But out there, it was his own will against that of nature. Survival was victory. The task was difficult, but it was straightforward.

A welcome change over his current life.

Weariness settled deep in his bones, a fatigue born of melancholy. He had dedicated his entire adult life to the preservation of the monasteries, but failure haunted his steps, just the same as it did the expeditions who returned from the mountains. He could fight against rebels, investigate every traitorous monk, but he stood in the way of an avalanche of change.

Since returning to the monastery, Delun had caught up on sleep, but his depression was as deep as ever.

He sensed Taio about the same time he heard him. They were all getting older, but Taio had aged well. The abbot had many years on Delun, yet he still climbed the stairs of the wall with strength and grace.

Taio stood next to him, calmly enjoying the view.

"It never gets old."

Delun agreed. If there was one place in the world where he could feel at ease, it was on this wall looking out over the untamed wild.

Home.

"You have spent little time with the other monks," Taio observed.

"I think both sides prefer it that way."

Delun's welcome had been less than warm. Ten years ago, in Kulat, Delun realized his mission wasn't just to protect the monasteries. Sometimes he had to limit them.

He'd seen firsthand what happened when a monastery seized too much power.

Threats against the monasteries were easier to track and simpler to crush. Extreme thinking within the monastery posed the far greater challenge. Very few monks went so far as to betray the vows of service they made to the empire when they completed their training. Most whispered to one another at night, or spoke softly around an evening fire.

A select few pushed too hard, though. They broke their vows, bringing Delun's justice upon them.

The work was necessary, but it earned him few friends

among his own kind. Even here at his home monastery, the monks avoided him.

"You don't have to continue," Taio said, understanding the direction of Delun's thoughts.

"Who else would carry on? No doubt many would volunteer to seek our enemies, but few would accept the other work."

Taio leaned against the stone wall, staring off into the distance. Delun had never seen him more hopeless. He didn't argue against Delun's cynicism.

"Do you ever fear that we cannot keep the peace?" Delun asked.

"Every day. But I refuse to surrender to despair."

"How?"

"There is some hope. Many monks still hold to the spirit of the vows. I think most just want to serve and be accepted."

Delun didn't share Taio's optimism. In his experience, more monks talked about controlling the empire than serving it.

"Have you been to Kulat recently?" Taio asked.

The shift in topic surprised Delun. "Not since Guanyu."

"Yang has done well as abbot. He writes us all frequently. His doors are always open and citizens come and go frequently. He isn't popular with many abbots, but sometimes I wonder if his ideas aren't worth pursuing."

Delun shook his head. Yang's ideas broke with tradition. They spit on the meaning of being a monk. Delun had been instrumental in Yang's ascension, but his feelings remained mixed on the subject.

Taio stood up, his back straight, command in his voice. "Don't judge Yang's ideas based on tradition alone, Delun. Think on this, if nothing else: For a decade you have traveled to every corner of the empire seeking justice. Yet you've never needed to return to Kulat."

The thought had never crossed Delun's mind. Once Taio mentioned it, though, he could think of nothing else.

The abbot turned to look down into the monastery. Monks hauled tables, and they set places in preparation for the Harvest Festival. The promise of this evening's celebration drove the young men of the monastery, lighting a fire in their eyes.

When Taio looked back at Delun, he no longer played the role of an old friend. He was the abbot of Two Bridges, one of the most powerful positions in the empire. "Your final task, Delun, is to bring a lasting peace to this land. You must bring together the monks and the citizens of this land so the empire can flourish. No longer can we react and control. We must lead."

Delun bowed, accepting the command, impossible as it was. He was nothing if not an obedient servant of the empire.

Taio softened and laid his hand on Delun's shoulder. "I know well the weight you carry, but I know you can show us a new way. Celebrate tonight, and tomorrow we'll discuss some of my ideas."

They enjoyed the view together for a few more minutes, but then Taio drifted off, other responsibilities demanding his attention.

Delun looked out over the view for a while alone, then went down the stairs to help with preparations. The younger monks didn't speak often to him, but they didn't turn down the assistance of another pair of hands.

It was early afternoon when Delun heard a disturbance at the gate to the monastery. Delun looked up from sweeping the grounds to study the interruption. He noticed little of concern except for the raised voices. The commotion passed in a few minutes, and Delun pushed the matter out of his mind.

A cart from Two Bridges soon came through the gates. Several casks rested within, the whole collection pulled by a pair of horses. The casks held wine and beer for the evening's festivities. The monks wouldn't partake much, if at all, but Delun wondered if even that longstanding prohibition was slipping. Most of the drink was for the people supposedly coming up from Two Bridges tonight.

Delun wondered at that. Although many citizens traded frequently with the monastery, few made the journey up the mountain for recreational purposes. But a large contingent was supposed to arrive in time for the evening meal. Delun's questioning had revealed that no one, not even Taio, knew more than that.

The cart driver deposited the casks and began his journey down the mountain. It seemed unusual that the cart would leave. The monks assumed most people would remain as guests overnight, given the difficulty of the journey up and down the mountain. Delun assumed the merchant would have remained until the celebration was over tomorrow morning to save himself a trip.

With nothing else to do, Delun returned the broom he had been using and climbed the monastery wall once again. Few tasks brought him as much peace as watching the mountains in their splendor.

He lost track of the time he spent on the wall. He breathed deeply of the cool mountain air. Slowly, his body relaxed.

Suddenly, his world exploded, fire accompanied by a deep, booming thunderclap. The blast threw him off the wall, cartwheeling through the air.

He barely managed to get his legs underneath him before he hit the stone. He felt his ankle give way as soon as he landed, but he kept his body loose and rolled with the impact. His body came to a skidding stop a few feet from the edge of a fatal drop-off.

He wasn't sure how long he lay there, unmoving. His breath didn't come easy, but it came. Perhaps he blacked out for a few minutes.

Concern for his brothers overwhelmed his pain. The explosion had come from the courtyard.

The casks.

How many had been hurt? He pushed himself to his feet, treating his left ankle gingerly. It didn't feel broken, but his stomach twisted whenever he put too much weight on it. He shuffled and crawled his way around the wall, grateful the builders of the monastery hadn't built all the way to the edge of the ridge. That decision, over a hundred years old, had saved his life today.

When he came around the corner that revealed the road leading up to the monastery, he stumbled at the sight of the desecration.

The gate and the surrounding wall no longer existed. The casks had been placed relatively close to the gate, but the explosion had torn a hole in the stone wall that looked like a giant's fist had made it. Delun shuffled to the gap that had once been a gate.

The damage to the wall was nothing compared to the devastation within. Evidence of the massacre was everywhere. Against a wall, a monk lay propped up at an odd angle, eyes open and staring. A dismembered arm stuck out from the snow, a brutal parody of a brother waving goodbye for the final time.

Delun wasn't the only survivor. Several monks wandered

the wreckage, looking for signs of life, eyes wide with disbelief.

He found Taio. The abbot lay, unmoving, out in the open, close to where the explosion had been. He didn't see any visible damage. Taio's bones had either collapsed or his organs hadn't withstood the pressure, turning to jam inside him. Delun knew the type of injuries intimately.

They were how a monk's attack killed its target.

Delun knelt down next to the man he had called a friend and master. They'd known each other for all of Delun's adult life.

Delun didn't have any tears to shed. A cold mountain wind blew through the wall where the gate had been, cutting through his robes. He glanced down the path, making sure there weren't others on their way to take advantage of the chaos and suffering.

The path was as silent as their departed brothers.

He felt nothing.

He was tired and empty. This had been his home, his sanctuary, the place where he could come and feel safe.

Now that was gone.

His friend was gone.

Delun just knelt there, keeping Taio company.

It wasn't enough, but it was all he could do.

6

———

Lei grinned as he bounced around in the rickety cart. It had been years since he had ventured farther than the small town of Galan below his village, and he was remembering how much he enjoyed traveling.

When he had come to the area many years ago the road that stretched between Galan and the larger city of Kulat had been near the edge of an expansive forest. In the intervening years, the forest had grown, swallowing the road and swaddling it in shade. Pine trees grew on both sides, their earthy scent permeating the air.

He was here thanks to Daiyu. When he told his wife that he had turned down an offer to visit Kulat, she immediately scolded him. The memory of her words had brought the grin to his face.

"You will not decline such an invitation on my account. I'm not going anywhere soon, so go."

Her encouragement represented a shift in longstanding beliefs. Once, they had pushed the world away enthusiastically. Doing so allowed them to escape the influence of the empire. The emperor and lords left them alone so long as Lei voluntarily isolated himself. His self-imposed exile purchased them a life lived in peace.

Now that she was dying, Daiyu desired his reengagement with the world.

She wanted him to live well once she passed.

He forced the thoughts aside. Merely visiting Kulat wouldn't violate his implicit agreement with Lord Xun, and Lei was curious about the developments Yang had spoken of. High in the mountains, Lei wondered about the changing relationship between the power of the monks and those who wielded the gifts.

Age and experience had increased Lei's ability by several orders of magnitude. But in recent years the nature of his ability had shifted. As a young man, he believed his gifts had been his own. The power had come from his body and will. Now the power he summoned felt more remote, connected to a source that defied description.

Lei's introspection was cut short by the cart coming to an intersection and turning toward Kulat. In a few minutes they rumbled out of the forest and into the grassy plain that surrounded the town.

Lei thought his first visit to Kulat in years would merit a greater reception, but not a single person noticed his arrival. He supposed that to most passersby he was just another old traveler. Lei slid off the back of the cart and thanked the merchant who had given him the ride. The cart turned a corner and disappeared, leaving Lei alone in the city.

Kulat had grown since he'd last visited, the streets filled with people in the aftermath of the Harvest Festival. Though Daiyu had ordered him out of the house, he waited until the festival was over to make the journey. Most people looked forward to the annual celebration. Lei dreaded the anniversary of his terrible battle with Fang.

Though the city had grown, Lei still knew the approach to the monastery. He made his way through the crowd, but was soon greeted by a young man pushing through the throng of people to reach him.

The young man stopped directly in front of him. "You must be Lei." The man looked eager.

"I am."

The man noticed Lei's confusion. "I'm sorry, I'm Wu, a student of Yang's. We sensed you approach Kulat, and they sent me to escort you to the monastery."

Lei hid his frown. He needed no escort. Old suspicions bubbled to the surface. Was Yang hiding something, or was he extending his hospitality?

Lei didn't see much harm in following the eager student. He gestured forward and Wu led the way. The young man couldn't stay silent for more than a moment. "It's a pleasure to meet you, sir."

"You can call me Lei."

"Thank you, sir, I mean, Lei." He took a breath. "It's a pleasure to meet you."

"So I've heard."

"Sorry, sir. It's just that we've all heard a lot about you. Master Yang says you might be one of the strongest people who has ever lived."

"I doubt that."

Wu gave him a knowing smile. "Of course, sir."

Lei sighed. He already regretted his decision to visit.

Wu LED Lei through the open gates of the monastery. He hadn't stopped talking the entire walk. Mostly, Yang's student was curious, and although Lei was tired from the journey, he didn't want to dissuade the man's enthusiasm. He answered questions politely, but remained eager to rid himself of his escort.

Nothing in Wu's behavior suggested anything but kindness from Yang. They had taken a straight route to the monastery, but Wu was more than happy to show Lei down side streets when he asked. The student's behavior put Lei thoroughly at ease.

Lei's first glance inside the walls of Kulat's monastery surprised him. Over a dozen people in white robes were in the courtyard, engaged in a dizzying array of tasks.

One woman was leading a group of what appeared to be elderly citizens in a series of stretches Lei recognized as the final part of a monk's daily training. The gentle movements eased the body after a long day of practice, or, it seemed, a long span of years.

In another corner a white-robed man led a group of children through the martial forms of the monastery. Lei recognized parts of the form, then realized they had altered it to accommodate those who weren't gifted. The mixed group of boys and girls were throwing themselves into the training with all the enthusiasm youth could generate.

This was Yang's dream, then. Lei felt a strange mixture of emotions at the sight. In many ways, Kulat was an echo of his own childhood. The forms were familiar; the movements memorized by his own muscles.

But this was not the monastery as he recognized it. This was a monk's knowledge and heritage, shared among all.

He was surprised to find he held a bit of resentment in his heart.

Lei agreed with Yang. The monasteries needed a new

way forward. He approved of what he saw and yet it was hard to see the secrets of the monastery laid so bare.

Lei calmed himself the way his masters had taught him as a child. A deep breath in through the nose, a slow exhalation through the mouth. He hadn't thought himself so petty. He recognized his resentment for what it was.

If the monastery's teachings were open to all, they no longer held the glamor they once did.

Lei knew the idea was foolish, yet there it was. He recognized his pride and let it go. After a minute in this place, he knew he was looking at the future.

He saw some awe on visitors' faces, but the fear the monastery usually inspired was gone. Citizens looked comfortable inside these walls, grateful even for the opportunity to be here.

Yang came out to greet Lei. On his home grounds the man radiated peace, even joy, as though he reflected the sun itself.

Yang showed Lei around the grounds.

"I never thought I would see the day when the monasteries would welcome so many with open arms," Lei admitted.

Yang sensed the discontent under his words. "The change is hard for many. I lost quite a few monks in the first years. They transferred to more traditional monasteries."

"Hard changes, but I think necessary."

"I agree. What you see is just the beginning, though. I know why you really came."

Yang led Lei into the training hall, where a group of students hastily gathered, no doubt in response to Lei's arrival. They all stood in a straight line. "Allow me to introduce my personal students."

The woman on Lei's far left appeared to be the oldest of

the group, but here that distinction meant little. She was in her mid-twenties at most. "This is Shu. She is the oldest and the first that I found," Yang said.

Lei could sense the woman's gift. She was strong, but not unreasonably so. Yang, as he so often did, understood the direction of Lei's thoughts. "Her powers are mostly in line with traditional monastic abilities. However, she can sense the gift over vast distances. She was the one who let us know you had arrived in Kulat."

That answered one of Lei's nagging questions.

Yang continued down the line. "You've already met Rong. She and several others here have abilities similar to Bai's. Of them, Rong's is the most developed. She's the strongest fighter of the group."

Lei didn't have to work hard to imagine that. He'd trained Bai and seen firsthand how dangerous she'd been with only weeks of training. Now he almost feared to imagine what she might be capable of. Rong walked in the master's footsteps.

"You've met Wu, too." The eager young man bowed deeply.

Lei stopped in front of him. He could barely sense the student. "What can you do?"

Wu gave Yang a questioning glance. Yang nodded.

Lei had no warning. The attack hit him, forcing him to bring a foot back to steady himself. The blow hadn't been strong, but Lei hadn't even sensed the power gathering. Lei stood there, belatedly realizing his mouth was hanging open.

Wu bowed again. "I have little strength, sir, but I can attack and defend without the signs."

If it hadn't just happened to him, Lei wouldn't have believed. Scholars believed that the signs weren't necessary, that they were crutches used by the monks to shape power to their wills. Lei had experimented himself, but for all the strength he could access, he couldn't focus the power without the signs. Wu's attack happened faster than Lei could react.

Lei's imagination exploded with possibilities. "That's an incredible gift."

Wu flushed with pride, and Yang finished introducing the rest of the students. They were young, but if their gifts were as varied as Yang promised, they were harbingers of something far greater.

Yang called for a demonstration between his students. Wu faced off against Rong.

Within moments, Lei knew Yang had uncovered the future.

Rong darted around Wu, but Wu's attacks were furious and unrelenting. No single blow did more than trip Rong up, but Wu was in full control of his gifts, and for all the speed Rong possessed, she struggled to break his defense.

His ability paled next to Rong's, though. He could delay her, but he had no hope of stopping her. She delivered a series of blows that brought him down, though Lei saw she held back.

Regardless, the demonstration impressed him. Though Rong was far superior in a duel, Lei would gladly bring Wu into a tense situation, especially against a monk with only traditional training.

Lei heard the commotion before he saw it, a loud argument just beyond the walls of the training hall where two monks stood guard. After a minute, the sentry escorted in a face Lei hadn't thought he'd ever see again.

It was Lord Xun's chief questioner. An assassin, spy, and torturer all rolled into one.

From the surprise on the man's face, he felt the same.

The sentry grimaced. "I'm sorry, Master, but he demanded entry. He claims he was sent straight from the emperor."

Lei decided he had chosen a truly poor moment to leave his village.

7

———

B ai wondered if there would ever come a day when she possessed answers to all her questions.

The world shifted beneath her feet, deep currents threatening to pull her in directions she didn't wish to go.

On the night of the Harvest Festival, while she waited for Hien to return, a massive explosion rocked the monastery in Windown. That evening Bai had been on a rooftop, taking in the festivities from a distance, avoiding any chance encounters with wandering monks. She had watched the flames lick the cloudless night sky, a dreadful certainty sinking deep into her bones.

War was coming.

For years tensions had grown between the monks, the military, and the people. The balance that had governed the empire for so long crumbled like a long-forgotten ruin, fading into decay.

No armies marched yet.

But they would.

Bai fought the currents. She didn't approach the

monastery to investigate. She remained hidden, refusing to provide the surviving monks a target for their anger.

At night she prowled the rooftops. Curiosity, and a healthy measure of self-preservation, drove her. The monks had been waiting for her. But how?

No one had known they were coming, and Bai was certain no one had followed them or sensed her power before the fight.

And now the monastery had been attacked. Bai feared suspicion would fall on her, though she hadn't been involved. Who had attacked the monks?

Questions without answers.

Her first step remained the same: Question the monks who had run from the ambush. The trail of answers began with them.

As a child, she had grown up with fear, had lived with it like a close relative. She looked down at the bracelet on her wrist, her last reminder of her mother. As a young seamstress, she had feared so much: wealthy men, soldiers, illness. But all those fears amounted to nothing when she caught sight of those white robes in her small town. Almost every time she'd seen a monk, she turned the other way.

Until the day she didn't, and her life had been forever altered.

No one should fear their protectors.

The explosion made her task more difficult. The surviving monks huddled within their broken walls, but it was days before she felt anyone gifted leave the monastery. Many people came and went in the interim, but no one aroused her interest.

Bai fought a mounting worry as well. Hien should have returned by now. She was only a day behind schedule, and any number of explanations existed, but Bai still fretted.

On the fourth night after the explosion, Bai finally caught a break.

She stood in the shadows upon a rooftop, watching the monastery from afar. Two monks left the monastery, casting furtive glances back and forth. She recognized them. They were the two she sought.

Bai followed.

She would have answers.

Bai leaped from rooftop to rooftop, the practice second nature to her now. The monks walked toward the outskirts of town.

She wished Hien were back. No doubt the woman would have half a dozen ideas for a clever ambush. Her mind skipped laterally across problems in ways Bai couldn't follow.

Direct solutions appealed more to Bai. She wanted to question the monks. Her imagination only came back with one course of action. She moved faster, closing the distance between them.

They hadn't made it far by the time she was above them. She dropped to the ground and sprinted the remaining dozen paces, pulling vast powers into her body as she did.

They sensed her then. They both spun around just as she launched herself at them. They had been traveling side by side, and as they turned, she slammed one palm against each monk's forehead, sending them sprawling onto their backs.

Her momentum carried her past them, and she channeled strength into her legs to absorb the landing. She spun around, surprised to find one monk had maintained enough focus to sign an attack and hold it as she struck. The monk released his power. The attack slashed at her, but she absorbed it with ease. With the extra strength, she darted forward and plowed a fist into the monk as he stumbled to his feet. As he doubled over, she brought her knee to his face. He crumpled to the street.

A flash of steel glinted in the moonlight as the second monk regained his feet. For a terrifying moment, she thought the monk had imbued the dagger with energy. Her hand still hadn't healed from the other night. She stumbled backward and out of the way, only to realize there was no energy attack. The monk used the dagger for its sharp edge alone.

The monk stabbed and swung, his movements untrained. No one had taught him how to fight with a blade.

Bai regained her balance and kicked at the monk. He backed up quickly, more than willing to give up ground to keep the dagger between them.

"How did you find me?" she asked.

He didn't answer. Instead, he signed an attack and launched it at her. She absorbed the energy without breaking stride. Desperate, he signed again, but this attack did no more damage to her than the first.

Bai matched the retreating monk step for step. She worried about the knife and was cautious about becoming overconfident. She wanted the monk to answer her questions, but she saw no hint of fear in his eyes. Only disgust.

And something else.

The monk knew something. Of that, she was certain.

"Why did you attack me?"

The monk snarled at her question. He leaped at her, launching another attack and swinging at her with the dagger.

She absorbed the energy and stepped into his swing, using his own momentum to throw him to the ground. With a quick movement, she broke his wrist, causing him to howl and drop the dagger.

Bai cursed. So far, the fight had been quiet. Screams would bring the overworked city watch.

She knelt over him and slapped him across the face, hard. He glared at her, the only recourse he had left. "Answer my question."

He spat at her. Bloody saliva hit her face, momentarily distracting her. He rolled over and grabbed the dagger with his good hand, swiping at her neck.

Her disorientation only lasted a moment, not long enough for him to strike true. She was awash with power, her limbs moving quickly. She blocked the cut and swung a fist at his face.

Her fist connected and broke his nose. His head snapped to the side and his eyes went dull for a moment.

Bai yanked on his tunic, bringing his face to hers. "How did you know we were here?"

She had jarred something loose in his head. His eyes were unfocused, his words broken and slow. "We summoned you."

The monk collapsed in her arms. His breathing was steady, but she wasn't sure even smelling salts would bring him around soon.

She searched his body, looking for clues. Monks didn't carry much, so she wasn't surprised when she didn't find anything that would lead her on, but she did notice a small tattoo on the underside of his forearm. She frowned as she bent closer to examine the symbol. It looked like a dagger stuck into the ground.

She wanted more light and more time, but the city watch gave her neither. She heard the sounds of men approaching and decided it was wisest to leave the scene. Filling her legs with power, she leaped onto the roofs just as the city guard came around the corner, discovering the unconscious monks. She could safely ignore them for the moment. Like everyone else, they'd never think to check above them.

Bai thought about the monk's last statement. On the surface, it made little sense. How had the monks summoned her? They'd come here at the behest of the woman in the brothel.

Sudden thoughts tumbled through her head. They'd come here at a woman's request.

What was to say that request had been honest?

What if it had all been a trap?

Bai's mind spun with the possibilities.

Then stopped.

Hien.

She still hadn't returned. If the monk had spoken true, it had all been set up.

The monks had captured Hien.

8

———

Every day, Delun imagined leaving the monastery. He stared longingly down the road that led to Two Bridges and the world beyond. He burned with thoughts of vengeance on the organizers of this attack.

Such dreams never took him even a single step beyond the gate, though. Revenge occupied nearly every waking thought, but duty held him in place.

A sense of duty to his brothers, both fallen and alive.

He refused to leave before they burned Taio's body, pushing the final remnants of his soul onto whatever awaited him on the other side of the veil.

Three full days had passed since the attack. Three days of tending to the wounded, of preparing the bodies of the dead, of dreaming of the suffering he would deliver. Whenever his gaze fell on a fallen brother, coals burned in the pit of his stomach, their heat never quenched. But that heat sizzled within a deep void, an everlasting emptiness that soaked up his anger and left him feeling hollow.

The ceremony for the fallen brothers was scheduled for tonight. Tradition demanded obedience, now more than ever. Some small part of the soul, or animating energy, still existed within the dead men. Fire released that fragment onto whatever journey awaited it. The truth was as old as the monasteries themselves.

Delun worked in a small cellar underneath the main hall. The dead crowded the room, making it difficult to shuffle around. He dressed Taio for his final journey, hands and fingers moving without conscious thought. His mind traveled the roads of the past.

Taio had been present for almost all of Delun's most important moments. He had welcomed Delun personally to the monastery over twenty-five years ago. The monastery had just reopened to students, the damage from the Order of the Serpent attack freshly repaired. Taio had been abbot for under a year, and they both felt like they had something to prove.

They had grown together. Delun became a feared warrior while Taio became one of the guiding lights among the abbots of the empire. Taio believed in the strength of the monasteries, but he still believed the monks were servants. His calm voice would be desperately missed in the weeks and months to come.

Delun pondered the circular nature of history. How hard would they have to fight to break the cycle of violence that trapped them? How often would his brothers have to die to prove their worth to this empire? Twice now the abbot of this monastery had been killed in an attack. Would another monk step forward as abbot, knowing the fate that had befallen his two predecessors?

Would they rebuild again, inviting another attack years from now? He couldn't stomach the thought.

This cycle had to stop.

The other monks already whispered about what came

next. Since the attack, decisions had been made by a nearly silent consensus. They cleared the shattered stone and piled it out of the way, ready to become material for new buildings. They gathered wood and built a large platform in the courtyard. Tonight they would douse the pyre in oil. The frames of the buildings the brothers had lived in would light their final journey.

After tonight were only questions. They needed a leader, but so soon after the attack, no one dared broach the subject and disrespect their lost abbot.

Delun wondered if he should volunteer. Unlike Taio, he had no desire for the position. He preferred being out in the world, not constrained by duties inside the walls of a monastery.

He also didn't consider himself a leader. Brothers had looked up to Taio, but even after the attack, Delun hadn't found welcome within these walls. Some glances even seemed accusatory, as though Delun had somehow failed them by allowing the attack to happen.

The glares cut deep, echoed by his own unspoken fears. If he hadn't traveled home and then stayed for the Harvest Festival, would he have stumbled upon the plot and stopped it in time? Reason told him no, but the possibility kept him awake at night.

He finished dressing Taio, certainty settling over him. He would leave in the morning. This monastery was no longer home.

Delun stepped out of the cellar just in time to hear a shout from the walls.

Like most of the monks, Delun ran toward the hole in the wall where the gate had once stood. He felt several monks prepare shields and attacks, suspicion overwhelming hospitality. Since the explosion, they had received no visitors, no support from the town below. The silence of Two Bridges said nearly as much as the attack itself.

But the visitors were not from Two Bridges. Four white-robed figures climbed up the path. Delun felt something break inside of him, a tension he hadn't even been aware of. He and the other monks weren't alone.

Other brothers appeared to echo his sentiment. A few began to cry.

The visiting monks stopped over a dozen paces away from the walls. Delun could see the grief etched on their faces. He knew then that Two Bridges had not been the only target. Sorrow connected them all. The four monks bowed deeply, and then the visitors stepped into the monastery, welcomed with open arms.

The monk leading them spoke. "I'm sorry, brothers." His voice shook with sorrow, his eyes on the verge of tears. "My name is Ping, and we have come to provide whatever aid we can."

The four monks joined the survivors, introducing themselves and diving into the work. Ping approached Delun. At first, Delun wondered why, then realized he was presumably the oldest survivor. The thought hadn't even occurred to him. He hoped Ping didn't assume he was in charge.

The monk bowed deeply to Delun. "I am sorry for your losses. How may we help?"

Delun returned the bow. "Thank you. I'm Delun. It is good to see a friendly face. We will honor our dead tonight. Assistance with the preparations would be appreciated."

At the mention of his name, Delun thought he noticed a slight shift in Ping's demeanor. "You are Delun? The same Delun who brought down the abbot of Kulat?"

Delun grimaced. "I am."

Unlike so many brothers, Ping didn't seem judgmental. He seemed more curious than anything else. "It's a pleasure to meet you. Perhaps, after the ceremony, we may speak again?"

Delun nodded.

The arrival of the other monks changed the attitude of the entire monastery. They didn't bring joy, exactly, but there was a lightness to the monks' actions that hadn't been present before. Delun hadn't realized how deeply the sense of isolation from the rest of the world was affecting them.

They prepared a feast, at least by monastic standards. For the first time in nights, conversation echoed in the halls that survived the attack. Delun didn't hear any laughter, but healing had begun. For today, that would be enough.

As the sun fell, the monks gathered in the courtyard. For a minute, they all shuffled around, and Delun realized they hadn't selected a monk to lead the ceremony. Traditionally, that responsibility was the abbot's.

He stepped forward. He was the eldest, but more than that, he wanted to speak for Taio. He received a few unwelcome glares, but no one objected.

Delun led them through the chants, the ritual that marked the end of a monk's life. As he did, he thought again of his long history with Taio. He glanced back at his master's body, the action causing his breath to catch.

When the last chants of the ritual had faded, Delun spoke. "Taio was my master, but he was also a friend. He taught me honor, and his words guided my path through many challenging times. He was one of the best of us, and we will miss him."

There was more he wanted to say, but he feared dishonoring Taio's memory. Less was more, as Taio himself had often said.

Delun invited the others to come forward and speak, and one by one, the monks did, remembering their fallen brothers.

Every story was a thread, a life woven among so many others. Delun listened to stories of friendship, of rivalry, and of sacrifice. The thread of a monk's life might be cut short, but their effect on the tapestry went on.

When no more brothers stepped forward to speak, Delun called for the flames. Typically, a single brother closest to the deceased lit the flames, but it had been decided that was not appropriate for tonight. The monks all joined, standing in a circle around the pyre, stepping forward as one and lighting the wood in unison. Only the four visitors stood apart.

Delun felt tears trickling silently down his cheeks. He saw the firelight reflected in the tears of the others. They stood in silence, watching their brothers complete their lives of service.

Hours passed before the flames burned low and the monks returned to their normal duties. Some retired to bed, but many had brewed tea and were sitting and speaking quietly in small groups.

Ping approached Delun. All day, Delun had tried to get a sense of the man. The visitors had thrown themselves into the preparations, but Delun suspected there was more to them than they appeared. He hated his cynicism at such a time, but old habits died hard.

"Thank you for the ceremony," Ping began.

"Thank you for your help. You've done more than you perhaps realize."

"If I may ask, what will you all do next?"

Delun looked around the courtyard, taking in the remains of the pyre and the monks scattered about. The monastery had been wounded, grievously, but it wasn't dead. They fought on. "I don't know. I suppose we must choose an abbot and have that abbot confirmed."

Ping looked surprised. "You don't know?"

Delun looked over at him. "Know what?"

Ping's face fell. "Your monastery was not the only one attacked. Many attacks were carried out the night of the Harvest Festival. It will be some time before the abbots can confirm new leaders."

Delun looked away, unable to meet Ping's eyes. He wanted to call the man a liar, but the sorrow and anger in Ping's voice was genuine. Delun clenched his fist, rage finally breaking through the void that had numbed him for so long.

Ping waited while Delun worked through the implications. He couldn't. His mind, already tumbled about by his personal grief, couldn't cope with the idea of losing so many brothers. "What's happening?"

"The monasteries don't have any organized purpose," Ping said. "We are all struggling with our grief in our own ways."

"Why are you here, then?"

"To offer what assistance we can. But also to make you aware that you and the monks of Two Bridges have options available to you. You needn't remain up here, isolated from the world. It would delight many monasteries to have you, and there is strength in numbers now."

Delun nodded, agreeing to the point. "Did you have a particular destination in mind?"

Ping shook his head. "Our own small group comes from several monasteries. But all of us have been brought together by this tragedy."

The two of them stood in silence for a moment, Delun

considering the other monk's offer. Traveling to another monastery might be a wise decision. They wouldn't be caught by surprise again, and it made sense for them to be together.

"May I ask a personal question?"

Delun looked over at Ping, surprised by the monk's forthrightness. He nodded.

"Do you regret your actions in Kulat?"

"I regret having to turn against my brothers. But I still don't believe there was a better choice." He'd asked himself that same question many times in the years since.

"Why not?"

"Because they were harming the innocent. I believe the monasteries can and should lead our empire, but those men were not fit to lead. They massacred citizens who had done them no harm."

"In response to an attack against them."

"And if they had killed only those responsible, I would not have blinked an eye. If we are to have authority, we must use it wisely."

"And what will you do now?"

"I will hunt and kill those responsible for these explosions."

Ping took a deep breath and unrolled the sleeve of his robes, revealing a tattoo on the underside of his forearm. A dagger stuck deep into the ground. "You've seen these?"

Delun nodded.

They called themselves wraiths. A group of monks who had promoted aggressive reforms the past few years. They'd been a concern of Delun's for a while. Many monks who broke their vows had some connection with the group, but Delun had never connected the crimes of an individual monk with the larger group.

Right now, he didn't care.

"You and I agree on what we must do. Come with me to Jihan. We know the Order of the Serpent has been reborn, and that they are based there. You and any brothers who are interested may join us."

A week ago, Delun would have turned down the offer. He fought hard to find a middle path, a place where monks possessed the authority they deserved but controlled their power.

Today, all that mattered was that Ping claimed he knew where to begin the hunt.

Delun would have revenge for Taio, for all his fallen brothers.

He looked around the courtyard, at the grief shared among them all. They needed a leader, someone to look up to and guide them through their grief and into a new purpose.

But he was not that man.

"I cannot speak for the others. I have no authority over them."

Ping nodded, as though he'd suspected that.

"I will join you, though."

9

The last time Lei saw the questioner had been ten years ago. The two hadn't parted on friendly terms back then, and Lei had believed he would never see the man again. The thought wasn't unpleasant.

Few people knew for certain that questioners even existed. Part detective, part assassin, part torturer, questioners solved the problems of the empire that most vexed the lords they served. The average citizen considered them rumors, a tale to frighten children with at night.

If only that were true.

Most citizens didn't survive learning that questioners were real.

The man who stood in the training hall was an excellent example of the profession. He was younger than Lei, although not by much. His features were nondescript, with a face one forgot a moment after looking at it.

The questioner wasn't gifted, but he radiated a dangerous aura. He carried himself with the calm assurance of a man who knew he held the power of life and death in his hands. Even Lei worried about the consequences of killing him.

A glance between Yang and the questioner confirmed that the two of them knew each other.

The questioner's attention was focused solely on Lei. "You are about the last person I expected to find here today."

"I feel the same about you."

Yang stepped in, explaining to the questioner. "I'd invited him a while back to observe a demonstration of my students' abilities. He finally accepted."

The questioner accepted the explanation with equanimity. "Perhaps the fates have a purpose greater than we can imagine. His presence is fortuitous."

The questioner looked around the hall with disdain. Yang understood. "Back to your regular duties, everyone."

He received some good-natured grumbling in reply, but everyone obeyed. Shu lingered for a moment, as though she had something to say, but decided against it.

When they were all alone, the questioner spoke. "I bring grim tidings, I'm afraid." He took a breath. "The most important is news I have just received. The monasteries have been attacked. Dozens, if not hundreds, of monks are dead. More are injured."

Lei frowned at the news, but Yang stumbled, physically rocked. "What happened?" the abbot asked.

"We are still learning the details," the questioner replied, "but the Order of the Serpent snuck barrels of black powder into many monasteries. They all exploded the afternoon of the Harvest Festival."

The earth tilted under Lei's feet. "Did you say the Order of the Serpent?"

"I did."

"How? I thought I destroyed the Order in Jihan."

Those terrible days had transformed his life. He had killed a student and a master, cutting short a plan that would have burned the capital to the ground. Although the fight had cost far too many innocent lives, the toll could have been far worse.

The questioner agreed. "We thought so, too. The original Order was just the two men. But the master left writings that have been discovered, collected, and shared. It has led to a rebirth of the organization. My colleagues and I have been gradually infiltrating them for over a year now, but we didn't know this was coming."

Lei relaxed his fist. Just the mention of the Order's name triggered his anger.

"That isn't the reason I came, though." The questioner looked uncomfortable with the admission. "I just found out this morning and wanted to let you know."

Yang's voice was soft. "There's more?"

"Disturbing news, yes, but not as tragic."

Lei saw Yang steel himself. "And?"

"The princess was attacked, days before the Harvest Festival." Before Yang could ask, the questioner continued. "She is shaken up but unharmed."

Lei's head spun. What was happening to the empire? "Was the attack linked to the Order?"

The questioner shook his head. "A wraith attacked her."

Lei's confusion increased.

Yang explained. "The wraiths are a group of monks who strongly believe that monasteries should be given more power in the empire. They've been a growing problem the last few years, but nothing like this has happened before."

"Monks attacked the princess?" Disbelief coursed through Lei.

The other two men glanced at one another. There was

another piece of information they weren't sharing. The secret brought a smile to their faces, despite the news.

"What?"

Yang seized the opportunity. "The princess is gifted."

Lei knew he'd heard Yang correctly, but he didn't believe. He'd learned too much, too fast, and this, more than anything, sent his head spinning. The implications staggered him.

Dozens of questions raced through his mind. Only one reached his lips. "How long have you known?"

The questioner answered. "About two years. Her power manifested gradually, but there were signs that alerted the emperor. Yang travels to Jihan several times a year to train her."

"She's not the strongest," Yang said, "but her gift is unique. She is skilled, and a very determined learner."

"She defended herself from the monks' attack. But if the wraiths harbored any suspicions, they've been confirmed," the questioner said.

Lei looked around the training hall, as though he could find answers or guidance along its bare walls. Isolated as he was, even he knew the princess would take the throne after the emperor passed away. For the first time in history, a gifted person might sit on the throne.

Would the people even accept her if they knew?

"I came," the questioner continued, turning to Yang, "to ask for your assistance. The emperor requests that you come, joined by your students, to protect the princess from further harm."

Yang bowed in acceptance. "We shall prepare to leave by tomorrow morning."

"Why Yang?" Lei asked. Kulat was a long way from Jihan. Why pass up the hundreds of monks between the two cities?

"Tensions between the government and the monks have been high," the questioner answered. "Knowing whom to trust is difficult. Yang is trusted, and if the wraiths attack, his students are the best equipped to protect the princess."

Of course. He wasn't thinking clearly. Against other monks, Yang's students were by far the best option. Bai would be better, but she had no friends in court.

The questioner turned to Lei. "I had not planned on visiting your village. But I know the emperor would extend his invitation to you as well."

Lei found himself tempted. A crossroads of history approached, and the questioner offered him the opportunity to play a role.

Thoughts of Daiyu overwhelmed all else, though. He didn't know the number of her remaining days. He would let the empire burn if it meant leaving her now. "I'll pass, thanks."

The questioner raised his eyebrow at that, but despite his profession, asked no probing questions.

Lei turned to Yang. "If it is permissible, I would stay here tonight, to see you off tomorrow."

Lei wanted more time with Yang's students. Not only were they uniquely gifted, they possessed impressive strengths. He could learn much from them in the time that remained.

The questioner bowed. "I will allow you two to continue your visit. You will forgive me if I cannot stay."

After the questioner left, the two men stood in silence for a minute. Lei's attention focused on the Order of the Serpent, a plague he thought he'd eradicated decades ago. Their return struck him as ominous.

Yang broke the silence, his voice soft. "I had hoped to have more time, both with them and with you."

"The world rarely provides what we wish for."

Yang gave a bitter laugh. "I've spent the past decade reforming Kulat, opening our doors to all. I suppose I should be grateful we were not attacked with the others, but I fear my work will be for naught if the violence spreads."

"Good work is never wasted," Lei replied. "It echoes throughout time, in ways we cannot imagine."

"I hope you are right, friend." Yang set his shoulders. "I have much to do tonight. But there is one question I have meant to ask you: where have your discoveries taken you?"

Lei affected a nonchalant look. "What do you mean?"

"I've heard the reports from monks traveling near Galan. They often assume the power is coming from the foothills. Most don't know how far away your village is. Your power has grown. I would like to know how much."

Lei debated. Yang's educated guess was correct. But Lei had reached his own conclusions.

Still, the desire to share his discovery burned within him. Perhaps it was just a selfish desire to leave a legacy beyond the disaster that was the Battle of Jihan.

Lei nodded. He'd not trained close to another gifted for years. "This... might hurt."

Yang backed up a few paces, as though that would make a difference.

Lei closed his eyes. He felt the currents of power running through the earth; the energy contained within Kulat, an enormous untapped reservoir.

He dove deep into the energy, opening himself up completely, a practice he'd been developing gradually year after year.

Lei didn't feel the power like he once had. Before, it had filled his limbs and made him feel like his strength was infinite.

Now it felt like sliding into a pool of warm water. The boundary between him and the energy dissolved. All that was left was his will, the ability to shape the energy.

He only allowed himself a moment, both for Yang's sake and for his own. High on the mountain, he had immersed himself for minutes at a time. Every time, though, he felt as though he risked losing himself. His experiences in that state had been confusing. Voices long dead called to him. He dared not remain too long.

When he opened his eyes, Yang was on the ground, arms up to ward against a power that never threatened to harm him. The abbot slowly cracked his eyes open. He didn't have words.

Lei helped him to his feet.

A commotion sounded at the door. The door crashed open. Yang's students stood there, prepared for a fight. They relaxed slowly when they saw no enemies. Their faces gave way to awe.

Yang finally found words. "I never would have guessed."

Lei nodded. What more was there for him to say?

Yang's eyes narrowed. "Will you pass this knowledge on?"

Lei shook his head. "I'd not really planned on even letting other monks know."

"I see."

Lei saw that Yang had more questions, but he also had more pressing concerns. "We must talk more, soon. Perhaps later tonight. But you swear that skill will remain yours alone?"

Lei nodded. "Don't worry, Yang. This technique will die with me."

10

Bai crouched on a rooftop, a strong sense of deja vu haunting her observations.

She'd been on this same roof just a week before.

The brothel squatted across the street from her, several windows open to cool the fiery passions burning within. Bai kept her eye on one window in particular, opened wide enough for a nimble intruder to pass through. A woman wandered back and forth just inside.

Bai waited until the woman left the room, then leaped across the gap, passing through the open window with room to spare. She landed and rolled, coming to her feet alert for danger.

The sun had set not an hour past, and the brothel hadn't reached peak capacity yet. Still, her footsteps were lost in the sounds of men grunting and women moaning.

Bai snuck to the door of the room and slid it open wide enough to peek through. The way to her target's room was clear.

Bai stepped out into the hallway and hurried to the other room. The lights were off and no sound came from within. She opened the door and melted into the shadows, awaiting the woman.

Several assumptions supported her task this evening. If the whole trip to Windown had been a setup, the woman they'd escorted out of town hadn't requested help. That led Bai to guess the woman would return to town.

Her first assumption seemed correct. Bai spotted the woman inside the brothel as soon as she bothered to look. The woman chatted amiably with the other women inside, and she carried no limps or bruises that indicated she'd experienced recent violence. Bai's observations supported her suspicions.

Bai's second assumption was that Hien lived. Bai's fight had been against monks, which implied Hien had only been the gate through which they hoped to ambush Bai. Hien only served their ends if she continued breathing.

The assumption provided Bai slim comfort.

The woman in the brothel would know more.

Bai settled in to wait, but didn't have to for long. She soon heard a pair of footsteps outside the walls. The door slid open, and the woman led a man into the room. Distracted as they were by each other, neither noticed Bai deep in the darkness.

Bai had no interest in watching the woman at work. She stepped out of the shadows and delivered a blow to the back of the man's head that knocked him immediately unconscious.

The woman barely flinched. Bai hadn't been this close to her before, but now the proximity made her hair stood on end. Not from danger, but from a sense of wrongness.

The woman didn't care one bit a gifted stranger had ambushed her in her own room. From her lack of reaction, she'd expected it. Her words confirmed as much. "I didn't think you'd come so soon. There was no need for that," she said as she gestured toward the man on the ground.

"What did you do with Hien?" Bai struggled to keep her voice calm.

The woman waved her hand dismissively. "No need for dramatics. She's being held in some shed outside of town." The woman walked over to a small desk and returned with a piece of paper. She held it out to Bai as though begrudgingly giving money to a street urchin. "Directions."

Bai stood, open-mouthed, staring at the woman. She opened the paper and held it up to the reflected moonlight coming in through the window. Detailed directions were indeed written on the paper. The woman had even expected this encounter.

The gall of it agitated her.

Bai imagined hitting this woman, making her suffer for her acts. But when she looked into the woman's eyes she saw only emptiness. Bai wasn't sure she even had the ability to reach whatever remained of this woman.

One fact was clear, though: if the woman had been waiting for her, the monks would be, too.

The fact didn't bother her. She looked forward to exacting vengeance.

"Could you leave, please? I need to call someone to clean this up." Bai bristled at the lack of care in the woman's voice.

She brought a sliver of power into her fist and drove it into the woman's stomach, sending her crashing to the ground, gasping for breath.

It had been pointless.

But it felt good.

THE SHED WAS A TRAP. The woman in the brothel hadn't

even pretended otherwise. The prepared paper was evidence enough of that.

The directions took her well off the main road that connected Jihan and Windown. The ground here was flat and covered in prairie grasses, browning in the dry autumn weather. Off in the distance a herd of cows contentedly chewed through the tall grass.

She figured life as a cow must be unbearably dull. All they did was stand around all day, chewing. Bai knew a few people who would have considered that a dream, but to her, such inactivity was a nightmare. She wished the herd well as she passed.

She spotted the shed easily enough. It matched the description on the paper exactly.

Bai didn't bother to hide in the tall grass. Out here in the open prairies, even a young monk could sense Bai's strength. Weak as it felt to most monks, without other people to hide it, she stood out.

She stopped, though, and considered the ambush. They knew who she was and probably had some idea of her gifts. One group had tried attacking her directly. She didn't think these monks would make the same mistake twice. Even monks eventually learned.

If she was in charge of the ambush, only one solution made sense to her.

Archers.

Bai chewed on her lower lip. A typical monk would cast a shield to protect themselves from projectiles. She had no such skill.

Where would the archers be? If they were ambitious, the monks might have stationed archers out in the tall grass, waiting day and night for her. Bai accepted the possibility, but found it unlikely. Such waiting was a lot to ask from hired help. She'd remain wary of other ambushes, but her instincts told her archers would hide within the shed.

They would fire from inside, from the shadows.

Bai continued on toward the shack, eyes darting left and right, watching for any movement that might be an archer or other warrior hiding in the grass.

She also walked a few feet off the beaten path, bearing the slight difficulty of walking through higher grass in exchange for avoiding any snares left upon the packed dirt.

When she was several hundred feet away from the shed, the door opened. Though the man didn't wear the robes of a monk, Bai could sense a little of his strength. He was gifted, even if he didn't wear the symbol of his status.

He pushed Hien out in front of him. Bai's friend's wrists were tied behind her. She'd been beaten, and beaten well. Bruises covered her bloody face, and from the looks of it, the woman could barely stand on her own. Her left leg kept giving out on her, forcing the monk to hold her upright.

Bai fought the urge to sprint toward Hien. More than likely, that was exactly what they wanted.

Bai stopped well over a hundred paces from the building. She still hadn't seen movement in the grass, but she summoned power all the same.

If her guess was right, they would want her to approach closer so the archers had an easy shot. How would they convince her to do so?

The monk pulled hard on Hien's hair, exposing her neck. Even though the move had to have hurt, Hien didn't make a sound. A knife appeared in his hand. "Surrender, or your friend dies."

Bai held up her hands.

"Come closer."

Subtle. Bai almost laughed. Did the monk believe he

was fooling anyone? She felt like she was engaging in a battle of wits with a toddler.

Still, she was too far away to do anything, and once she got closer, it would spring the trap.

Before she could act, chaos erupted, as it often did with Hien in the mix.

The warrior's hands suddenly came free, sunlight glinting off steel in her hand. Before the monk holding her hair could react, she drove the blade into the side of his neck.

Distracted by the action, Bai's barely noticed the sudden movement from within the shed.

Bai slid to the side, power filling her legs as she ducked and weaved toward the building. Two arrows hissed wide past her.

She felt a sudden swelling of power. A moment later the door blasted off the shed, slamming into Hien and knocking her to the ground.

Another monk stood tall inside the shattered doorway.

She could feel his strength.

Nothing else moved outside the building. All her enemies remained in the shed. She knew she faced at least two archers and one monk.

The archers were her true threat. Bai angled toward the shed, moving away from the two open windows in the front. Another pair of arrows searched for her, but her speed and distance made her a difficult target.

The monk stood tall spin the doorway, summoning a powerful attack. Bai suspected he was trying for the fifth two-handed sign. An impressive accomplishment. No doubt he assumed his power would be the one that finally overwhelmed her gift.

But even the fifth sign was utterly useless against her.

The blast of energy struck her twenty paces from the door.

The world slowed as her body absorbed the immense energy.

She saw the arrow leap from the shadows behind the window, then tilted her head as it whizzed past her ear.

Her punch, powered by the monk's own energy, collapsed his rib cage. He died with his eyes wide with shock.

Then she was in the house. The two archers weren't gifted like the monks, but their aim was true even in the confined spaces of the house.

Bai twisted to avoid one arrow, but the other grazed her torso.

Both archers dropped their bows and drew daggers.

But Bai still had power to spare. She attacked before they could even set their feet against her. She showed them no mercy, ending the battle in a moment.

Bai paused to look around. Her heart pounded in her chest and she battled tunnel vision. In such a state she could easily overlook an important detail.

She saw blood in the corner, but otherwise the house was barren. This had only served as a temporary hideout.

Bai gazed cautiously out the window, looking for assailants she might have missed. The grasses were quiet.

When she was satisfied it was safe, she ran to Hien. Up close, Hien's injuries were worse than Bai had thought. No doubt, the blood in the corner had all belonged to her.

And Hien had still surprised them.

Hien gave Bai a weak smile. "They never even searched me."

Bai shook her head. "A shame none of them lived to learn from the experience."

"A real shame."

Hien wasn't unconscious, but her awareness drifted in and out. Bai didn't think any of the warrior's wounds were fatal, but she needed care. She took a moment to search the bodies for clues that might lead her on, but the monks had carried nothing. She saw the tattoo on one monk that indicated he was a wraith, but that was a slim surprise.

For now, her investigation could wait.

It was time to take Hien home.

11

———

The monks left the monastery at Two Bridges two days after the pyre was lit.

Several would have left sooner, but they all had responsibilities that could not be shirked. Food needed to be prepared. Possessions needed to be packed. And although the damage to the monastery couldn't be repaired in a day, they all felt an unspoken desire to clear the rubble and leave their home presentable for those who came after.

The whole monastery left at sun's first light. Ping's invitation had found fertile ground among the grieving monks. Delun guessed that some traveled for vengeance, but most traveled to Jihan simply to be with other monks, to build a new community.

They walked the road in their traveling clothes. As a large group, they probably fooled no one, but Ping insisted the choice of clothing would keep them safer.

Delun spent most of his traveling time with Ping. The young monk was the head of their small expedition, and he took a deep interest in Delun.

In many ways the two men were opposites of one another. Delun had twice as many years on him as Ping, and the difference in their experiences separated them. Ping angered quickly. The young man brimmed with enthusiasm for the change he sought to make in the world. Barely a mile would pass in silence before he'd launch into another long-winded speech about the rights of monks and the fight ahead.

Delun bore the monologues with patience. The monk's earnest manner prevented Delun's cynicism from rising much. He considered the young man a fool, but a well-intentioned one.

The others latched onto Ping's enthusiasm, though. Ping's leadership was natural, an extension of his youthful exuberance and unwavering determination. Ping drew followers like spilled honey drew ants.

Delun saw no hypocrisy in the young man. Ping trained daily, waking early in the morning to hone his considerable skills. He asked nothing of others that he didn't expect from himself.

Despite their differences of opinion, Delun slowly reached the conclusion that young Ping might be a monk worth following.

They debated frequently on the road. Both monks wished to see the monasteries imbued with more authority than they currently possessed. Delun's aims were more modest. He believed the monks should have a seat on the emperor's ruling council, the small body of lawmakers that ran the empire day to day. Ping wanted to see monks exempt from every law of the land and dreamed of a day a gifted warrior sat on the throne of the emperor.

By the time they reached Jihan, Delun's opinions of the

wraiths had changed. He remained concerned the monks demanded too much, but Ping impressed him.

Ping had another quality in his favor, one that colored the rest of Delun's perceptions.

He supported Delun's self-proclaimed quest to root out and destroy the Order of the Serpent. Several times a day, Ping reassured him that once they reached Jihan, their hunt for the criminals could begin.

A day outside of the city, the fellowship split into several smaller groups. Ping worried about passing through the gate in large numbers, alerting the guards to the flood of monks settling in Jihan.

Ping asked Delun to join him, to wait until the other groups had all passed the gates and made their way to the monastery or to various safehouses. Delun agreed. They passed the extra time in yet more conversation. Ping had no shortage of questions and thoughts to discuss. Delun rarely met young warriors who thought so deeply about so much. He admired the trait, but worried that someday Ping might think himself into an early death.

Eventually they received word that all the monks had safely entered Jihan. Ping and Delun resumed their journey and passed through the massive gates of the city without a problem. Delun turned to walk toward the monastery, but Ping stopped him with a gentle hand on his shoulder.

"My master has set up his command in another part of Jihan. The monastery is watched too closely."

A pang of regret seized Delun, but he shoved it aside. Ping said Jihan's monastery had also been attacked in the Harvest Festival explosions, and Delun had several friends within he wanted to check on.

But there would be time. As soon as the walls of Jihan

had come into view, almost all of Delun's thoughts had turned to vengeance.

Ping led him to a rather nondescript house, one of many unremarkable homes in a section of the city Delun had never visited before. Delun paid careful attention to their route, but wasn't certain he could find the place again. As they approached the door, Delun sensed two monks inside.

Ping entered without knocking. Delun followed, passing a monk standing guard inside the door. The guard gave him a glare meant to be intimidating, but it slid off Delun. Ping led Delun through the first room in the house to one in the back, where another monk kneeled at a desk shuffling through piles of papers.

Delun didn't recognize the monk, and nothing about his outward appearance gave Delun a sense of danger. He'd rarely met someone so perfectly nondescript. The man was gifted, there was no doubt of that, but not nearly so strong that Delun feared for his safety.

Ping bowed. "Master Chao, this is Delun."

Delun's name served as introduction enough. Chao smiled, but his gaze was calculating. "It is a pleasure to meet you at last, Delun. Stories of your deeds have spread far across the empire."

Some aspect of the man's demeanor made Delun's hairs stand on end. His appearance might not be fearsome, but Delun recognized a dangerous man all the same. Delun bowed, choosing to remain silent.

Ping continued, "Delun survived the attack on the monastery above Two Bridges. After speaking with him I offered him an opportunity to join us."

Delun noticed the sharp eyes behind Chao's relaxed face. "I see." He paused, considering. "Ping, you may leave us. Thank you for bringing Delun."

Ping looked surprised, but bowed and left without question. Chao's authority wasn't questioned here. Delun realized he wasn't just standing in front of a local authority for the wraiths. Chao led the movement. For years Delun had searched for this man, and now Ping had brought them together.

The two men each took the measure of the other. Chao spoke first. "Given your history, it seems unlikely that you would join us. You have punished several of our sworn brothers."

"Our goals aren't as far apart as our methods. They broke their vows to serve the empire."

Chao didn't appear offended at the challenge. "You believe your methods are effective? I know you are no fool. I know your past. You've traveled all over the empire for, what, fifteen years now? Twenty? You produce results. But are you any closer to your goal than you were when you started?"

Delun shook his head, unable to speak, not wanting to show Chao how deeply the words cut at him.

"So what is *your* grand plan, Delun? It is easy to criticize another, but if you truly believe what you have been doing matters, explain how. What is this deep strategy that will free our brothers from the chains that envelop them?"

"My way doesn't kill innocents." Half a dozen instances of wraiths going too far surfaced in Delun's memories.

"A noble sentiment. One I agree with, though you may find that difficult to believe. Those you've punished deserved their fate. But again, I ask, specifically, what would you do to give monks the authority we both believe they deserve?"

Delun had no answer. He'd thought on it for years, but had never created a realistic answer. It was another reason he preferred taking orders. Such problems were beyond him.

"I respect you, Delun. You've done more than most to protect the monasteries. Certainly more than most understand. But you haven't gone far enough. For all your efforts, you have not given us freedom, and our freedom is all that matters."

Delun, unused to being berated, turned the question on his host. "What do you propose, then? Shall we kill all our enemies until the empire lays at our feet in tatters?"

Chao smiled, as though that was the exact question he had been waiting for.

"Did you know that Guanyu approached me when he first started planning his little takeover of Kulat?"

Delun frowned, both at the fact and the sudden change of the conversation's direction. In the brief time he'd known Guanyu, the rebel abbot had never mentioned Chao's name. Delun still didn't know who Chao was. The wraith wasn't an abbot, but that was as much as Delun knew.

It didn't surprise Delun that Guanyu reached out for support. Even the rebellious abbot hadn't been so proud that he believed he could have conquered the empire by himself. But why Chao?

Chao continued, visibly enjoying the opportunity to relate a secret history. "I didn't join with Guanyu for one simple reason, the same reason so many coups fail: force is a temporary solution. Lasting change happens in the hearts of people, and hearts are rarely changed through coercion."

Delun's eyes shot up. This was the last thing he had expected to hear from the leader of the wraiths.

Chao rolled up his sleeve, revealing the all-too-familiar tattoo. "Do you know why our symbol is a blade embedded in the ground?"

Delun shook his head.

"It represents two key beliefs. The first is that the monks serve as a sword to bring justice and peace to the land. But it is vital that this sword springs from the ground. Our roots must be deep, and we must work with the land to rule."

Delun raced through the possibilities. "I didn't expect the wraiths to be focused on cooperation. How will that bring us the authority we seek?"

He couldn't imagine a world in which Chao's vision came true, but the man's certainty shook him. Chao's stated ideal stood almost directly opposed to the current reality. In any other man, Delun would have expected madness. But Chao's eyes were clear and piercing.

"I cannot tell you now," Chao said. "You must forgive me, but until you earn my trust, my faith in you is incomplete. For now, suffice it to say that the empire is rotten at its very core. Soon enough, everyone will know, and they will look to us for leadership. You won't doubt my word on that day."

Delun didn't know what to think. Part of him was beginning to believe, though. Chao's claims struck him more as the calculated gamble of a master general than the ravings of a madman.

Delun's willingness to believe frightened him.

He needed to understand.

Chao changed the direction of the conversation again. He pushed a small pile of papers over to Delun. "If you want to know more, start here. This is all we know about the Order of the Serpent. We never imagined they had the resources or organization to pull off the attacks. But we are certain they are based here. This is all the information we've gathered. It's slim, but it will get you started."

Chao motioned at the tattoo on his arm. "Take down the

Order of the Serpent, and if you wish, you may join our cause."

Finally. The wraiths intrigued him, but they mattered little compared to the opportunity to hunt the Serpent. Now he could track down those responsible for murdering his brothers. He didn't hesitate. It didn't matter if this tied him more closely to the wraiths. He grabbed the papers.

"I'll begin today."

12

————

Morning dawned on Kulat, the skies overcast and threatening a late-season rain. For all that, though, Yang's students sounded excited to have a mission handed down straight from the emperor.

Lei understood. He too had once been young and eager to tackle the problems in front of him. His primary problem as a young man had been finding money for drink, but still, he understood.

Shu rounded up all the students before Yang arrived in the courtyard. Lei watched her as she did. The woman wasn't an instinctive leader. The others looked to her because of her age, but their respect didn't seem to go much deeper. Lei considered mentioning his observation to Yang but held his tongue. No doubt the abbot had already noticed the same.

When Yang arrived, he inspected them briefly, then turned to Lei. "What do you think?"

"They're eager."

"That they are. You'll join us on the way out?"

"I'll leave you at the intersection."

Yang looked tired but excited. The mission given by the questioner presented his students and his cause an incredible opportunity. But leaving the monastery required no small amount of preparation, especially for Yang. Abbots didn't have the freedom to pack up and wander around the empire. The monastery still needed guidance in his absence.

For the moment, though, excitement overwhelmed whatever exhaustion Yang suffered from. With a gesture, the monks walked toward the gate.

Lei took up a position near the rear of the loose column. The students would walk out of Kulat, then take a horse and cart the rest of the way. The journey to Jihan was a long one.

Lei noted the manner in which Yang's students interacted with the citizens of Kulat. The journey out of the city was much slower than he expected. The monks stopped frequently to speak with a shopkeeper or answer a question from a child. Yang never hurried a disruption. He answered Lei's impatient look with a smile. "This is our true work. Protecting the princess is vital to the empire, but I doubt the difference of an hour or two will matter much. Every connection we create or strengthen today brings us that much closer to peaceful coexistence."

Lei agreed. He had spent little time in Kulat, but Yang's words rang true. His philosophy worked. Lei knew he was seeing the result of a decade of dedicated effort, but Kulat gave him hope where none had existed before.

Monks and citizens, living and working side by side.

Lei hadn't thought he would see the day.

The procession worked its way down the main thoroughfare of Kulat, still a solid half mile away from the gate.

A flash of fabric above them was the only warning Lei

had. On distant rooftops to each side of the street, archers appeared, arrows already nocked. Lei's instincts kicked in, a shield covering him in an instant.

He shouted, but too late.

Arrows split the air. Some found flesh while others skipped off the stone of the road. Two slammed against Lei's shield and broke.

"To me!" Yang cried.

Lei advanced, his eyes roving back and forth as citizens and students alike scrambled for safety. The students ran toward Yang. The citizens fled to side streets and houses.

Certain that he wouldn't hurt anyone, Lei dropped his first shield and cast another, this one almost as wide as the street itself. It surrounded all the students, even the ones unmoving on the ground.

A dozen arrows hit the shield before the archers realized what happened.

Lei figured he could ignore them for a moment. His shield was cast and he could hold it for some time. The immediate danger had passed.

Yang and Shu both shouted orders, herding the dazed students closer together. Four lay on the ground. Lei couldn't sense anything from them.

Yang had an arrow sticking out of his arm, but he barely seemed to notice. He looked at Lei. "Thank you."

Lei just nodded, allowing Yang to continue his work gathering the students. Within a moment they were all huddled together. Lei considered casting a smaller shield but decided against it. They were safe enough.

His attention turned toward the rooftops. He'd expected to find them empty.

They were anything but.

A dozen men stood calmly about a block away on the roofs, bows held loosely, arrows nocked and ready for use.

What were they waiting for?

They had set their ambush. Wise men would have left as the monks gathered.

So why hadn't they?

The archers looked expectant. Were they waiting for his shield to drop?

Lei's thoughts raced. That made little sense. His shield was invisible to them. The only way to test it would be to fire arrows at it. No one did. They weren't waiting for his shield.

He looked around. Something tickled the edges of his attention, but he couldn't bring the detail to his conscious mind.

Then his eyes settled on a cart ten paces ahead of the huddled monks. Its owners had abandoned it when the attack began.

And it was filled with barrels.

Lei swore.

He took a quick step into the center of the huddled monks and cast another, smaller, shield around them. He kept his first, larger shield up, too.

That much powder would destroy the buildings in the immediate vicinity. Anyone inside was as good as dead. That was why the archers had kept their distance.

But holding two shields required incredible strength and focus. Lei gritted his teeth as his will focused his power.

Even inside the second shield the force of the explosion threw unsuspecting monks to the ground.

Lei had caught the barrels between his two shields. He protected the living students and the buildings outside his larger shield.

Lei barely kept his balance as the ground trembled

underfoot. The force of the blast slammed against his shields with an almost living rage. Lei groaned as his shields threatened to buckle. He hadn't been prepared to channel this much power.

The air beyond the smaller shield filled with fire. For a moment, it blotted out the sun. An inferno surrounded Lei and the students, burning against the invisible wall Lei held.

Smoke quickly replaced flame, and Lei released his outer shield. The smoke and dust began to clear, revealing the incredible damage the blast, focused by Lei's shields, had done.

The road beyond Lei's small shield was destroyed, a circular moat carved into the stone all around them. It ended in a sharp cutoff where Lei's larger shield had held.

It destroyed beyond recognition the bodies of the four who had fallen. Lei glimpsed shattered remains and looked away.

Lei still held on to the second shield. It was all that protected them from the dangers beyond. A few arrows struck the invisible wall, but after the inferno, he barely noticed. After a minute the arrows stopped falling, the archers realizing monks still lived and were protected.

A high-pitched wail escaped from one of Yang's students. The horror of the past few minutes finally dawned on her. Her friends were lost.

Lei looked up at the rooftops. Now the archers were gone, their horrible ambush complete.

LEI SAT on a bench at the monastery. For all his strength, he had no skill in healing. He'd bandaged a few wounds and helped how he could. Blood from Yang's students stained his clothes. Yet his efforts felt pathetic. Outside of a fight, what good was he?

Evening had fallen when Yang stumbled out and collapsed on the bench. If he'd been exhausted before, he now looked like a walking corpse. He was dead on his feet, but Lei didn't doubt the abbot still had work to be done.

"How bad?" Lei asked.

"Five dead. One in no condition to travel."

Lei did the math. "Six are ready?"

Yang nodded. "I will send them in the morning. The princess still needs protection."

"They know?"

Yang nodded again, too tired to speak.

"I will escort them to the intersection." Lei knew his offer wasn't much, but it was still all he was willing to give.

Yang stared at his palms, as though they had answers for him. "How can you have so much power, see so much, and still not act?"

They'd spoken of this before. Yang already knew Lei's answer. He just didn't believe it held even after the ambush.

Lei had unleashed his power in Jihan over thirty years ago. Thousands of lives were saved that night, but dozens, if not hundreds, were lost. To unveil his full ability now risked far more. But no rationale would ease Yang's anger. Lei's quick reactions and incredible strength had saved all who still breathed, but Yang only thought of those who were gone. Lei couldn't fault the man for that.

Yang took a deep, steadying breath. "I will remain here with those who are injured. I must heal the wounds of my students and of my city. Shu will lead the students to protect the princess."

Lei thought of her trying to gather the students that

morning. Protecting the princess seemed a responsibility beyond her. "You trust her?"

"I must. There is no one else." He gave Lei a pointed glance. "That is unfair of me. She struggles to act as a leader should, but she will not fail."

A long silence stretched between the old acquaintances. Lei hesitated, unsure about bringing up the topic that had troubled him since the attack.

But the abbot had to know. "Yang, few people knew we were leaving. You only decided last night."

Lei left the rest unspoken. Besides the questioner, every person who had known of the departure was within the monastery. More than likely, the information for the ambush had come from someone close to Yang.

"The same problem troubles me."

There was little else to say. This wasn't Lei's fight, and Yang knew the risks. He'd taken many others over the years. Anything Lei might add was meaningless. Yang would seek whoever had betrayed them. Lei almost felt sorry for them. Yang's ideas were ahead of his time, but he knew well the use of violence.

Still, Lei worried for the abbot. "Be careful."

"I will." Yang stood up, the effort appearing to take much of his remaining strength. He started walking away, calling softly over his shoulder as he did. "You can't hide in exile forever, Lei. Soon you will have to choose."

13

———

Hien walked steadier than before, but her injuries still bothered her. She tried to hide her pain and discomfort, but Bai's eyes were sharp. They missed little, and Bai worried for her friend.

The journey back to the village was not a short one. Galan sat on the opposite edge of the empire from Windown and Jihan. Even though the two women made good time, the journey still took longer than either of them wished. Hien rested in the back of a cart most days. The inactivity made her irritable, but her long experience taught her that rest was vital. She bore the forced relaxation as well as she could.

Bai feared Hien's injuries were worse than they appeared. They'd determined Hien's captors had cracked several of her ribs, left her bruised from head to toe, and possibly caused damage to her head when they captured her.

Hien's tale of the ambush was brutal. The monks had been expecting her. They hid well and barely restrained their attacks. Hien described herself as a leaf blown about by competing tornados.

Bai was just grateful Hien lived. She didn't care to contemplate the loss of her friend.

Hien's injuries forced her to consider her own decisions.

For the past few years she had wandered throughout the empire. Hien summoned her occasionally to help with a task, but most of Bai's life was lived on the road. She sought monks who terrorized communities and brought them to justice.

Her wanderings only brought her into conflict with one or two monks a year, though. The empire was vast, and she was only one person. Her odds of running into any specific behavior were slim. She also believed that word of her deeds was spreading. The monks in Windown represented an extreme, but she'd been tracked down twice before.

Her decision to wander the empire came from her own experiences growing up. Monks had held Galan in the grip of fear before the Massacre of Kulat had brought the monastery crashing to the ground. Continuing that work had seemed a natural choice.

The path had also been easy. What good were her gifts if she didn't fight monks?

Hien made her doubt.

The woman had been Bai's closest ally for ten years. While Bai enjoyed being at her physical peak, the years relentlessly stripped away Hien's strengths one at a time. The warrior would be dangerous for many years to come, Bai knew that. But the signs were already clear for anyone to see. A younger Hien would have healed from these injuries much more quickly. She was getting too old for this work, but what else did the warrior have left?

Hien had a home in Lei's village, but she spent little time

there. She'd never found a purpose that included time at home. And it almost cost her everything.

Bai loved Hien, but she didn't want to be fighting in her fifties.

She yearned for something more.

Hunting monks had its place, but it made little difference. Citizens appreciated her efforts, but the empire still crumbled beneath her feet.

Perhaps she should travel to Kulat and visit Yang. Hien's hope for her future wasn't without merit. If others like her trained there, as the rumors suggested, the possibilities were tantalizing.

The idea didn't thrill her, though. Bai detested taking orders from anyone. She had spent her entire youth under the thumb of wealthy clients who demanded much but rewarded little. Though she respected Yang, the very thought of monastic life chafed at her own vision of her future.

The tops of the mountains of their home range came into view. Bai shook her head to clear the thoughts away. Someday she would solve her life. Today, she was home.

THEY CAUSED a commotion when they entered the village, as Bai expected they would. Hien was a local hero, and no small number of women in the village were here because Hien had brought them to start a new life.

Together, they carried Hien home. Bai breathed easier knowing her friend would receive more care and attention here than she would ever want.

When the commotion died down, Bai stood alone on the path that ran through the village. She was about to return to her own small room when she felt his presence outside his house. Every time she visited, she felt his power reach deeper. Being near him was like looking down a bottomless well.

"Trouble?" Lei asked.

Bai turned. Lei was the closest she had to a master. He had started her down this path, had shown her just how much she was capable of. "More than usual."

He gestured toward his house. "Come on in. Daiyu is preparing supper."

Bai never turned down Daiyu's meals. Lei's wife cooked better than anyone Bai had ever met, and even her simple meals tasted like feasts. After days and days of basic food on the road, the offer made her mouth water.

Inside, Bai sipped from a cup of wine while she related recent events. Lei listened attentively, leaning forward and only asking a few questions.

When she finished, a long silence settled over the table. Lei stared off in the distance. Something more was at play here.

"What's wrong?" Bai asked.

"Too many coincidences," Lei answered. He told his own story of visiting Kulat. His revelations rocked her not once, but twice. First to learn she wasn't alone, then to hear of the ambush they had suffered.

"If you hadn't been there..."

Lei nodded. "It bothers me, too. The more I think about the ambush, the more I think my presence was the only piece they didn't anticipate. Yang could have cast a shield, or Wu, perhaps, but neither of them are gifted with much strength. I think the barrels of black powder would have overwhelmed them. We might have lost all of them."

"Who could have been behind it?"

"That part bothers me, too. They had to possess

information from inside the monastery. It's been well over a week, and I think I've suspected everyone at some point. Perhaps the whole mission was a setup by the questioner. Maybe one of Yang's students betrayed him. But I can never get all the facts to fit together, and there's no solid evidence implicating anyone."

Bai raced to assumptions of her own, but she held onto them. No doubt Lei had already tested every possibility.

The larger pattern worried her, too. An attack on the princess, the explosions at the monasteries, and the ambushes of both Yang's students and her? Try as she might, Bai couldn't draw any line between the events. But she shared Lei's apprehensions. Too much was happening for it to be mere coincidence.

Daiyu interrupted Bai's gloomy thoughts. The matriarch of the village brought out an oversized bowl of noodles that found its way in front of Bai. The steaming broth was filled with meat and vegetables, all of it no doubt from the community gardens.

Bai bowed to Daiyu in appreciation.

Daiyu smiled. "I imagine you haven't been eating well, as usual."

Bai heard the reproach in Daiyu's voice. "I'm sorry, Mother."

Lei chuckled at that.

Daiyu disappeared for another moment, then came out of the kitchen again carrying two more bowls for her and Lei.

Bai noticed Daiyu's movement then, the slow and cautious steps that were not the woman she remembered. She hadn't been here in over a year, but she knew something was wrong. "Daiyu?"

She gave Bai a weak smile and turned to Lei. He gave a small shake of his head.

Daiyu sat down with her bowl. "I'm dying."

Bai's stomach knotted. When they had first met, the two of them hadn't seen eye to eye. But for years Bai had counted Daiyu as one of her closest friends.

And if not for Hien's injury forcing her return, Bai might never have known of Daiyu's illness. Shame flushed her cheeks.

She almost stood up to run around the table and embrace the woman, but Daiyu pointed her chopsticks at Bai's bowl. "Eat. There's no point in worrying about what can't be changed."

Bai sat frozen, torn between the earnest desire to embrace her friend and Daiyu's request.

It was so like Daiyu to refuse comfort. Lei never could have married anyone else. The woman had enough steel in her to gird the hearts of an entire army. Bai surrendered to Daiyu's command.

The noodles were almost good enough to wash away Bai's despair.

As they ate, Daiyu told Bai of her disease. Her voice rarely wavered, and only once did she pause to compose herself.

Bai's heart went out to Daiyu. Death came for them all, of course. But Bai had the luxury of being a warrior. She suspected that when death came for her, it would be sudden, one final surprise to cap off her tumultuous life.

To see it coming, though, to know every day was another step towards the end, that took a courage Bai didn't know if she possessed.

Her respect for Daiyu had never been greater.

Bai offered to help in any way she could. The gesture felt hollow even though the words were heartfelt.

She didn't expect Daiyu to pounce on the offer.

"You should take Lei and go to Jihan."

Bai glanced at Lei. His jaw was set. Her sense of danger lit like a signal fire. She had unwittingly stepped into the middle of an ongoing argument. No one with an ounce of wisdom desired to be stuck between two people of immense will.

He put his chopsticks down and took a deep breath. "I will not leave you, Daiyu. That is final."

Bai imagined the air between the two twisting with tension. Lei was the strongest warrior Bai had ever met. Perhaps he was the strongest history had ever seen. But Daiyu's will matched his own.

Daiyu sighed, indicating her acceptance of Lei's wishes. Knowing Daiyu, though, Bai suspected the acceptance was more a strategic retreat than a surrender.

Lei turned his attention to Bai. "Although I know Daiyu wishes me to move on with life, her idea isn't without merit. If there is a larger pattern to the events unfolding, the center of that pattern lies in Jihan. Your presence there could tip the scales of whatever occurs. You could meet with Yang's students. He gave me directions to do so, in case I changed my mind."

The decision wasn't a hard one. She would need to say a difficult farewell to Daiyu, but little else held her here. Even if she remained for her friend, there was nothing she could do to influence the outcome. The chance to meet others like her was a temptation she couldn't ignore.

Someday she would find a way to settle into a new life.

But not today.

14

———

Delun began his investigation into the Order of the Serpent inside the city's taverns. What the method lacked in originality, it made up for in effectiveness. Someday men would learn that alcohol and secrets didn't mix. Until that day, Delun planned on visiting plenty of drinking holes. He sipped at his beer as more men came through the door wearing the uniforms of the city watch.

This was his third tavern in six nights. So far, Chao's information hadn't yielded results. Patience had never been so difficult or so necessary.

It hadn't taken long to locate the establishment, one of a half dozen found within Chao's papers. These were places where sympathizers gathered. In the previous locations, Delun had found plenty of citizens upset with monks, but he had observed nothing more suspicious than drunk and bitter men.

This tavern gave a different impression. Delun's eyes wandered over the crowd. Almost every patron was a young man, full of the energy that comes from being drunk with companions who were closer than blood.

Delun ignored a slight pang of envy. Alcohol was not permitted for most monks. Despite also being part of an order of warriors, Delun would never know the camaraderie that formed from intoxication with a fellow brother. The friendships formed through training and duty were only strengthened over a strong tankard of ale.

At least, that was what he believed.

Sitting along a wall, Delun felt old. It was more than his years, though. There were a few commanders in the group tonight, men nearly his age. It was the exhaustion deep in his bones. He sat surrounded by youthful energy, but he didn't feed off of it.

He finished his beer more quickly than he intended. Many years ago, it had taken him months to acquire the taste for beer, but his willingness to drink was one of the small details that made him uniquely suited for the task at hand.

The details mattered. The art of investigation was the art of relationship. If he didn't drink, or if he asked too many questions, suspicions surfaced. It was why so many monks failed utterly in their attempts to root out the conspiracies that haunted the monasteries. The monastic system created excellent monks, but it didn't create men who made friends easily. Robes identified a monk at a distance, but even a blind man recognized a monk when he encountered one.

He could say the same of the city watch. Although the young men in the tavern varied in many ways, identifying them as soldiers took no skill at all. Even out of uniform the men had straight bearings, their bodies all right angles. Delun didn't think he saw more than a handful of men slouching in the place.

He mimicked them, almost unconsciously. He sat up straight and drank his second beer with a hint of stiffness.

For the first part of the evening he smiled, said hello when greeted, but mostly kept his eyes and ears open. He joined in a game of dice, losing a few silver pieces with good grace.

He didn't ask questions.

The moon had been up for at least three hours when Delun found the first hint of what he was looking for. A group of young men had taken a table in a corner and were whispering to one another. When he casually stumbled by, they glared at him and fell into silence as he passed.

The evidence wasn't conclusive. The men were too wary to listen in on, nor did he dare approach them and try to ingratiate himself into their conversation. Doing so would only increase their suspicion. He memorized their faces, then paid his bill and left the tavern.

Delun found a dark alcove that gave him a view of the tavern entrance. He pushed himself deep into the shadows and waited.

He risked failure.

But even failure served as information. Chao's sources identified the tavern as a spot for dissension. The city watch would have connections to black powder. A group of men conspired about something. Perhaps the talk had been as meaningless as a discussion about one of their member's marriage prospects. But perhaps they were part of something greater.

Only time would tell. If his instincts misled him, tomorrow was a new night.

The four men exited the tavern together.

After speaking in hushed tones for a few minutes, the group split apart. Two left together, with the other two traveling in other directions. Delun followed the pair that remained together.

Following the men proved challenging. The streets of

Jihan were eerily empty, as though citizens understood a storm was brewing and hid themselves indoors. Without a crowd for cover, Delun ran a higher risk of discovery while trailing the men.

Fortunately, while the men glanced backward occasionally, they didn't seem concerned about being followed. Delun worried his intuition had guided him wrong.

The two men stopped outside of a house in a residential area. Delun's heart sank. He'd been so sure of his instincts, but tonight looked to be a false lead.

Another brief discussion was held, the watchmen looking up and down the streets cautiously, then stepped inside. Delun hid in the shadows, wondering if the night was a loss.

A few minutes later, a third man stepped out of the house. The monk memorized the face in case they met again.

His suspicions returned. The house held at least three men, and from the look of the third, all of them were members of the city watch. Why would so many watchmen be entering and leaving a residential house? If they were unmarried, they had bunks back near the center of Jihan.

The streets were perfectly quiet. The moon hung high in the sky, illuminating Jihan with a milky, pale light.

Delun waited.

A city watch patrol marched down the street, four guards evenly spaced. Their eyes were sharp, but they missed Delun motionless in the shadows. They didn't seem to make a special note of the house, but Delun couldn't be certain.

Less than an hour later another patrol marched by.

Delun's eyes narrowed. In a city this large, two patrols so close together was unlikely.

Eventually, Delun's curiosity demanded satisfaction. He crossed the street and tried the windows of the house. They were all closed, locked, and covered. Hidden deep in shadows, he tested the locks of one window. It didn't budge. He tried another with similar results.

Should he enter? He risked discovery. Word might spread and he would lose any element of surprise against the Order.

At the moment, he didn't mind the risk. His patience waned. Weeks had passed since the explosions and the perpetrators still ran free.

He creeped to the front of the house, checking to ensure the street was still deserted. Then he pushed the door open a crack.

It opened without a sound. Delun crouched next to the door, his head tilted, listening for sounds. He heard voices, but they sounded as though they came from a far room.

When he was fairly certain that the front room wasn't occupied, he pushed the door open the rest of the way. He stepped inside, checked the room, then shut the door.

The room was unoccupied. It was also bare. It held no furniture, no decorations, nothing. Delun's suspicions grew.

The voices continued, coming from a room in the back. Delun sneaked forward, able to make out two distinct voices.

"It's not enough?"

A short pause.

"How much more?"

"Two barrels, at least."

Delun clenched his fist. They had to be speaking about black powder. Was it being stored here?

"When?"

"Our next shipment arrives at the end of the week. The captain will make sure the paperwork is in order."

"I'll let the men know to be ready."

Delun heard the creaking of wood. The men were returning to the front room.

Hide or fight?

There was no place to hide. The room was devoid of any cover.

Delun drew a knife from a sheath hidden in his robes. These men had sacrificed their own lives the moment they attacked his brothers. Monks weren't allowed to carry blades, but Delun had started after his fight with Bai ten years ago. He wanted every advantage, and the use of a weapon would disguise what happened here.

The men stepped into the room, surprise painted on their faces when they found Delun standing there. Delun stepped forward, the knife coming up and under the first man's jaw. His eyes went blank. The other man reacted, but Delun was too fast. He pulled the knife free of the first man and drove it through the second man's hand and into the wall behind, pinning him there as he screamed.

The guard's free hand went for a weapon. Delun intercepted it without a problem. The man stopped screaming when Delun drove his knee into the guard's stomach. He coughed and spit, and Delun used his free hand to pull the man's head up by his hair. He leaned in close.

"I've got questions."

The sun rose on a brisk day by the time Delun left the house. He left bloody footprints outside the door, an unavoidable problem. He had considered lighting the powder stored in the back room. Too many innocents lived nearby, though, and he had a better idea. He would return soon with help to remove the black powder. The Order's greatest weapon was about to be stolen and used against them.

And thanks to the helpful guard, he now knew who to hunt next.

15

Lei walked a narrow path leading away from his village. It came out on a small ledge that provided a spectacular view of the empire stretching to the horizon and beyond.

From this altitude, the world appeared so peaceful. The tensions that threatened to shatter the empire weren't physical. They couldn't be seen like an advancing army or billowing storm clouds pierced by lightning. But the invisible threat posed more danger than armies or the forces of nature. Ideas were as dangerous as swords, if not more so. Shields could deflect or block a sword, but ideas were nearly impossible to contain.

Lei focused on his breath. The events of the past two months caused him to doubt his decisions, the path he had set for himself. Yang's question, asked amid overwhelming grief, echoed in his memories.

How can you have so much power and not act?

Yang hadn't understood. But he also hadn't been in Jihan, all those years ago, when Lei had first fought Fang and the original Order of the Serpent. Their duel had caused incredible destruction and changed the course of history. Decades later, Jihan was still a rallying cry for citizens across the empire, a symbol of monastic power taken too far.

Most today didn't know that for all the lives lost, he had saved many more. The Order's plan to light the capital on fire had never become public. Lei saved the city, but that day still became equivalent in most people's minds with the Massacre of Kulat.

He couldn't predict the ripples that spread from his actions. The stronger he became, the wider those ripples expanded. If he truly believed his decisions would change the world for the better, he might not have voluntarily gone into exile. But even well-intentioned actions brought horrible consequences.

Daiyu had shown him a better way. She reminded him that a modest life could be a pleasurable and rewarding one. They ran the village, gardened, and had a close-knit group of neighbors and friends. The empire went on without them, and Lei woke up early in the morning looking forward to the day.

Let the young attempt to change the world. He wouldn't trade his life for anything.

But life changed.

Somewhere down there, far out of sight, Bai made her way to Jihan, set on making a difference. Off to his right, also beyond view, Yang mourned in Kulat, rebuilding his dream on top of the bones of his beloved students. In the village directly behind him, Daiyu's fate grew ever nearer, as inevitable as the changing of the seasons.

He turned away from the view and wandered to his house, nestled near the center of the gathering of buildings. A quick look through the small house revealed that Daiyu wasn't inside. He exited through the back and hiked a well-worn trail that led to a terrace. There he found Daiyu, tending to their garden.

Even after thirty years together, she looked gorgeous. The illness sapped her strength, but her appearance remained unchanged. He still thought she was the most beautiful woman he'd ever met.

She looked up at him and gave him a soft smile.

He considered reminding her she needed rest, but what good would it do? She loved being outside in the garden, loved watching the plants grow through the seasons. It was far better that she enjoy her time than strictly follow the healer's orders. The end of the story was the same, so why not enjoy the journey?

Lei finished hiking the path and joined her. She harvested the last remaining vegetables, the ones determined to finish growing before the weather turned too cold. Their village hadn't had a frost or snow yet, but the time was soon coming.

Daiyu dropped the vegetables in a basket and brushed her hands off. "How was the view?"

Lei chuckled. He didn't know how Daiyu knew where he'd been. But the woman's gift of observation was second to none. Long ago, Daiyu had worked for the triads, and habits died hard. She collected information the way others focused on money.

"Quiet."

Daiyu kneeled next to another patch of late-season harvest and went to work. "You're torn."

"Perhaps."

In their years together, secrets had disappeared. She knew his mind too well for him to hide from her, and she trusted him with everything.

"Has your decision changed?"

"No. I remain here."

His response agitated Daiyu. Her outward expressions were almost invisible, but they had been together too long. The slightest tic was enough for him to know the course of her thoughts. For a few moments, the only sound was that of the breeze through the trees. They no longer rushed to fill the silences between them, content instead to give each other time to find the words they meant. As they had gotten older, time itself meant something different to them.

"Do you have regrets?" she asked.

He looked back at his life, contemplating her question earnestly. "Yes. I know my decisions have led me here, to you, but if I could go back, I wouldn't do the same."

She nodded. When they'd been younger, such a comment might have angered her. But honesty meant everything now. When Lei had been a boy, he lost control of his power and killed a young girl from Two Bridges. He could trace a path of cause and effect from that to him sitting in a garden with the love of his life, but that didn't mean he would sacrifice the girl's life again.

"I feel selfish," Daiyu admitted.

Lei gave her a quizzical look.

"If not for me, would you have retreated from the empire?"

Lei had thought about that question on and off over the years, but had never come to a satisfactory answer. He'd never considered himself a hero. While he'd been blessed with great strength, all he'd ever wanted was his own happiness. He didn't have any desire to sacrifice his life for some greater good, or seek trouble that wasn't his own.

He clasped Daiyu's hands between his own. "I made my choice, the same as you."

"But you might have made a different choice, and now the empire might not be in this state."

"There's no way of knowing. You could also argue that if I'd remained in the empire, anger at the monasteries would have increased. You'll recall I wasn't a very popular man after Jihan. Perhaps this all would have come to pass years ago."

She smiled at him again. "I know, but I *feel* selfish."

"You've done more for this village over the years than anyone else. Perhaps it hasn't changed the course of the empire, but think of the people who can live here without fear thanks to you."

The statement was no exaggeration. Daiyu, though not nearly the oldest in the small village, had acted as its elder from day one. They accepted those who sought shelter from the empire, or those seeking a quieter life. Hien had brought no small number of women here over the years. The village was a haven, but Daiyu rarely gave herself enough credit.

She twisted the conversation. "What would you do if Yang came after I die? Would you have the same hesitations?"

Lei opened his mouth to deny the inherent accusation, but a look from Daiyu silenced him. He took a deep breath and imagined what he would do. He sighed. "I would probably go."

She nodded, no doubt expecting that answer. "Then I am holding you back."

"These are still my choices."

Daiyu stood up, and Lei followed suit. They held hands as they walked around the garden, Daiyu lost in thought. When she spoke, her question surprised him. "Do you remember the Heron?"

"The inn where we met in Jihan?"

"Yes. Did you know that it is still open?"

He shook his head. He did not understand how Daiyu knew that, but then again, she always knew far more than he suspected.

"I would like to visit it again. It has been far too long, and it is one of my favorite places in the world."

Lei stepped in front of her. He knew what she was doing and was frightened by what she implied. His worst fears wrapped their shadowy fingers around his heart. "It's a long journey, there and back."

Her smile was sad. "I do not think I will be coming back, my love."

Lei's heart broke, his fears confirmed.

"You can't give up," he mumbled. He looked at the ground, unable to meet her eyes.

She lifted his chin with one hand, forcing him to look at her. Her eyes were bright, even though they glistened. "I'm not giving up. But I feel weaker every day. I don't have much longer left, and I love the Heron. It is where we began our life together. I'd be overjoyed to be there, at the end."

Lei wiped a hand across his eyes. "And then I'll be in the center of the chaos."

Her hand wrapped around the back of his head and pulled his face gently towards her. Their lips met, and after all these years, his heart still beat faster when they kissed.

She gently released him. "I think it's where you belong."

16

—————

Bai swore the shadows sought her out. In her travels and adventures she had developed a fair degree of caution. One didn't interfere with both monks and triads without learning to look frequently over one's shoulder. She had always prided herself on avoiding paranoia, though.

In Jihan, she wasn't sure which side of madness she fell on.

While the sun burned its way through the sky, she had no problems. But at night, when only the moon and the stars illuminated her paths, ethereal creatures haunted her. She had arrived in Jihan two days ago. She had yet to seek Yang's students, preferring to explore the city on her own first. Tomorrow she would go to them. Tonight, she sought answers.

Every night she felt the hairs rise on the back of her neck, certain she was being watched. Even when she wandered the roofs, she saw shadows that didn't belong. Whenever she approached, though, she found nothing of interest. Nor did she sense another gifted.

She didn't believe she was mad, but after two nights of chasing shadows, she began to wonder.

Tonight's full moon would reveal her answers. Someone followed her. By the time the sun rose, she planned on knowing who.

Bai leaped over an alley separating two roofs, her footsteps light on the tiles. Her eyes wandered restlessly over the surrounding buildings, looking for misshapen darkness and unnatural shadows. She paid attention to the streets below, judging the mood of the city.

Bai imagined Jihan as a thread pulled taut. The city watch patrolled the streets more than anywhere Bai had ever been. Some merchants refused to open their stalls and shops for business.

The thread was in danger of snapping. During the day, people bustled to their destinations, hurrying from shelter to shelter. At night no one left their homes. Even now, the street below her sat perfectly empty.

When she first realized how empty the nighttime streets were, Bai worried a monk might detect her nocturnal wanderings. She had some advantages, though.

Jihan was an enormous city, and most monks struggled to sense the gift in others when surrounded by other people. Bai didn't understand why, but the more crowded a space was, the more difficult a monk's power was to sense. She had made great use of that fact in several cities. Her presence was naturally light, and within the walls of the empire's most populous cities, she practically had to be on top of a monk before they sensed her.

With the streets empty, it was another story entirely.

She had yet to see a monk in the streets, though. Jihan's monastery had been attacked like the one in Windown. Bai had seen the damage to the walls with her own eyes. The monks huddled inside their shattered sanctuary, licking their wounds.

Who knew what they planned?

She leaped to another rooftop, finding a deep recess to hide within. The odds of anyone spotting her standing in the open were slim, but why take a chance? She closed her eyes and focused her senses, focusing on her breath the way Lei had taught her.

Nothing.

After a few minutes, she opened her eyes. As soon as she did, she thought she saw a shadow move, three buildings over.

This was her chance.

Desperate for answers, Bai broke from cover, leaping across roofs, arriving at the spot only seconds after she had seen the movement.

She saw nothing that explained what she was sure she had seen. Bai squatted and examined the area. This rooftop didn't connect to any others. If someone had been watching her, they either jumped down three stories or leaped across a fairly wide street.

She *had* seen something.

She clenched her fist. Either she really was going mad, or she was missing something.

Bai calmed her breathing. She relied too heavily on her sight.

Eyes closed and breath steady, she noticed a sense of someone else. It didn't feel like a monk. The feeling was much softer, like the difference between a single candle near the bottom of its wick and a raging bonfire.

They were close.

She opened her eyes, focused on where she thought the presence might be. At first, she saw nothing. She waited.

Eventually, a shadow moved on the rooftop across the street.

Bai's worldview shifted, as though she had been looking at her problems upside-down.

The answer was simple, but so unlikely it hadn't occurred to her.

Bai remained still. There was no reason to move until she'd planned her actions.

Catching her shadow required fast moves and sharp senses. Her tail was talented.

Bai grinned. She hadn't faced a challenge like this in some time.

She took one final deep breath, then burst from the roof, pulling energy as she did.

Bai couldn't track the shadow with her eyes. As soon as she ran, the shadow melted away. When she reached the other roof, the shadow was gone, leaving no evidence of its passing. But Bai kept her other senses open and questing and felt a subtle energy coming from below. It was no wonder she had missed it before. Her shadow moved like her.

Bai dropped off the rooftops, chasing her mysterious target.

If she'd had any doubt that her own power was being sensed, it didn't last long. Her shadow sprinted, almost as quick as her.

Bai followed like a bloodhound after catching a scent. She kept her focus on her sense. Whoever she chased was adept at hiding, moving from shadow to darkness, loose robes indistinct in the middle of the night. At first, Bai wasn't sure she could catch up. Her target was fast and agile, changing directions without warning.

After taking a tight corner too quickly and slamming her

shoulder into a wall, Bai bounded up onto the rooftops, her speed increasing as fewer obstacles hampered her. Her target realized what had happened and jumped up, too.

It was like chasing a mirror image of herself.

Her target's change in elevation came too late. Bai had already closed most of the distance between them. She gained on her target, her pursuit relentless. Bai's leaps between rooftops were a little smoother, a little farther. So long as Bai remained close enough to sense the shadow, they had no place to hide. She vowed to run her prey to the ground.

They came to a large gap, a leap across one of the main thoroughfares of this neighborhood. Bai felt the way her target shifted their power as they leaped. By the time Bai understood what was happening, she was already in midair behind the shadow.

As soon as her target landed they stopped, grounding their weight and swinging a back fist at her. Bai saw the blow coming but could do little about it. Her leap took her directly into the strike. Bai got an arm up, the block hasty and poorly performed. The strength of the blow, combined with Bai's own momentum, sent her spinning, the back of her head rushing straight to the roof.

Bai twisted, taking the impact on her shoulder rather than her head. Agony flared in the shoulder, but Bai pushed the pain down. Her assailant didn't give her a moment to recover, aiming a powerful kick at her head. Bai raised her arms to block, funneling energy into them, and the kick caught her across the forearms. Her injured shoulder flared in pain. The blow caused her body to crater the rooftop.

Bai kicked up at her assailant, catching her enemy by surprise. The kick knocked the hooded figure back several feet.

Bai scrambled to her feet, pulling desperately for more energy. The assailant attacked again, unleashing a series of blows almost too fast to track. Bai's eyes widened as she fought to keep up. Even with all her strength, her defense barely held.

Her heart raced as she completed blocks closer and closer to her body. Then she missed a block, and the punch sent her off the roof.

Transferring energy to her legs, Bai landed on her feet, then immediately jumped back into the fight. She caught her opponent off-guard, already turning around to flee.

Bai unleashed her own attacks, a series of punches and elbows that would have killed any monk. Her challenger gave up ground but blocked or avoided every strike.

The two of them split apart, each preparing for the next exchange. Bai pulled more power in, studying her opponent. They had a slight build and were covered from head to toe in dark black robes, revealing only their eyes.

Bai had never fought anyone like herself. She'd never even considered it. The techniques she relied on against monks, or against warriors that weren't gifted, were of little use here. What remained?

No clever answers came. Her only thought was to be faster and stronger. She took a deep breath, centered herself, and approached her opponent.

Their first exchange had been fast, the uncontrolled power of two warriors crashing into one another for the first time. Their second was more orderly, each relying on their techniques to surpass the other.

Bai led with a series of jabs, then blocked a snap kick aimed at her leg. She pushed closer, switching to her elbows. The strategy disoriented the other warrior. Bai landed two glancing shots, then used the momentary confusion to grab her opponent's robes and throw them off the roof. She followed.

They fell together, Bai above the masked enemy. Bai focused her energy into her legs and feet. She sensed the other person shift their energy to their back and torso, protecting them from most of the impact. They crashed into the ground together.

Her enemy didn't get up. Bai didn't recover quickly, either. Drawing power gave her strength, but a body still had limits.

The shadow tore off the fabric around their head, revealing a young woman's face underneath. Her nose trickled blood from one of Bai's elbows, but her lips were turned up in a smile. "That was excellent!"

Confusion flooded through Bai. She stood, tensed, ready to fight. The other woman stood up and brushed herself off, as casually as though she'd just tripped.

Bai stepped forward, but the woman held up a hand. "There's no need to fight. I only wanted to test you. You know I've been watching you for a few days?"

Bai nodded.

"My name is Rong. Would you like to meet the others?"

Bai didn't understand. What others?

Then it clicked. Rong's gifts. Her welcoming demeanor. Others. Bai didn't need to find Yang's students.

They had found her. And if Rong was any indication, they were strong.

She followed the mysterious warrior deeper into the shadows.

THE JOURNEY TOOK LONGER than Bai expected. The two women rested for a few minutes by walking the streets, but then took to the roofs. Rong led her all the way through the city. Bai didn't mind. For the first time in her life, she shared her gift with another.

Hien was as close as a sister, but the differences in their abilities created a wall between them that couldn't be broken. How could Hien know what it felt like to arc between buildings, the wind snapping through your hair?

Rong knew.

She understood the freedom that Bai couldn't put into words, the lightheartedness that came from traveling paths most people weren't aware of. In all of Jihan, only the two of them were truly free.

Rong led and Bai sensed the competitive spirit within. The woman moved fast, bounding across buildings with obvious confidence. Bai, not to be outdone, remained no more than a pace or two behind.

They came to the wall that surrounded Jihan, but Rong didn't slow. Bai sensed the incredible power the woman funneled into her legs, her leap taking her up and over the wall.

Bai had never attempted such a large leap. But she wouldn't capitulate. She pulled and channeled the necessary energy, jumping just as Rong had. She cleared the wall with ease, passing two oblivious sentries. Their backs were to her as they walked the wall. They didn't even hear her passing.

Bai used most of her remaining energy to land on the other side of the wall. She saw Rong ahead of her, running further away from Jihan. Bai followed.

Eventually, Rong came to halt on the outskirts of a copse. The other woman wasn't even out of breath. Their eyes met, and Rong smiled.

"I've never been followed so well."

Bai understood the implication. "There are others?"

"A few."

"I didn't know there was anyone else like me."

"More are discovered every year."

Bai had a thousand questions, but none of them escaped her lips. She didn't know where to begin.

A part of her had always hoped to meet others. The empire was vast, and it seemed unusual that she would be the only person with a certain ability. But that hope had waned as year after year passed without meeting a kindred soul.

She wasn't alone. That thought silenced all others.

Rong stepped into the copse. "Don't be nervous. No one here will hurt you."

Bai was about to ask why when she realized Rong's meaning. Monks were in this copse. In the excitement of following Rong, she'd let down her guard.

They soon came upon a small camp. Bai sensed those sitting around the fire were gifted, but any similarities to monks ended there. The group was small, but consisted of both women and men dressed in heavy traveling clothes. They possessed an ease never found in monasteries.

The first morning rays broke over the horizon, but it appeared everyone had been awake for some time. Cook fires crackled while the group prepared to break their fast. Everyone moved with a quiet competence born of experience. They were young, Bai saw.

When the others noticed Bai, the attention of the entire camp focused on her. Bai gave a small bow in greeting.

A woman, older than the rest, spoke. "Welcome."

Rong replied, "This is Bai."

Her name seemed to be introduction enough. The older woman gave Bai a deep bow. "I'm glad Rong brought you.

I've wanted to meet you for some time, but you aren't an easy woman to find."

Bai looked around the group. "You're from Kulat?"

"We are. My name is Shu. Master Yang asked me to lead this expedition."

Bai gestured to the camp. "Why are you camped out here? I planned on finding you at the palace this very day."

Shu looked pained. "When we arrived, we reported to the palace. Yang was supposed to lead us. Although we possessed a sealed letter, the guards did not allow us entry without Yang."

"Why not?"

"It's a question we have all asked ourselves. Regardless, we did not feel that staying inside Jihan was wise. The situation is far too tense, and we are not welcomed by other monks. I decided it was prudent to remain outside the walls. I've sent messages to Yang and others, hoping to resolve the situation. Until then, we wait."

"Leaving the princess unguarded."

Shu grimaced. "We do what we can. I go into town every day to sense if monks approach the palace. Others do what they can, limited as we are. Our precautions helped us to find you."

Bai had wondered about that.

"Would you care to break your fast with us?"

That had been Bai's other pressing question. Her body hungered for sustenance. Fighting and following Rong had taken much out of her. "I'd be delighted."

As Rong introduced Bai to the remaining students, Bai returned to the thought that had kept her spirits high since Rong had introduced herself.

She no longer fought this war alone.

17

Delun returned to the safehouse where he now lived with a handful of other wraiths. The evening had been long and uneventful, but at least the morning sun promised rest.

The past few weeks had been relentlessly calm, much to Delun's dismay. He had hoped that his impromptu raid and murder of the guards would shake the bees from their hive. Chaos created fertile ground for enemies to make mistakes.

The captain of the city watch, if he was the head of the Order of the Serpent, made no such errors. Wraiths had carried out the black powder the same night Delun struck. Others then watched the house for a week after.

The bodies were discovered within a day by other watchmen visiting the house.

Delun had waited for another attack. Wraiths quietly guarded potential targets, but the days and nights passed without explosions, raids, or any other sign that Delun's capture of the powder had worried the Order.

News of the murder of two watchmen spread throughout the city. Delun prepared for a public backlash against the monasteries, but none came. The watch treated the killings like any other. Watchmen combed the neighborhood, asking those who lived nearby if they had seen or heard anything suspicious. Posters went up offering rewards for information.

Delun knew the Order had to suspect what had really happened. But if they did, they gave no evidence of it.

After all his efforts, Delun found himself at a bit of a dead end. He had no new leads to follow up on.

Delun himself helped watch the captain, but never had his time been spent so fruitlessly. The captain, by all appearances, was a paragon. His men loved him. After his shifts ended, the captain went home and rarely left. He had two young sons he trained in various martial skills. The captain never met with shadowy figures or spent his nights drinking in taverns.

In short, he was the most uninteresting man Delun had ever tailed.

The only gap in Delun's observations was the man's headquarters. He kept his command post in the middle of the city watch's fortified barracks. No admittance to the grounds was permitted unless one was a member of the watch. The hours the captain spent within his post were largely a mystery to Delun.

Delun's fruitless observations left him with two possibilities.

The first was the simpler of the two. The captain was exactly how he appeared. Delun had either misheard or misunderstood the watchmen in the house. He chased after imaginary enemies.

Otherwise, the captain was the most devious of enemies Delun had faced.

The evidence strongly suggested the former possibility was correct. Delun hoped for the latter.

Regardless, he couldn't continue on for much longer without something to show for his efforts. The other wraiths had been called to other duties. Delun continued his investigation alone. He lay in his bed feeling the weight of failure sitting on his chest.

Exhaustion soon took him.

He woke to the sounds of conversation outside. He wiped his eyes and rolled himself into a sitting position. Judging from the position of the sun, he hadn't slept for very long. He rarely did anymore.

He stepped into the main room of the house. Chao stood there, talking with some other residents. When he saw Delun he finished his conversation. He gestured to Delun's room, and they both entered.

Delun remained impressed by Chao. The man seemed to have his fingers everywhere in the empire, yet Delun had never seen him overwhelmed. His calculating eyes never wandered, and Delun suspected the man played a game much deeper than anyone realized.

Even more frustrating, Delun couldn't dig up who Chao was. The leader of the wraiths was a monk, but he possessed no noteworthy strength. Delun would have passed him without a second thought in any monastery in the empire. Yet here he was, coordinating the wraiths with strategic purpose and the force of his considerable belief.

"How goes the investigation?"

Delun glanced down at the floor. "Not well."

He didn't need to say more. Chao kept a close eye on the activities of every wraith. He knew the problems Delun's investigation faced.

"Perhaps you need a break." Chao handed Delun a folded piece of paper.

Delun unfolded it. The paper contained a detailed sketch of a face he hadn't expected to see again. He closed his eyes, knowing Chao's request already.

"Watchers at the gates recognized her entering Jihan several days ago. Our informants believe she is here to track down wraiths and kill them. She killed a handful a few weeks ago in Windown."

Delun opened his eyes and studied Chao. The man had spies everywhere, it seemed. Delun only caught bits and pieces, but he believed Chao knew virtually everything of importance that happened throughout the empire. His information probably rivaled that of the questioners.

Delun had pried, once, about a week ago. Chao told him in no uncertain terms that where the information came from was Chao's alone. The secrecy made sense. Information was power, and Chao's information gave him considerable leverage.

The more time Delun spent with the wraiths, the more he understood the value of Chao's information. The wraiths possessed more knowledge about troop movements, watch schedules, and the comings and goings of vital personnel than any monk normally would. Perhaps that network, more than anything else, gave the wraiths the advantages they enjoyed.

Delun had no cause to doubt Chao's information. The leader of the wraiths hadn't misled him yet.

"Why me?"

"Because you have faced her before. Her skills are unique. Every monk I have sent against her has failed. Somehow, I do not think you will."

"And my investigation?"

"Our brothers will have their justice. I trust your instincts, and I am seeking information to use against the beloved captain. I only need time."

Delun studied Bai's sketch in his hands. Over a decade had passed since they had parted ways. They had never been allies, exactly, but they hadn't been enemies either. Delun had long suspected how Bai had spent the intervening years. Other monks spread rumors of a monk-killer. Delun assumed if the rumors were true, Bai hid behind them. In all his years, he'd never tried to track her down, though.

He told himself it was because she had rendered him aid in Kulat. Without her, the rebellion would have set half the empire ablaze.

Seeing her again, even as a sketch, made that story a lie. Chao was right. He had prepared to fight her, knowing that someday he might have to. If nothing else, the intellectual challenge had been worthwhile.

But he had hoped never to use the skills he'd practiced.

He respected her. In the short time they had known each other, she had acted with dignity and respect. Many monks could stand to learn from her.

Chao's piercing gaze never left him. He had little choice in the matter. Taio deserved justice. They all did. If he was going to deliver it, he needed the wraiths and Chao's information. Killing Bai was the price.

He nodded. "I'll do it."

"Good. And one more challenge. It must be done two nights from now."

Chao turned and left, leaving Delun with the piece of paper and more questions than answers. Delun stared at it.

He thought of the view of the mountain from the walls of the monastery. The wild still called to him.

He had no allies to turn to, no one he trusted.

He would give his life for the monasteries, but he had no one to rely on.

Delun crumpled up the paper and tossed it into a corner of the room. If Bai was in town, she was most likely the closest person he had to a friend.

And he would kill her.

18

———

Jihan was not the same city Lei ran from so many years ago. He felt constantly disoriented, the familiar blending with the new, lost in a place he once knew well.

Over thirty years had passed since he had last been here. From where he currently stood he could see the tall tower where he and Fang had fought their final destructive battle. It still stood, a silent testament to Lei's victory that night. The sight of the tower brought back memories of that fight, of Fang's submission at the end.

Lei didn't feel regret, exactly. He wished events had unfolded differently, but once he'd passed through the gates of Jihan he'd done his best. For as many times as he'd relived the experience, he couldn't imagine better decisions than those he'd made.

Lei wondered, as the guards watched him and Daiyu enter the city, how they would react if they knew who he was. Would they try to kill him, or would they flee in terror? As they passed the gates without incident, he was glad he didn't have to find out.

Since his fight and subsequent escape, the city had rebuilt and grown, eating up old buildings and constructing new ones. Even the gates were in a different place than they had been before, the wall torn down and rebuilt to accommodate the ever-expanding city. The symphony of hammers, saws, and blacksmiths could be heard at every intersection.

Lei figured their return was poetic, in a way. When they'd last been here, they'd been running away from the monastery in Jihan, beginning their lives together. Now it seemed their mutual journey would end in the same city.

They wandered the streets aimlessly for a time. Traveling lifted Daiyu's spirits as it wrecked her body. They had been content in their little village, but their journey reminded them how many wonders the world contained. Even little details, like the items for sale in local markets, were unexpected treats. Daiyu walked from stall to stall, lost in exploration, while Lei watched the streets with a wary eye.

He hadn't seen any monks since passing the gates, a fact for which he was grateful. The news heard from other travelers was that the attack on the monastery had convinced the monks to remain firmly behind their walls. The Heron wasn't located near the monastery, but it eased Lei's heart to know he wouldn't happen randomly across many monks. His strength wasn't easy to find in a crowd, but Shu's demonstration of her ability in Kulat made him nervous.

He felt the tension in the streets, though. The events of the past few weeks weren't enough to bring commerce to a halt, but Lei expected the markets to be busier. Merchants glanced constantly around while patrons walked quickly to their destination. The market was busy, but it felt empty.

Lei assumed Daiyu noticed. Her perception was sharper than his, but she made no comment. Her joy at shopping Jihan's markets drove away most of Lei's nerves.

They brought enough gold for a comfortable stay in Jihan, although not enough for opulence. Daiyu bought a necklace that highlighted her eyes, and Lei was reminded again how fortunate he was to have her in his life.

That afternoon they arrived at the Heron. They were shown to a room, and Lei marveled at how similar the place was to his memories. For all Jihan had changed, the Heron had remained the same. No doubt the building had endured multiple renovations, but the effect was one of agelessness. They ate that evening in the skywell where Lei had found Daiyu all those years ago, and Lei felt at peace with the world. The troubles of Jihan seemed far removed from their meal.

As night fell, Daiyu took a turn for the worse. Perhaps they had been too active that morning, but Lei said nothing. The experience had been worth it, for both of them. As she lay in bed recovering her strength, she turned to him. "You could seek out Yang's students. There's no need for both of us to be stuck in this room."

"I'm here with you."

She shook her head, as though she was arguing with a fool, but she didn't complain.

The next day dawned bright, the sun driving away autumn's chill. They visited a well-regarded tea house, then walked along a canal, discussing their past history with the city. Daiyu had lived in Jihan for a while, back when she worked for the triads. Lei had only ever visited on random occasions, but often enough he felt familiar with the labyrinthine streets.

Jihan made him feel his age. Some was the same, but his

memories were of a different place. The city had gone on without him. It would continue on long after his spirit joined with his ancestors.

For lunch they returned to the Heron, where Lei found Bai waiting. He swore softly, and Bai hurried to explain.

"I made contact with Yang's students. Shu sensed you as you came into the city yesterday. After how much you two spoke of the Heron, I figured I would find you here."

The reunion was sweet. Bai looked worn, and she carried a fresh set of bruises, but she smiled easily as they caught up with one another. The meal passed quickly, most of the time disappearing as Bai regaled her hosts with tales of recent adventures.

Despite the interruption of his time with Daiyu, Lei enjoyed the company. He almost couldn't see the young, fearful woman he had trained anymore. She was older now, confident in her powers. He was glad he had taken a chance on her so long ago when she'd shown up in his village.

They sipped at wine as they finished their meal. The Heron never disappointed. Lei almost thought they might finish the meal without problem, but Bai's concern for Daiyu broke the unspoken truce.

"How are you feeling?" she asked Daiyu.

"Weak," Lei's wife admitted.

Bai gave Lei a pitying look. Lei imagined she meant to hide it from Daiyu, but his wife noticed it anyway. "My time is coming. I've made my peace with it. I expect you to keep an eye on Lei after."

Daiyu's voice was calm, but Lei saw the effort she hid from Bai. Daiyu accepted her fate, but she wasn't at peace, not yet. As it did every day, his heart broke knowing their remaining time together was so limited.

Bai smiled. "Knowing Lei, he's going to end up looking after me."

The resulting silence was surprisingly awkward for people who had known each other for years. Bai didn't seem to know how to speak with the dying. Lei had felt the same way for some time, before he realized no change was necessary.

Bai turned to face Lei. His stomach twisted in knots, knowing what was coming. "We could really use your help."

Lei felt his muscles tense at the suggestion, but he forced himself to take a deep breath and relax. "I don't want to hear it. I'm here to be with Daiyu."

Bai sighed, knowing him well enough to be sure that nothing she could say would change his mind. He knew she was frustrated, but they all tried to move forward. They finished the meal with that gentle tension sitting between them.

Daiyu and Bai had a protracted exchange after the meal. Lei gave them some distance. They were saying goodbye, again.

He didn't know how accurate Daiyu's sense of her illness was. The healers hadn't been able to say exactly how long she had, but she was convinced she didn't have many weeks left. She'd done the same in the village before they'd left, saying goodbye to everyone for the final time. She didn't plan on returning.

Though he'd watched a dozen similar exchanges, each still tugged at his heart. They were just another reminder of his approaching agony. Another reminder that there were battles he couldn't win.

That afternoon was quiet. Daiyu napped for a time, but in the evening they took to the city again, finding a restaurant Daiyu remembered. The fish and rice were superb, and the meal passed quickly.

"Do you wish we would have done more of this?" Lei asked.

She finished her last bite. "No."

Lei grinned. "I was always surprised you seemed content in our little village."

Her smile matched his. "The same could be said for you." She paused. "Although I imagine you enjoyed not having to look over your shoulder every minute."

He conceded that point. They'd only been in the city for two days, and already his constant vigilance exhausted him. Peace of mind was a priceless commodity.

She changed the subject on him again. "Bai was disappointed you didn't join them."

"She'll be fine."

"What about you?"

"I'm with you."

She sighed softly at his refrain. "The empire needs you."

"No, it doesn't." He watched the subtle play of expressions over her face. "Why is this so important?"

She clasped her hands and bit her lower lip. Whatever the reason, Lei realized she wasn't entirely comfortable sharing it. He waited patiently.

"I've had a strong feeling, one that's been growing lately."

Lei frowned. Already this didn't sound like Daiyu.

"I can't explain this, so please don't ask me to, but I feel certain that you are the one who will shape the next generation of the empire. When you insist on accompanying me, I fear you will miss your destiny."

Lei leaned back. Daiyu didn't usually believe in fate.

Still, her confession didn't change his mind. He reached across the table and held her hands.

"I'm not going to leave you."

Daiyu squeezed his hands. "I know. Sometimes, I wish you would leave so I could spare you the end. But that's too selfish."

They left the restaurant and enjoyed the view of the stars above. Watching the constellations crawl across the sky had been one of their favorite hobbies back home. They held hands as they walked, Lei enjoying the warmth of her hand in his.

They returned to their room and began undressing one another. Lei drank in the sight and scent of her body. Their lips met and lingered. Then she smiled a mischievous grin. "I hate seeing you put off the entire empire because of me, but I'm glad you're here."

"I am, too."

Her hands ran down his torso, tracing his scars with the tips of her fingers. She looked up at him. "You're a good man, Lei."

He thought then of duty and responsibility, what a true son of the empire would do. Then Daiyu took a step back, her figure silhouetted by light from the window. All thoughts of duty fled. "I'm no hero."

She held out a hand to him, inviting him. "But you are no hero," she agreed.

With that, she pulled him toward the bed before he could respond.

19

B ai perched on the edge of a roof, thinking about Lei, Daiyu, and the empire. Below her, Jihan's heart beat slow and steady as the evening wore on.

Lei occupied the most prominent place in her thoughts. His refusal grated on her. She understood, in a way. His obsession with Daiyu was endearing, most days. But the empire crumbled while the two of them relived their early days. The lives of tens of thousands of people hung in the balance, and Lei, perhaps more than anyone else, could shape the course of the future. The blood of an empire would be on his head because of his inaction.

Bai slammed her fist against the roof, shattering one of the tiles. People were foolish. Often, they resorted to violence when no need existed. The monks and lords were perfect examples. But sometimes they didn't stir to action even when they should.

Were Lei's choices based in love or cowardice?

She didn't know.

Part of her anger was turned inward. She didn't know what she should do. Yang's students had started to look up to her, but she remained at a complete loss. They might follow her, but what could she do?

She had hoped Lei would provide some guidance.

Instead he pushed her away, forcing her to wander this maze of conflicting interests on her own.

She should be grateful for his trust.

But she felt abandoned.

A tremendous surge of energy interrupted her musings. Bai was more sensitive than most gifted to the power of monks, but for her to feel a blast at that distance, within Jihan, meant it had been an incredible power.

Like a moth drawn towards light, Bai traced a path across the rooftops toward the blast. That power had been incredible, obtainable by only a few. It signified danger within Jihan, and if Lei would do nothing, Bai would act.

As she hopped lightly across the rooftops, she kept her senses focused for other monks. Surely she wasn't the only person in Jihan who felt that? But as she neared the place she believed she'd felt the power, she remained alone. That set her nerves on edge. Why hadn't the monks come? Were they that scared to leave the walls of their monastery?

She stopped, scouting the area before jumping down. The source of the blast was obvious enough, though the sight of him stole her breath for a moment. He stood alone in the center of a large abandoned square.

Delun.

She hadn't seen him since Kulat, and had sincerely hoped their paths would never cross again. He was a good man, but they stood on opposite sides of an old conflict. No doubt he detested her. She had hunted and killed several of the men he called brothers.

Though she recognized him, she made no move to approach. Everything about this encounter screamed danger. She didn't see any damage nearby, which meant the huge expenditure of energy hadn't been an attack, at least as far as she could see. What other purpose could it serve?

Had it been meant to draw her in, or someone like her?

The only way to find out was to ask.

Bai kept her distance from Delun. "It's been a long time."

Delun didn't reply, and Bai's sharp eye picked up on worrying details. Delun held a stone in his right hand and a small pouch hung at his hip. From the way the cord that held it strained, she guessed it contained something heavy. His left hand gripped a staff, treating it like a walking stick at the moment. It would double as a weapon, though.

She remembered Delun as an intense man, but the way his eyes bored into her now made her uncomfortable. His silence increased her unease. She couldn't begin to understand his intent.

He didn't speak. He never provided his rationale. He just attacked.

Her caution saved her. She felt the power focus in his right hand, similar to the second attack the monks learned, but the shape of it was slightly different. Delun's hand snapped up, aimed at her head. The rock shot out of his grasp, blurring with speed.

Bai twisted away, the rock grazing her temple. Bright lights swam across her vision, momentarily blinding her.

When her vision returned she saw Delun closing the distance between them, staff whirling in his hands.

She fought her disorientation and pulled in more energy, preparing for battle.

One end of the staff snapped at her head. She dodged, but then the other end attacked her torso. She funneled energy into her arm, barely protecting herself.

Delun attacked relentlessly. The staff spun and snapped, and Bai struggled to follow the unfamiliar weapon.

The monk knew his energy attacks wouldn't work against her. He'd seen her power firsthand.

She dodged backward, giving up ground in exchange for safety.

He never allowed her an opening.

Understanding dawned on her.

He had been training for this, possibly for years.

He had prepared for the day when they might have to fight.

Anger filled her heart. They had once risked their lives for one another. She had helped him when no one else would. And in repayment, he learned techniques specifically designed to kill her.

She blocked his next attack, then stepped forward. She punched at his face, her frustration building as he retreated, using the staff to prevent her from closing with him. He knew she couldn't use energy the same way the monks did. She couldn't attack from distance. So long as he maintained his separation, she couldn't hit him.

Bai might as well have been fighting a ghost.

She leaped at him, trying to get inside the guard of his staff.

As soon as she did, he brought up his right hand, a rock held firmly within. She felt the same attack as before, that same unusual shape. The rock sped at her, but in midair there was no way to dodge. The stone slammed into her chest, shooting a deep throbbing pain through her ribcage and sending her sprawling to the ground.

She stood up a moment later, grateful Delun didn't press his attack. She rubbed at her chest where the rock had landed. Never had she seen a monk use their gifts to manipulate objects in such a way.

Before tonight, she had believed herself virtually invincible against monks. Certainly, they could get lucky, but the battles were hers to lose. Delun made her wonder if she'd been too confident. She hadn't even hit him yet.

She didn't want to fight Delun. They held different beliefs, but Delun was a decent man. Her quest was against the others, the monks who didn't understand the consequences of their abuses of power. She'd seen him torn by the horrible actions of other monks.

"Why?" Bai cried.

His only answer was the focusing of his energy.

He ran forward. The staff twirled with deadly grace in his hands, and Bai lost all hope of a peaceful resolution.

She pulled in more energy, fortifying her arms as she stepped into Delun's attack. She blocked with one arm and attacked with the other. But Delun had mastered the use of distance.

Monks traditionally fought only with their hands and their energy. Bai's skills had developed in response to that style. She could block Delun's staff, but he kept enough space between them to prevent her from mounting an effective counterattack. While she struggled to break his guard, he attacked with ease with the greater length of the staff. In a small space she might have had options, but in the wide open courtyard, Delun had plenty of space to give.

He knew it, too. He never even allowed her to drive him too close to one of the buildings surrounding the courtyard.

For the first time in a decade, Bai felt completely powerless.

Two more blows bounced off her arms, ineffective but tiring. She countered again, striking nothing but air. The stalemate couldn't last forever. One of them would tire or make a mistake. Bai worried it would be her. Delun looked calm and focused, in control.

Whenever she tried to retreat, to gather herself and think, Delun attacked with the rocks. None of them were big or fast enough to kill, but they had no problem dazing, bruising, and distracting. As he sent another stone at her face, she wondered how many he had left in that pouch. He grabbed them with a quickness that displayed many hours of consistent practice.

Another two passes resulted in nothing more than two more strikes for Delun. He wouldn't make a mistake.

Hopelessness settled under her skin. The warrior she had fought so hard to become was being easily dismantled by Delun's patient attacks. If she couldn't fight the monks, what good was she?

She dodged a small stone aimed at her face, hopelessness morphing into rage.

How dare he take this away from her?

She felt the power welling up inside of her, her body's natural response to anger. Already, she had pulled in much tonight and knew she would regret it come morning. Energy masked pain, but didn't eliminate it. Every hit Delun had landed would ache as the bruises formed, and her muscles would soon groan in agony.

Right now, she didn't care. She wanted Delun's blood.

Bai screamed, power flooding through tired muscles. The world sharpened and Delun's motions slowed. Not much, but enough. She feinted towards him, moved back as he responded, then darted into the opening he left.

Even with her enhanced speed and senses, the opening closed quickly. Delun retreated a step, bringing the staff around and at Bai's head. But she was close enough, and her fist landed before the staff. Her punch caught him in the stomach, doubling him over as she kicked at him, sending him sprawling backward.

She had hoped to bring the fight to a stop, at least, but her hope was futile.

Delun absorbed the blows and rolled to his feet, attacking with renewed vigor.

Bai's anger, relieved by the blows she had landed, no longer focused her.

She tried to block but found herself too slow. The tip of the staff found her chest, knocking her several steps back. She kept her feet, barely.

Bai coughed up blood, the idea that she was beaten rooting itself in her mind, as deadly as any cut. She'd never been defeated, not like this.

Her thoughts turned suddenly to retreat. She didn't need to fight Delun, not now. Wincing with the effort, she pulled more energy in from the city, knowing she would deeply regret the decision later.

But regret was better than death.

She turned away from Delun, muscles tensing to jump, when she heard a brief shout behind her. "No!"

Bai felt the focus, but her gift couldn't track the rock. Without sight, she wasn't sure where he aimed.

Pain shot up her leg as the stone drilled into her calf. Even with energy pulsing through her legs she could feel it, a red-hot burning that radiated upward.

Bai stumbled, catching herself against the stone wall of the building she had meant to leap on top of.

She turned in time to feel Delun focus another attack, this one more familiar to her.

She grinned viciously. Finally, he had made a mistake.

He had forgotten, even if just for a moment, her gift. She would absorb his energy and use it against him.

His attack wasn't aimed at her, though. The blast of energy crashed against the building she leaned against. She fell backward, her stone support suddenly gone.

Walls and supports cracked, and the building groaned like a giant old man about to stumble and fall. Bai felt Delun prepare another attack. The building had no chance.

She clawed for more power, and Jihan, always so generous, gave more of itself.

But it was too late. Stones shifted and wood split as the building gave up, finally overwhelmed. Bai only had time to close her eyes as Delun buried her alive.

20

———

Delun sat on top of a roof, overlooking a random street in Jihan. Unlike Bai, he couldn't leap on top of buildings. He'd had to climb the structure like anyone else.

Coming up here had been an impulse, a decision he didn't fully understand himself.

He turned a stone over in his hand.

He'd only had three left, at the end.

Despite his victory, exhaustion left him feeling empty inside.

Or perhaps the feeling was due to the victory against Bai.

They never had seen eye to eye, but they had respected one another. Delun believed that was true.

Her question still stabbed at his heart.

Why?

Because she had made enemies in the past decade, enemies who knew how dangerous she was.

Because she stood in the way of justice for his fallen brothers.

He knew the explanations. But they meant little to him.

They satisfied his mind, but they left his heart wanting more.

He hadn't refused to answer because of some cruelty.

He hadn't answered because he didn't know.

Delun gripped the stone tightly in his hands. How much time had he spent preparing for that fight? He'd never wanted to use those skills, but a part of him had always known Bai might someday stand against him. He had always believed in preparing for every possible opponent. But he'd seen the betrayal on her face. She had never expected them to be enemies.

Up here, Delun understood why Bai took to the rooftops. Height afforded a different perspective. Up here, insurmountable problems resolved themselves into mere challenges.

He didn't know if he had killed Bai. He hoped not. Someday he hoped she would understand, would know that it had never been personal.

Someday.

He took a deep breath. None of these doubts mattered. What was done was done. Time only marched forward. He'd completed a task for the wraiths. In exchange he hoped Chao would deliver him the captain of the guard. If the man was responsible, he would know agony beyond understanding.

Delun put the rock back in the pouch. There was no room for doubt, no room for turning back. Not anymore.

HE'D HOPED Chao would visit the next day, but he was disappointed.

Ping came instead.

The enthusiastic young man could barely sit still. He

rocked back and forth on his feet. Delun wondered what had him so excited.

Ping launched directly into his questions. "Did you kill her?"

"I think so."

Ping's face turned in a moment, excitement suddenly replaced by doubt. "You think?"

Delun waved away his doubt. "I could not recover the body. In the course of our fight, I dropped a building on top of her."

Ping raised an eyebrow, impressed.

"I remained for a few minutes after. I saw and sensed no one."

"We had hoped for a body."

Delun shrugged.

Ping studied Delun. The older monk suspected Ping wasn't used to others treating him so rudely. Eventually, Ping capitulated. "Very well. This evening, Chao is gathering all the wraiths in Jihan. Tonight, we strike the head off the Order of the Serpent."

Delun leaned forward. "You've found information on the captain?"

Ping nodded. "While you fought Bai, other wraiths completed another mission last night, designed to expose the Order's leaders."

Delun noticed Ping's deliberate vagueness.

"It worked, even better than we expected. The Order has been forced into hasty action. They plan on assaulting the monastery tonight and murdering the monks within. Tonight we don't just cut off the head, we kill the entire snake."

Delun didn't understand. How could so much have been accomplished in so little time? Whatever the rest of the wraiths had done last night, it must have been significant to bring about such a response.

He found he didn't care. If it brought the Order out of hiding, into the light where he could hunt them, he approved.

His fight with Bai had served as a distraction from Chao's larger plan, then. It took Bai out of the fight, permitting Chao to focus his resources on other problems.

Ping left, spreading the news to the other wraiths in the house. Delun lay on his bed, staring at the ceiling. Chao's accomplishments intimidated him. Chao thought several moves ahead of everyone else, and it had put the wraiths in a powerful position.

What Chao's ultimate plan looked like, Delun had no idea. He knew Chao's goal, but how he expected to get from here to there was far beyond him. But he would follow, if it meant justice for his brothers.

Delun closed his eyes and attempted to rest. He would need his strength this night.

THE WHOLE SMALL group of monks left the safehouse shortly before the sun set. Ping had insisted they wear their robes. Delun put his on, grateful for the familiar comfort. He hadn't worn them in weeks, and he realized how little he felt like himself without them. The robes were only a symbol, but they were a powerful one. He felt stronger just wearing them.

The city was abuzz with activity. City watchmen patrolled the streets, nailing up announcements in every square. A curfew had been established by order of the emperor and the city watch. Anyone found in the streets after curfew would face immediate imprisonment.

Crowds gathered around the signs, whispered murmurs passing between fearful glances. Other posters offered rewards for information about the destruction of a building in a square in a different part of town. The city watch searched for Delun.

The tension had been building in Jihan for weeks, but it had been a slow, creeping thing, resting somewhere in the background, a terror easily dismissed like a nightmare in the morning. Now it sat at the forefront of everyone's minds, haunting their waking thoughts.

Delun struggled to focus. Bai, Chao, and the Order of the Serpent all blended together in his thoughts. They each had their purpose, and a convergence of enemies gathered on the board, but to what end? He had spent so much time obsessed with seeking the Order and bringing it to justice that he had lost track of the bigger picture. He would need to solve that problem soon, after the Order was eliminated.

He followed Ping, surprised when the younger monk led him to a large building clearly designed as a warehouse.

Delun stopped outside the doors. He sensed the monks within, a gathering of power larger than any he had felt since approaching the monastery up in Two Bridges. His brothers gathered here in preparation for decisive action. The air quivered with possibility. There were far more wraiths here than he expected.

So much strength, finally gathered together.

The Order of the Serpent would regret its rebirth. None would stand in the way of the monasteries.

Delun stepped inside the building, impressed by the sheer size of the place. Barrels were stacked up along the walls, indicative of the original purpose of the building. The majority of the building was one enormous room. Near the back, several rooms had been built out of stone. In more normal times, Delun imagined they served as the rooms where the men who ran the warehouse would work and possibly sleep.

Nothing struck his attention more than the gathering of monks, however. From living in the safehouse, Delun had imagined the wraiths only numbered about a dozen in and around Jihan. Instead he counted close to four dozen. An entire monastery's worth of monks and then some had come covertly to Jihan. Unless the Order of the Serpent had more members than a lord's army, Chao's plans clearly extended beyond the elimination of the Order.

Ping left Delun to himself, and Delun reunited with a few monks he knew well. The wraiths' membership had grown over the past few months, the explosions forcing monks to choose action or pacifism. He was surprised at the sight of several monks. The attacks had forced otherwise moderate monks into decisive action. The Order would regret their mistake.

He didn't have long to reminisce with acquaintances. Soon the crowd hushed as Chao approached a small raised dais to speak with the assembled monks.

"It is good to see you here, friends. The time of our revenge is at hand. Tonight, we expect the Order of the Serpent to gather and strike at the monastery in Jihan."

A startled murmur rose from the crowd.

"Tonight, we stop the Order and destroy it." Chao held up a scroll in his hand for all to see. "We have a decree from the emperor himself. The Order is found guilty of treason against the empire. The punishment is death."

Delun found himself nodding along with all the rest. It was about time. They'd waited more than long enough to avenge their brothers. The emperor's support only made the action that much sweeter.

"You will be placed into groups. My lieutenants will have plans and details for you all. In short, though, the Order will gather in hideouts all around the city in preparation for their attack tonight. Thanks to our information from spies inside the Order, we know where many of these gathering places are. We will attack, and we will wipe the Order out with one clean move before they can strike again."

A cheer rose from the crowd, building in volume as a fervor swept over them.

Delun's voice was loud among them.

Chao stepped down from the dais and men began to circulate, collecting the wraiths into their groups for the evening.

Ping himself found Delun and brought him to Chao.

The leader of the wraiths gave Delun a grim smile. "Does our work tonight please you?"

Delun bowed. "It does. How did you achieve such a feat?"

Chao grinned, and Delun saw a hint of pride. Chao's plans were coming to fruition, and they delighted him. "Fate played a role, but last night Ping led a group of monks in a daring mission while you distracted Bai. Tonight, I want you and Ping to work as a pair. The two of you will pursue the captain himself. I've finally confirmed that the captain is behind it all. Are you up for it?"

Delun nodded. "I am."

"Good. Here are the details." Chao passed a stack of papers over to Delun. Delun looked through them with mounting disbelief.

"How have you learned so much, so fast?"

Chao leaned forward and spoke in hushed tones. "Last night, we met with some questioners, sent by the emperor. When I spoke, I spoke the truth. The emperor knows how much we are needed. It was the questioners who provided the information. They've infiltrated the Order at the highest ranks."

Was that how Chao had obtained so much information? It would make sense. The secretive questioners maintained the empire's deepest collection of spies and informants. It made much more sense than Chao building his own collection without so much as a whisper reaching Delun's ears.

The information also settled Delun's quiet fears.

Chao had been cooperating with the emperor the entire time.

The land was on the path to redemption. Delun could almost see the peace ahead.

Delun left Chao, eager to find the captain and end his life.

21

Lei and Daiyu broke their fast early in the afternoon at the Heron. Daiyu had woke up feeling weak, so they kept close to their room throughout the morning. When her strength finally returned, they made their way to the dining room just as most were eating lunch. As they ate, Lei's gaze kept wandering over to Daiyu, his chest constricting.

She was too young. Both of them had seen over fifty years, a full and healthy life by anyone's measure. But it was still too early to say goodbye.

She noticed his attention and shot him a glare. "Stop looking at me like that."

He gave her a short smile and focused on his food. As usual, the Heron's cook had prepared an incredible meal. Lei dug in and took another bite, but he possessed little appetite to sate.

Their meal was interrupted by hushed voices at the door. A man in a military uniform entered the dining area, ignoring the protestations of the Heron's owner.

Eventually the officer made it past the owner. Despite the owner's valiant attempts, he had no choice but to capitulate. Very few people could afford to defy the empire in any meaningful way.

The officer made a direct line for the two of them. Lei met the man's gaze, warning him away.

The officer was either dense or obstinate. He never broke stride until he stood above the couple and held out a scroll sealed with the personal mark of the emperor. He treated the paper as gently as a newborn babe.

Lei didn't take the proffered scroll, shocking the officer. "How can I help you?"

The soldier, flustered, sputtered, "I have orders direct from the emperor to escort you to the palace, master."

Lei raised an eyebrow, then turned his attention to Daiyu. She gave him a small nod, saying volumes with that small gesture.

She would be fine.

There was no point in causing more trouble than necessary.

He should go.

Lei sighed, stood up, and kissed the top of Daiyu's head. "I'll be back soon."

She nodded with the nonchalance of one who already knew.

Lei grabbed the paper out of the officer's hands. He followed the man out into the street, where a full unit of uniformed men stood at ready attention. Lei shook his head in disbelief, but the officer, with his duty again in progress, didn't notice.

They traveled through town, Lei surrounded by guards. What must people think about him as they passed by?

He'd never been to the palace before, but even from a distance it appeared appropriately majestic. The walls were tall and thick, the stone menacing.

They passed the thick gates without problem and Lei was treated to his first uninterrupted view of the seat of the emperor. The palace itself sat beyond an incredibly large courtyard, and the structure was the largest building Lei had ever seen.

Stone and wood combined to form a building four stories tall. Additions, terraces, and balconies jutted from the edifice, and the rooftops seemed a maze one might never escape from. He couldn't even guess how many rooms the building held.

He noticed two facts immediately.

The first was that the courtyard leading to the palace was nearly empty. He and his escort made up most of the expansive area's population. Of the people he could see, he was the only one not in uniform.

The second fact was that the palace was being repaired. Off in the distance, almost hidden from where Lei stood, was a hole in the wall. Workers in uniform swarmed around the blemish.

Lei's eye was drawn toward the figure of a man walking quickly toward them. He shook his head. Of all the people in the world.

Lord Xun's questioner stopped about ten paces away from Lei and his escort. It seemed Lord Xun and his retinue had moved into position as one of the emperor's top advisers. Lei couldn't imagine another reason he'd be seeing so much of the man.

"Lei, it is good to see you again."

"I wish the same could be said for you."

The man smiled. No matter how Lei tried, he couldn't offend him. That lack of offense was a powerful tool in the questioner's line of duty, Lei imagined.

The questioner turned to the officer who had escorted Lei. "You may return to your normal duties. Thank you."

The officer gave a doubtful look, but he wasn't the type of man to question orders. He saluted, bowed, then marched his unit away.

The questioner swept his hand in the direction of the palace. "Shall we?"

Lei walked at the questioner's side as they crossed the enormous courtyard. "How did you find me?"

The questioner answered the unasked question. "You weren't followed. I suspected either you or Daiyu would spot a tail. We had watchers, both along the possible routes of travel and within Jihan. You couldn't have spotted them, and it was unlikely you would make it past them."

It was too much to ask that they travel in anonymity, Lei supposed.

Within the walls of the palace grounds, the questioner traveled with impunity. They passed several sets of guards without so much as a question. They entered the palace building itself, and Lei's pace slowed to a complete stop.

He'd never imagined such a structure was possible. All the furniture was lined with gold, and the wood floors were polished to a shine. Dust found no home here, and the spaces were so large as to cause Lei to look up and expect to see open sky above him.

Lei had grown up in a monastery, an impressive structure by most accounts, with thick walls and stout buildings. They had been clean, but the spaces within were small, and there had been no opulence. Monks shunned such affectations.

Even when he'd founded his own village, the buildings were simple wooden constructions. He'd thought his house large, but his whole home would have fit in this single room.

He hadn't even believed such wonders possible.

The questioner gave him a knowing smile. "It's quite something, isn't it?"

Lei could only nod.

The questioner resumed their journey and Lei followed. He could tell the questioner was impatient, but this architecture was too much to just pass by. Lei suddenly felt small and provincial, a novel feeling for his age.

They passed through room after room of wonder, Lei taking as much of it in as possible.

Finally, they reached a thick double door. A set of four guards stood outside it, and Lei assumed the room held the emperor. Despite his own beliefs, he felt a sense of awe. Part of it was the enormity of the palace, but part of it was just coming face to face with a new type of power.

Lei could destroy cities, if he so chose, but the emperor could command an entire land. What would the emperor be like?

He noticed the questioner studying him. "I imagine you don't know the first thing about court etiquette?"

Lei shook his head.

The questioner gave a sigh. "Just bow when you enter."

Lei gave him a skeptical look. "I don't serve the empire."

The questioner looked as though he'd swallowed something sour. "If I die for this, I'm haunting you for the rest of your days."

The questioner nodded to the guards, who opened the thick doors. They stepped into a room which made all that had come before pale in comparison. The room was a long rectangle, with thick columns running up both sides. On the other end of the room sat a throne, currently occupied.

Lei's first look at the emperor didn't impress. The ruler of the land was in conference with a few other men, and the price of all the clothing worn between them would have fed a village for months.

The questioner bowed when he entered the room, even though no one acknowledged him. They advanced halfway to the throne before stopping.

A few minutes later, the men ended their conference and left. Lei got his first full view of the emperor.

He saw a man little different from any other. If anything, the man seemed spoiled by his lifestyle. He wasn't fat, exactly, but carried more weight than most men Lei knew. If the man had ever served in the military, that past was long behind him now.

As soon as the emperor's gaze fell upon them, the questioner prostrated himself, bowing all the way to the ground. Lei looked at the man in disbelief. Such actions should only be used to express the deepest of emotions. Lei remained standing.

He saw a flicker of annoyance pass over the emperor's face. Apparently the questioner's behavior was expected. Lei's was not.

Lei felt the fear radiating off the questioner, but he remained standing. A knife remained hidden in his robes. Throughout his journey, no one had thought to ask him about a weapon. He didn't serve the emperor, and if the worst came, Lei wasn't particularly worried. He would still be back to Daiyu before the evening meal. As impressive as the palace's walls were, they couldn't withstand his gift.

She would criticize him, call him a proud fool, but at his age, he just didn't care anymore.

"You don't bow to your emperor?" Lei heard the anger in the man's voice and chose to ignore it.

"You aren't my emperor."

The emperor made a gesture, and Lei heard the sounds

of bows being drawn all around him. He signed a shield, just in case the situation deteriorated. He spoke calmly, soothing the tension. "You can't harm me. I could tear this building down in minutes, killing you and everyone here. This has been true for decades, yet you still live. I am here, peacefully and of my own choice. Why have you summoned me?"

For a tense moment, Lei thought he might have to follow through on his threat. The emperor looked angry enough to test him.

The anger turned to cold, calculating fury. The emperor's next words were spoken without emotion.

"I need you to find my daughter."

Another gesture allowed the archers around the room to relax, and the questioner finally looked up, standing slowly.

Lei didn't understand. The princess was gone? How could such a thing have happened with her protection increased after the first attempt? "What happened?"

"We believe she was kidnapped by a group of monks who call themselves wraiths."

Lei knew the group well enough. Yang spoke of them as a scourge. Lei didn't realize they would be so bold. Monks swore an oath to protect the empire. How did they fall so far as to kidnap the princess? And what did they hope to accomplish?

"You've heard nothing from them? They've given no demands?"

The questioner shook his head. "This all happened last night. We have not yet heard from them."

Another thought crossed Lei's mind. If Yang's students had been permitted entry to the palace, none of this would have happened. He wondered if the emperor and the questioner thought the same.

Lei felt a twisting in his stomach. Something in this

room was off, something below the level of his conscious attention. He studied both the questioner and the emperor. Both had their gazes fixed on him like teachers waiting for a student to give their answer. What thoughts ran through their minds?

The emperor spoke again. "I will not allow my daughter to come to harm, Master Lei. I have summoned Lord Xun's army to the city, and they will be here in less than a week. If the princess is not found by then, I will order the army into the city to search for her."

Lei hid his frown, realizing these men played a deep game where appearances were not as they seemed. Lei knew his history. He didn't think a sitting emperor had ever allowed an army into Jihan. The disruption to lives and business would be monumental.

"I do not want to resort to such measures," the emperor continued. "But if she is not found, I will. Find her before then."

There was no question in the emperor's voice. He expected obedience, though Lei had shown little thus far.

No small part of Lei wanted to turn away from it all, to spend Daiyu's final days in peace. Yet he felt the confluence of forces gathering around him. Could he live with himself if he didn't play at least some role? Could he live in peace if he refused the emperor?

He figured he had little choice. He could fight if he chose, but that only complicated his life. Better to follow the currents where they took him, for now. He gave a small bow and followed the questioner out of the room.

22

———

Bai's heart pounded in her ears as she fought against the weight of the building. Dust filled her nostrils, but she couldn't expand her chest to cough. Unable to breathe, she pulled in more energy, the process sluggish and unnatural now. Her body neared its limit, pushed too hard for the last time. She channeled energy into her arms, pushing against the weight of stone pressing her inexorably toward death.

For a terrifying moment, nothing happened. Even with her gifts, her arms lacked the strength to push the stone away. Then something gave and she created a small space. The weight shifted and settled in a new position.

Cool air burst upon her face. She sucked greedily, coughing as more dust coated her throat.

All things considered, she'd been fortunate. She'd forced an enormous amount of energy into her body as the building collapsed around her. Her legs were pinned, but not tightly. If she had more room to work, she thought she might be able to free them. As it was, there just wasn't enough space.

But she'd created a gap, and air was reaching her lungs. For the moment, she was safe.

Her memories flashed back to some of her earliest training with Lei. After the battle of Kulat, they had focused for months on mental discipline. Her lack of focus had almost killed her in Kulat and Lei didn't want the mistake repeated.

That training brought her some measure of ease now. She closed her eyes and focused on her breath. She released most of the power she held, slowly, ensuring her small cave wouldn't collapse without her supporting its weight.

The focus on her breath kept the panic at bay. She had no love for small spaces, and even with her last effort, all she had done was clear a space about a hand's width wide. She could breathe but little else.

Exhaustion crept through her aching limbs and she fought the urge to close her eyes. She needed to escape this rubble, but she had so little left to fight with. She'd pulled in strength to run across the roofs, then even more to fight Delun. Her body could only take so much.

With every passing moment, hopelessness settled heavier on her shoulders. She didn't know how deeply she was buried. She couldn't see the sky. Even if she summoned more energy, she wasn't sure pushing at the walls of her coffin was wise. She had no way of judging the risk. But if she did nothing, her odds were even worse.

Thoughts of dying, trapped under the ruins of a building, made her heart race. Again, she focused on her breath. There had to be a way. She moved her head, looking around as far as the space would allow.

Her attention shifted when she felt another gifted approach. Bai cursed. She was defenseless. Had Delun come to finish what he started? That seemed low, even for him.

She soon decided it wasn't Delun. The monk felt very different, his power obvious even from a distance. As soon as she focused her attention, she knew who had come. She breathed a sigh of relief.

Rong stood just beyond the pile of stone.

Bai licked her lips. "Here!"

She had meant her voice to be louder, but it came out as a strangled croak.

Rong heard her, though. She approached closer to the rubble. "Bai?"

"I'm here."

Bai felt Rong's power grow, and she could hear the sound of rock being moved. From where she lay, though, she couldn't feel any difference in the weight.

"Are you okay?" Rong asked.

"I think so. I'm trapped."

"Hold on."

Bai had never thought the sound of rock against rock could be so beautiful. Rong worked methodically, and after a few minutes, had uncovered Bai's face.

"Hello."

Bai laughed, relief flooding through her. She felt euphoric. Her breath came easier.

Bai summoned some more power, the effort twisting her stomach into knots. Working together, the two women freed Bai from the broken depths of the building.

Gingerly, Bai tested her mobility. She would have plenty of bruises, but she thought she would be otherwise uninjured. She'd been fortunate to have enough wherewithal to reinforce her limbs as the walls collapsed around her.

Rong escorted her out of the courtyard to safety.

They made it to the outskirts of Jihan without problem.

Instead of leaving through the gate, as they had before, this time Rong led her to a small house near the wall. Together they stepped in.

Yang's students were inside. Questions struggled to find purchase in Bai's mind, and nothing settled. At the moment, all that mattered was that she was safe.

Rong led her to a room with a bed, where Bai immediately lay down and fell asleep.

WHEN SHE WOKE, her head pounded and her body complained. Groaning, she sat up and looked out the window. Daylight filtered through it. Despite the hammering in her head, she felt rested, if stiff.

Her muscles spasmed when she tried to stand and she tumbled to the floor in a heap. The noise brought Rong into the room. The woman saw Bai up, left for a moment, then returned with a pail of water and a ladle.

"Drink slowly," she said.

Bai didn't need encouragement. Her throat felt like it was cracking open. She took one sip, then another. She wasn't sure water had ever tasted so wonderful. "Thank you," she croaked.

Rong flashed her a sympathetic smile. "How are you feeling?"

"I used too much energy. Far too much."

Rong nodded. "We were worried about you for a while, earlier in the day. Your breathing slowed so much we thought you were near death."

"Not yet."

Rong sat in silence while Bai sipped more water. Now that her thirst had been slaked, she realized it had been a long time since she'd eaten. Her stomach rumbled loudly, asking the question Bai was ashamed to.

Rong didn't seem to mind. "We've got food, too."

The next hour was one of the most glorious of Bai's life. Rong and her companions prepared no small amount of food, and Bai ate with a ravenous hunger. She was certain she had never eaten so much in one sitting before. Near the end of her feast, she wondered if she worried her hosts at all.

Rong, at least, seemed to be the type of person who took all things in stride. Nothing disturbed her calm and friendly nature.

Eventually, Bai felt like she was ready to be up and about again. She struggled to her feet, wondering if this was how it felt to age. Each of her muscles obeyed her commands, but they did so against their will.

Rong invited her for a walk. Bai shot a questioning glance outside. "What about threats?"

The younger warrior shook her head. "Given all that's been happening, I don't think we have much to worry about."

Bai wasn't so certain, but Rong had earned her trust. She owed the mysterious woman her life.

They stepped out into the street together, and Rong led the way, kindly moving slowly for Bai's sake. Bai's legs protested the effort initially, but after they had walked for a while, they began to feel much better. A gentle walk had been exactly the remedy she needed.

Rong led the conversation as well as the walk. "What happened in the courtyard? I felt the energy, although I'm sure almost every monk in Jihan did, too."

"I had a run-in with an old friend." Bai recounted the story.

"Why didn't other monks show up? I worried at first, but I was the only one who approached the area."

Bai shrugged. "Delun probably set the trap so we wouldn't be bothered. He had a decent amount of authority in the monasteries a decade ago. I can only imagine he's developed more over the years."

Bai could tell Rong had several things on her mind, but she let the woman take her time. Rong shuffled her feet, her head down. "Do you mind if I ask you a personal question?"

Bai shook her head.

"What was it like, when you found out?"

Though it had been ten years, the memory was as fresh as those from this morning. "I don't remember the actual event. But when I learned the truth, I was devastated. I had harmed many people I knew and cared about. You?"

"Ecstatic."

"Do you remember the moment?"

Rong nodded. "It wasn't very dramatic, actually. I was making a living as a thief. A monk grabbed me by the wrist once, right after I'd made a mistake and was running from the watch. I felt the power surge through me, and I was able to throw the monk and run faster than I ever had before. That was the incident that brought me to Yang's attention."

Rong spoke of the moment with affection in her voice. Without hearing an explanation, Bai created her own version of Rong's history.

A thief, probably struggling to get by, scraping together the money needed to live. One didn't turn to crime unless the need was high. Bai had no trouble imagining Rong's past life: bargaining for day-old bread, fighting the temptation to grab food from the market and run, hiding what little coin she had.

In many ways, Rong's story wasn't all that different from Bai's.

Bai had never crossed that invisible line that made her a criminal, not until she discovered her power. But it had always beckoned.

And now?

Bai saw herself in Rong. They were both criminals, she supposed, although the word didn't quite fit. But they no longer worried where their next meal would come from. Their sights were set higher than survival, now.

Bai watched the other woman out of the corner of her eye. Though they barely knew each other, she felt at ease around Rong, like they were friends from childhood. At the moment, the other woman had a question on her mind she hadn't found the courage to ask. From the way Rong nibbled her lower lip, Bai suspected it was the question she had really been meaning to ask the whole time.

Finally, it came, spilling out of her like soldiers crashing through the collapse of a besieged wall. "What was it like, attacking Kulat?"

Bai searched for the best answer. "Terrifying. Thrilling. Foolish. I had just discovered my powers and had people telling me my purpose in life was to fight monks. I believed them."

Rong gave her a funny look, noticing her tone. "Aren't you proud?"

Bai looked off into the distance, considering the question. She'd spent years thinking about those days, but she wasn't sure she had answered that for herself yet. "I am proud that we stopped the plans that were in place. I know we saved lives that day, that we prevented a war." Her memory traveled back to her final fight with the abbot of Kulat, his mangled body a sight she could never unsee, the damage caused by her own fist. "I have always wondered if there was a better way. We created a martyr that day."

"You created a legend for yourself, too. All of us talk about that day. We want to be like you."

Bai almost laughed, but caught herself before it escaped. The sincerity in Rong's voice was almost painful to hear. "I do not feel like a legend. I was caught up in the moment, and while I did what I could, it felt more like being caught in a powerful stream, following the current."

"Almost like now."

Bai nodded. "Exactly like now."

23

———

Delun and Ping worked their way toward the building Chao believed would host the Order's leaders this night. The description and directions they'd received were detailed, and the two of them made quick time.

They arrived well before evening and found a roof across the street where they could watch the building. The location appeared to be an old shop that hadn't been open for years. Their vantage point allowed them a full view of the building while providing concealment from wary eyes.

While they waited for the leadership to arrive, Delun's mind finally had time to wander. After weeks of pointless investigation, events had suddenly moved quickly.

The captain of the watch was on the forefront of his mind. For weeks, he'd seen nothing but the behavior of a dedicated soldier. Delun believed the captain was guilty, but he'd yet to see any suggestion of guilt firsthand.

All he had was Chao's word that the man was the traitor Delun suspected he was.

Delun knew the danger of accepting any opinion that

agreed with his preconceived notions, but his instincts told him the captain was too good to be clean.

Tonight would be evidence enough. If the captain appeared, Delun considered that an admission of guilt.

The two wraiths didn't speak much, mostly content with the silence between them. Delun watched the area. Beside him, Ping quivered with nervous energy. After a while, Delun began to wonder about his compatriot.

"Are you ready?"

Ping looked offended, but Delun gestured toward Ping's hands, which hadn't been still for over an hour. The younger man blushed. "It's my first combat." He spoke the words as though they were an intimate secret.

Delun controlled his reaction. It wasn't unusual for a monk not to have seen combat. For the majority of monks, days consisted entirely of training and monastic life. But given Ping's rhetoric, he'd always assumed the monk had fought before.

Tonight seemed a poor time to start.

Shadows lengthened as evening fell, the streets slowly falling into peacefulness below as citizens hurried to get home before the new curfew.

The moon had just begun to rise when the captain of the city watch came into view. Delun's heart beat faster. Any lingering doubts dissipated. The captain looked both ways down the street before entering the building.

Shortly thereafter, four others joined him, trickling into the building singly.

All five of the highest leaders of the Order of the Serpent were gathered, exactly the number Chao's intelligence had predicted.

Delun glanced at Ping, who nodded. Neither saw much point in delaying the inevitable. Moving like their namesakes, the wraiths slid down to ground level without so much as a whisper of fabric.

Tonight Delun carried a dagger. Unlike some, he didn't possess the ability to fill the dagger with energy. It was nothing more than a blade in his hand. But sometimes a blade could make all the difference in the world. He'd spent the past decade training with weapons, moving beyond the traditions of the monasteries.

The abandoned shop had two entrances. Delun paused near the front while Ping made his way to the rear. Delun would be the hammer and Ping the anvil. Delun gave Ping a minute to get in position, then focused energy into his hand and blasted the door off its hinges.

Delun formed another attack even as he stepped through the doorway. Dust clogged the air as the door clattered to the floor in the center of the room. Delun ensured the first room was clear before stepping deeper into the house.

He took three steps inside. A man stepped into the doorway from the next room, sword already in hand. Delun lifted his hand and released the attack, blasting the man off his feet until he crashed into the opposite wall ten feet back. The blow probably didn't kill the serpent, but he would be stunned for several valuable seconds.

Delun formed another attack and worked his way into the second room. Another sword-wielding soldier greeted him with a deadly shout and an overhand cut. Delun released his attack into the man's exposed torso, sending him crashing into a different wall.

He needed to kill the men, and quick. Five against one in a small space was poor odds, even for a monk. Delun darted over to the first man, who was working his way back to his feet. Delun slammed his knee into the man's nose, shattering the soft bone underneath.

Finally, he drew the dagger and stabbed it deep into the man's neck.

When he turned around, the second man was already back to his feet, advancing warily on Delun, sword held out straight in front of him in a defensive stance.

Delun knew time was against him. Ping guarded the back door, but the longer a fight went on, the more time there was for things to go wrong. Delun sheathed his knife with one hand while the other signed an even more powerful attack.

The soldier saw the motion and darted in, aiming for a fatal wound before Delun could release his attack.

The traitor never had a chance. Delun released his power. The soldier, and the wall behind him, collapsed from Delun's attack.

Delun darted into the hole he'd just made, seeking out his final opponents. He swore when he saw the back door open.

A moment later he stood in the alley behind the abandoned shop, surveying the scene before him. Two of the men were clearly dead, their bodies twisted at unnatural angles. The final man, the captain, still lived. His face was broken and bloody, but there was no mistaking the rage in his eyes.

For all the captain had done to convince the world he was a man of honor, Delun saw the truth reflected in the man's eyes.

The captain hated monks. In other circumstances, Delun might have questioned the captain, but face to face with his most detested enemy, he saw no point. They already knew the captain led the Order. All the serpents' plans would fail tonight. What else was there to know?

Ping looked calm as ever. He bowed and took a step away. "I figured you might want the honor."

Delun found himself moved by the gesture. They had all lost friends in the explosions this man had orchestrated, yet Ping was willing to sacrifice his vengeance for Delun.

Delun bowed toward Ping. Words failed him.

He stood over the captain and drew his dagger. The mere sight of the man tinged his vision with red. Justice wasn't enough. This was the man who had planned Taio's death and the deaths of so many. Any end was too good for the man.

Delun drove the dagger into the man's stomach. He stabbed once, twice, three times, his arm moving back and forth of its own accord. The captain grunted but made no other sound.

The captain tried to spit at him, but Delun saw the motion coming. He backhanded the man's face, snapping it to the side. The spit ended up against the wall that supported the man.

Delun crouched down next to him. "Any final words?"

The captain grinned. "Someday, you'll be betrayed too."

Delun shook his head. As far as final words went, he wasn't impressed.

He drove the dagger into the man's heart, giving him a few more seconds to contemplate his failure.

The captain closed his eyes, and Delun nodded to Ping. He wiped the dagger on the captain's clothing and sheathed it. Ping gathered his energy and shot it into the air.

Delun felt the answering signals burst into the air throughout the city. The signal spread throughout Jihan. The captain was dead, the head of the serpent decapitated. Now it was time to destroy the rest of the body.

Their evening of vengeance was just beginning.

DELUN AND PING'S orders were to meet up with another group of wraiths before they began their own assault. The other team consisted of two younger wraiths, eager but unused to the rigors of combat. The younger team took point while Delun and Ping provided support. Delun began to suspect that Chao was using him as a battlefield mentor.

Their assigned target was a large, squat building. The two young monks who staked out the building reported that nearly a dozen men were inside, possibly with powder.

Delun stepped back, letting Ping take charge. The younger monk craved the responsibility. Ping would lead them inside while Delun waited nearby outside in case anyone escaped.

The wraiths moved in without giving warning. Off in the distance, Delun heard an explosion. Somewhere, at least a barrel of black powder had gone off. Delun thought he saw the glow of fires reflected off the low-hanging clouds. Parts of Jihan might burn tonight, but when the fires burned out, a healthier community would be left behind. Fire cleansed and prepared the way for the next generation of growth.

Sounds of fighting soon escaped the building, the whole structure groaning as the monks within unleashed their gifts on the surprised traitors. Delun heard footsteps and drew his dagger. He stabbed the first man out through the door, barely glancing at his target as he moved to the next man escaping.

There was a shout from within. Delun sensed the three monks running back toward him, toward the exit.

The rear of the building suddenly erupted, sending chunks of stone and wood high into the air. The blast knocked Delun off his feet, but he had the presence of mind to cast a shield over himself as the debris crashed down around him.

When the dust finally cleared, Delun saw two of the monks hiding under a shield. He looked more closely. Ping had cast the dome over them, protecting them from the explosion and the collapse.

The final wraith was nowhere to be seen. His fate was certain.

The serpents had blown themselves up instead of fighting like honorable warriors.

Delun's hatred of the Order deepened. How could they act in such a way? Were they completely without reason?

Ping dropped the shield, his face ashen. He looked around. "Where?"

Delun picked his way through the rubble. He kneeled down next to Ping. "Are you okay?"

Ping didn't seem to hear him. "Where is he?"

Delun put his hand on the younger man's shoulder. Their eyes met and Delun shook his head.

Ping bent his head.

The older monk gave the others a few minutes. But there was more to do. Delun felt the energy rippling throughout the city. The battle hadn't been won yet. "Can you fight?"

There would be no shame in saying no, but Ping nodded.

The three of them took off into the night.

There was much work yet to be done, and another life that called for vengeance.

24

Lei and the questioner walked the polished hallways of the castle. Lei wondered if it was possible to become used to such opulence. The feats of architecture and design inspired him, reminded him that people were capable of great deeds.

The questioner didn't push Lei to hurry. Lei knew he wouldn't be back in time for the evening meal, so he forced himself to relax and study the palace. Lei inspected the paintings, the gold-leafed furniture, and the displays of weapons. To him, the empire had always been more of an idea than something physical. It was a set of laws he largely ignored, a system of power and control he had little use for. But here, walking these halls, the empire represented something different. History was tangible. Lei saw gifts that had been sent from rival lords hundreds of years ago when the empire had first unified.

Eventually they came to a room with two guards standing watch. The guards let the questioner through without a second glance. They gave Lei searching looks, but accompanying the questioner was enough.

The room they entered was a study in contrasts. Like the other rooms in the palace, fine art and decoration adorned the walls, but the resulting emotion was different. Other rooms and halls were packed with items, overwhelming the visitor. In contrast, this room felt spacious and considered. Whoever lived here took great care in arranging their space.

The effect was considerably diminished by the gaping hole in the opposing wall, and the destruction of nearly half the room.

"The princess's chambers," the questioner announced.

Lei stopped a few paces into the room, letting himself soak this place in. He wasn't sure what the emperor or the questioner expected from him. He was no investigator. But perhaps there were clues.

Lei sniffed the air. A faint whiff of incense tickled his nostrils. A calming scent still clung to the space. He found that unusual. He turned to the questioner. "The hole is from the attack several weeks ago. Did the princess still use the chambers after?"

"She did. She hosted visitors elsewhere, but otherwise, she was often found here. She slept here, also."

The bedroom was unharmed, a room set apart from the rest of the chambers. Lei supposed nothing prevented the princess from a comfortable night's rest there, but he imagined having a hole to the outdoors in the next room over would be odd.

These rooms meant something to her. Lei noted it and moved on.

His hair stood on end. Some detail bothered him, but he couldn't put his finger on it.

The first half of the main chambers, the part he'd seen when he first stepped in, was pristine, a study in the character of the princess. Lei looked at her space and saw a calm, determined woman. He knew next to nothing about the imperial court, but if her room was a reflection of her character, Lei was impressed.

He focused on the other part of the room. Here, the evidence of a fight intrigued him. He saw broken furniture, torn tapestries, and gouges along the walls. Repairs had begun on the outer wall, but the original damage was still visible. The scope of the damage indicated the strengths of the warriors involved.

The hole drew his attention, and Lei gave in to his mounting curiosity. He walked to it, leaning out until he saw the ground below. Broken stone lay in a pile of rubble below. Outside, the sun had just fallen below the horizon.

"The blast was from inside?" All evidence pointed that way, but Lei wanted to be sure.

"Yes. Flying debris killed a guard. All of that is from the first attack."

Lei frowned as a thought occurred to him. He stepped back to take a look at the hole again. The wall of the palace was another ten paces past the wall of the princess's room. To blow stone large enough to kill a man, and to make a hole that size, required impressive strength. The monk who made that hole had to be strong and had to have used at least the fourth sign. That sign only had one purpose: to kill.

"Was there anyone else in the room for either attack?"

"No."

Lei turned to face the man. "What do you think happened here?"

The questioner thought for a moment. "There are no secrets here. A couple of weeks ago, the princess met with a group of monks who turned out to be wraiths. The monks, unwilling to accept that the princess was gifted, attacked. The princess killed most of her assailants, but we know at least one escaped. No doubt the wraiths planned revenge. We still don't know how they captured the princess last night, but no other suspects seem reasonable."

Lei wondered at that. The explanations sounded reasonable. But something about them rubbed him the wrong way. He couldn't see why the monks would kidnap the princess. If they hated the idea of her, Lei imagined they would try to kill her. But they hadn't. Or, if they had, they had gone to a great deal of trouble to hide it. He sensed that there was more happening underneath the surface, something he didn't understand.

He also wondered how the monks had gotten to the princess. If she'd survived the fourth sign in her first encounter, her training was beyond what Lei had assumed. Why didn't she fight the second time?

He backed up, taking in the whole room again, this time with new eyes. What were her powers? Now that his attention had a focus, more details emerged from the chaos. He saw how some of the furniture had been broken by the monk's attacks, the blunt damage familiar to his eye.

Other details didn't make sense, though. A tapestry hanging on the wall caught his eye, the design cut in two with a single sharp stroke. "Does the princess know how to use a sword, or a dagger?"

"No."

Lei approached the fabric. The tapestry hung on a stone wall. From a distance, the cut looked like a clean sword cut. When Lei came closer, he saw that whatever had cut the tapestry had cut the wall behind as well, the stone gouged with a narrow gash. Such damage required more physical strength than even Lei possessed.

At both the beginning and end of the slice, the cut was shallow, deepening near the middle. It made no sense.

Cutting through stone required the gift, but if the power of the gift had made this cut, the cut would be more uniform. Lei didn't understand. "How much do you know about the princess's gift?"

The questioner shook his head. "Neither Master Yang nor the princess ever shared that information."

Lei stood back from the wall. He wouldn't understand the princess's gift, not today. It was unique, and it was strong enough to defend against monks. The information wasn't much, but it would get him started.

A plan for recovering the princess began to form in his mind. If her gift was this strong, there were ways to find her. He turned to the questioner one more time. "Are you certain she is still in Jihan?"

"As much as we can be, yes. From the moment her disappearance was discovered, all the gates have been watched as closely as we can. Nothing and no one is leaving without our knowledge."

The comfort was slim, but it would have to be enough. He could begin the search.

Lei was just about to dismiss himself when he felt tremendous surges of energy throughout Jihan. He started. He'd never felt so many flares of energy. If he could feel them all the way from the palace, the power being released was incredible.

The questioner's sharp eyes noticed Lei's expression. "What is it?"

"Jihan. Something is happening."

The questioner didn't seem concerned, but he couldn't feel what Lei felt. So many monks coordinating their efforts meant disaster.

Memories of thirty years ago came rushing back, the explosions of energy that tore apart a city.

Daiyu was there.

Lei didn't have time to explain. There was little the city watch could do against such a force, anyhow. Lei needed to be down there. He bolted from the room, beginning the long run to the city.

LEI WISHED, not for the first time, that he had some small measure of Bai's gifts. For all the strength he could summon, he still couldn't move faster than a run, and at his age, he didn't run like he used to. His legs were strong, but his age was undeniable. It took him far too long to exit the palace, cross the courtyard, and reach Jihan.

Distant rumbles of power kept him moving, fear for the city and one visitor in particular pushing him far past his normal boundaries.

In retrospect he should have stolen a horse from the palace, but the thought hadn't occurred to him and it was too late now.

The streets of Jihan were eerily quiet once he arrived. Of course, most people wouldn't feel the surges of energy, but Lei had expected more chaos. If not for the power manifesting throughout the city, he almost would have guessed the night was no different than any other.

Lei ignored the wells of power that surrounded him. He wasn't looking for a fight, only Daiyu. Whenever he felt powers gathering nearby he angled away from them.

His luck ran out about a half mile from the Heron. Two groups of wraiths were coming together. Going around would take too long. Lei pulled in power, feeling the energy rejuvenate his tired limbs. He cast a shield over himself and kept running. With any luck they would ignore him and move on to other targets.

The wraiths came into view. Lei saw the blood on their clothes. This wasn't their first encounter of the evening.

He ignored them, but the groups focused on him, following him as he ran.

Lei wouldn't bring six monks to the Heron. He refused to allow fighting to approach the inn.

So he stopped and turned. He raised his hand to stop them, but the gesture was misinterpreted as an attack. Several waves of energy crashed against his shield, but it held. Either they weren't aware of his strength or they were fools.

In other times Lei might have had the patience for a different approach. But tonight he thought only of Daiyu's safety. He dove deep into the rivers of power flowing around him and called upon them. Then he replied to their attacks, sending blast after blast of energy at them. His attacks furrowed ditches in the road as they roared toward his enemies. Four of the six monks crumpled to the ground before the others ran.

Lei didn't care about the fate of the wraiths. They had initiated the violence. The consequences rested on their heads.

Lei turned and ran toward the Heron.

25

Bai and Rong returned to the safehouse that evening, the walk through the city having done wonders for Bai. Her body was still sore, and her limbs still felt as heavy as iron, but she was up and moving. The rest would heal in time.

Shu stood outside the safehouse. She spoke to Bai. "May we talk for a moment?"

Bai could smell the meal being cooked within the house. Her stomach, amazingly, still craved more food.

"We'll be done in time for supper."

That was all the argument Bai needed. She'd been wanting to speak more with Shu, also. Rong went inside to help with the preparation.

Shu led Bai on a short walk around the block. "The others look up to you."

Shu's voice wasn't accusatory, but Bai still felt the weight of the woman's suspicions. "They are too kind. If it concerns you, I have no desire to lead this group."

Shu didn't respond immediately. They walked for a

minute in silence. Shu's next question caught Bai by surprise. "You love your gift, don't you?"

She'd never been asked such a question. "I suppose. I can't imagine life without it."

That wasn't strictly true. Bai knew well the path her life would have taken if her gift had never manifested. She'd still be in Galan, poor and hungry and mending clothes for men who leered at her. She would have turned into her mother. But knowing her life now, she couldn't imagine returning to that role.

Shu stopped. "I wish mine had never manifested."

Bai turned so she was facing the woman. "Really?"

Shu gave a small shrug, as though to say it didn't really matter. The gesture didn't fool Bai, though. "I had a family."

Bai noted the tense. "What happened?"

"When I realized I was gifted, I ran away from them. I didn't want them to know, and I didn't want to put them in danger." She gave a grim smile then that Bai didn't understand.

"I'm sorry."

Shu's eyes came up to meet Bai's. They held a sudden, unexpected intensity. "I think you should lead Yang's students."

The offer took Bai aback. The thought of giving commands was even more reprehensible than having to obey them. She had no desire to order others about. She shook her head. "Thank you, but no. If you don't want the position, why not ask someone else?"

"There is no one else. The others look up to Rong, but her blood boils with a desire to fight. She cannot keep them safe. If you won't, I'm not sure anyone can."

Bai didn't know how to respond, but Shu saved her the

difficulty. She walked quickly away, back to the front of the house. After a moment Bai followed.

The food that had been prepared smelled delicious enough to make Bai's mouth water. Though she'd eaten no small amount of food when she'd woken up, her body still demanded more. She figured she could eat all the food in Jihan right now.

Bai pushed aside her conversation with Shu. She could understand the other woman wanting to shed the responsibility, but Bai was not the one to pass it off to.

The more Bai learned about the other warriors Yang had taught, the more comfortable she became. They all shared a common physical language. In the group, Shu acted like an overprotective mother. Rong typically sat apart from the others, quiet and with her eyes focused on some distant point.

Wu was the heart of the group. He was young, not just in age, but in spirit. Life was an adventure to him. Bai didn't think she ever saw the young man without a smile on his face. Being among them made her feel at home in a way she never had since her mother died.

As much as she enjoyed them all, Bai found herself drawn to Rong's company. Gliding across rooftops with the other warrior had sealed a bond Bai couldn't articulate. She'd never had a sister, but perhaps this was how it felt. Even their temperaments were similar.

The food and company lulled her into complacency.

They all sensed the monks. As gifted warriors inside Jihan, there was no mistaking the waves of power reaching into the sky. The whole city suddenly came alive with power. Bai tensed up, her body as taut as a bowstring. She couldn't even count how many attacks she felt.

None had felt particularly close, but that did little to

ease Bai's concern. The attacks could only have come from the wraiths. They had spread throughout the city. To what purpose?

Rong gave voice to everyone's fear. "What was that?"

As one, the group turned to Shu. Bai still felt like a guest among the group, so she preferred to remain outside decisions whenever possible. Shu looked stunned, no answer coming from her lips. Her eyes darted from person to person, as though searching for answers on their faces.

Then Bai's blood turned to ice.

She sensed four monks encircling their house.

Bai cursed. From the looks on the others' faces, they sensed the impending danger, too.

Shu should have noticed them earlier, but she must not have been paying attention to her surroundings.

The monks approached closer, but Shu still didn't give commands.

Bai refused to wait any longer. Somehow, the monks had found them. There was no point in questioning how, not now. Survival was all that mattered.

She turned to Rong. "Come with me. Everyone else, pack up what you can and be prepared to run. You have five minutes."

She didn't have time to see if the others followed her orders. The monks were close now, their powers building as they prepared attacks.

Rong followed Bai to the entrance. Bai looked over her shoulder as she slammed open the front door. "Kill them. I'll go left."

Rong nodded. Bai thought she saw a grin on the woman's face.

Bai had fought Rong before. She knew the woman's strengths and knew most monks wouldn't stand a chance against her. They were the students' best hope of surviving the evening.

The two women sprinted out of the house. Bai turned left and Rong went right.

They were just a few seconds too late.

Blasts came from every direction. Bai leaped in front of one, absorbing the energy meant for the safehouse. On another side of the house, she felt Rong do the same. Two of the walls cracked as power crashed against them, but the house stood.

Barely.

Bai threw herself at the first monk, the man whose attack she'd just absorbed, pummeling him with fists filled with power. He fell to her assault in only a moment, surprising Bai. She imagined the ambush had been specifically targeted for Yang's students. Why hadn't the wraiths sent their best?

Bai continued around the house, searching for the next monk. She was surprised to find Rong already there, a long knife in her hand. Bai had never seen the weapon before. Rong slid the blade into the monk's vitals, demonstrating a deadly competence. As they stood across from one another, Rong wiped the blade off and returned it to a hidden sheath. She looked unarmed once again.

Bai was grateful Rong hadn't used the blade when they had fought.

Their eyes met, Rong's searching Bai's for judgment. She had none to offer. The monks liked to speak endlessly about honor and the use of power, but when it came to a fight, all that mattered was winning. If a blade helped with that, Bai had no complaints. The two women turned to the house.

After being buried underneath a building once already

this week, Bai had no desire to enter one that was crumbling. She looked to Rong. "Get them."

The young warrior nodded and stepped inside the building. Bai wondered if Rong had any fear at all.

Soon the whole group was gathered again, safely outside the house with everything they needed. Yang's students looked to Shu for guidance, but she stared off into the distance. Bai wondered if something inside the woman had finally broken.

Bai looked around. Powers still rumbled throughout the city. The wraiths' work, whatever it was, seemed far from over. She turned to the group in front of her. They were young and unprepared for the storm that raged around them. She was exhausted from the small effort she'd just exerted. Her body needed more time to recover.

They were in no state to fight. They needed protection.

Lei.

He was in Jihan, and Bai had some inkling of the power he could access. They would be in the Heron tonight. She was certain.

Bai called the group close. "We're going to the Heron, a nice inn across the city. Lei is there. He will keep us safe tonight."

The students all nodded, except for Shu, who continued to stare off into the distance. That was a shame. They could have made good use of her ability tonight. Bai just hoped she hadn't lied to the students.

Lei would be in the Heron. He must.

They made their way through the streets of Jihan. If not for the flickering of flame reflected against the undersides of the clouds, it might have been any other night. Thanks to the curfew established by the city watch, no one walked the streets. The timing of the curfew seemed too unlikely to be coincidence, but Bai didn't have time to think about that.

She focused on her sense as she began the long walk from their safehouse to the Heron. Avoiding enemies took precedence over speed. Whenever she felt another power she altered their course until they were safe.

She lost track of time. The moon went behind the clouds. They might have walked for minutes or hours. She did not know.

They were over halfway to the Heron when Bai felt another power, greater than any other. It overwhelmed her sense, causing her step to falter. But at the same time, it brought a smile to her face.

Lei had joined the fight. And he was close.

Bai directed them toward Lei. The others didn't need any encouragement. Once she told them that power could protect them this evening, they followed her like cubs.

As quickly as Lei's power appeared, it vanished.

Bai didn't worry. Although Lei could access powers she couldn't even imagine, when he stopped he was difficult to sense. She refused to believe he'd been defeated. No doubt he had accomplished whatever small task had stood in his way.

The wraiths seemed to feel the same way. Bai felt at least one group approaching the place where Lei had unleashed his attack. She urged Yang's students on, picking up the pace. They were close. They just needed to reach him first.

Three blocks later they found him. He was walking down the street toward the Heron. He saw Bai and her entourage. She didn't need to tell him why she was there. He gave her a small nod and she waved the students toward him.

They were just in time.

Less than a minute later another familiar power came around the corner. Delun led the group of wraiths closing in on Lei, the one Bai had sensed earlier. The two groups stopped in the street, less than a hundred paces separating them. Bai felt Lei prepare himself. His energy wasn't blinding, yet, but he could access it in a moment. Though she knew she would regret it come morning, Bai summoned her own strength.

Bai stepped forward, ready to attack. Lei held a hand out, stopping her. She looked up and saw his eyes were locked with Delun's.

"I'm disappointed in you, Delun. I thought you a better man than this."

If Lei's words had any effect on Delun, Bai didn't see them. The wraiths gathered attacks in their hands. Delun traveled with strong company, Bai noticed. The fight ahead would be difficult unless Lei stepped in.

After a few tense moments, Delun motioned for the others to drop their attacks. He snarled and turned around. The other wraiths, not sure what had just happened, took a moment to follow.

Bai gradually released her power, holding on to just enough to get her to the Heron.

Lei looked as though he'd just killed a friend, but when he glanced down at Bai he seemed to snap himself out of his depression.

Together, they walked to the Heron to take shelter for the rest of the night.

26

Delun wandered the deserted streets as the sun came up over a new day. The turbulent feelings gripping his heart were not those he had expected when the sun had fallen last night.

The Order of the Serpent was no more. Delun did not doubt that some members had escaped the wrath of the wraiths, but the leadership had been killed and the structure of the organization burned to the ground. The lucky few that survived wouldn't be able to reorganize. Those that tried knew the consequences.

The work he'd spent so long on, the desire that had drove him, was done. The man who had planned the death of so many had suffered the same fate himself.

Delun felt no sense of satisfaction.

In the pale pink light of the early morning Delun could see several plumes of smoke rising into the now clear sky. Several small cells had decided blowing up the powder was the best course of action. They sacrificed themselves for any opportunity to kill a monk. Still, for the amount of fighting that had taken place last night, Jihan seemed surprisingly intact. The wraiths had struck at their targets and struck true.

His gaze traveled down to the bloody dagger clutched in his hand. He and Ping had engaged in no fewer than half a dozen battles throughout the evening. The Order had been larger than anyone expected, but the work was done and the monastery remained safe from further attack.

But if the night had been such a success, why did he feel like a failure?

He knew the answer. He just didn't like contemplating it.

Bai and Lei had been together, and they loomed large in his memory. He supposed he was glad Bai had survived his attack.

He remembered walking up the steep path that led to Lei's village, bowing on his knees before those same two warriors to ask for their assistance in fighting against a rogue abbot. That act led to him and Bai fighting together, a short-lived alliance.

Ten years ago they had fought Guanyu and his rebel monks because of the violence the monks had committed against citizens. Delun had watched, helpless, as the monks massacred the citizens of Kulat.

Tonight he had been part of a group of monks. His dagger and robes were evidence enough of the work he had done. Was he different?

These citizens were guilty of their own crimes, perhaps, but questions plagued his mind.

Lei's words echoed in his head, cutting deeper than any dagger could have.

He respected Lei and he respected Bai. Neither understood what drove him. Was that their fault or his?

He *was* different than those monks from a decade ago. The Order of the Serpent had committed heinous crimes against the monasteries. Delun and his fellow wraiths had not committed murder, they had executed traitors. There was a world of difference between those two acts.

Wasn't there?

Delun's certainty from the night before eroded away, replaced by frustrating doubt and questions that had no answers. Lei and Bai both detested him. He'd seen it on their faces. What did they see in him that he did not see in himself?

Ping had been disappointed in him, too. He'd argued against Delun's decision, insisting they could fight Lei and the warriors he protected. The younger monk had been flushed with the glory of his easy victories against the Order.

Delun had saved him from himself, but it would take some time before Ping realized that, if he ever did.

Not long after that incident, Delun had split from the rest of the group. He'd wanted privacy and they weren't interested much in his company. Since then he'd meandered through the streets, searching for answers in the quiet morning.

His wanderings eventually led him back to the large warehouse where the various wraiths now returned from their evening's work.

As he approached, Delun first noticed the sentries standing guard on the buildings that surrounded the warehouse. They were like guards on a castle wall, just removed and placed in a commercial district of the empire's largest city. They allowed Delun to pass without issue, no doubt sensing him the same way that he sensed them.

When he opened the warehouse doors, he was surprised

by the wave of sound that buffeted him. He stepped inside a downright jovial scene. Throughout the large space, monks ate and drank together. Some were in small groups, others gathered into large circles. Most of the wraiths looked like they had seen combat that evening. Robes were dirty and torn, and more than a few still wore the blood of their enemies.

Despite the long night, the room buzzed with enthusiasm. Some of it came from the mere presence of so many other monks. The effect was well-documented in some of the larger monasteries. Simply being around other gifted gave one a sense of euphoria. Monks within some of the larger monasteries needed to be careful to ensure they got enough rest. Their bodies and feelings misled them.

But that wasn't the sole explanation. As Delun watched the crowd he saw a deep sense of satisfaction, of a job well done, of a community being built around the events of the evening. It jarred against his own doubts.

Delun's felt like a stranger moving through a foreign land. These were his peers, yet he was no part of this. He walked like a ghost, wondering if they even saw him.

As he worked his way through the crowd, Delun noticed that many of the younger monks weren't just drinking water. They were actually drinking. Some of the barrels stacked along the walls of the warehouse were apparently filled with wine, and several of the monks imbibed freely.

Delun drank. Learning how to do so had not been an easy task for him. The prohibitions against intoxication were strong, and it had taken Delun months simply to reach the point where he could drink alcohol with the same enthusiasm as the average tavern goer. His attention to such details was one of the reasons why he was good at his work. But he had always considered it a sacrifice. He broke the guidelines of the monasteries so that he could better protect them.

This was not the same. Many of these young monks drank with ease, giving away the fact that this behavior was not unusual. Delun made his way to a quiet corner of the building, searching for time and space to think.

He sat there, head held in his hands. Nothing was as it seemed.

They had killed this night.

It felt as though they celebrated at a funeral.

After a while, Chao found him. Their eyes met and Delun was grateful that Chao, at least, hadn't drank. His gaze was sharp and clear. Chao took one glance at his face and saw that something bothered him. "What troubles you?"

He couldn't admit his doubts. Among these men, such a choice lacked wisdom. His mind searched for an appropriate answer and found one quickly enough. "I ran into Bai again tonight. She survived my attack. And there is something worse. She has met with Lei. I believe they are working together."

Delun wondered if he needed to explain Lei's history. Most abbots, at least, were aware of the man's history, but Delun still didn't know where Chao had come from and didn't know how much he knew.

From the reaction on his face, he knew enough. "So that is who you ran into. That explains why you held Ping back. A wise choice, if what I've heard is true."

Chao considered Delun's information for a moment longer, but then a smile returned to his face. "That is serious news, and we will have to figure that problem out. But try to let those concerns go. We won a great victory today, and more are coming. You are one of us now."

Chao bowed deeply to Delun.

Had the same lines been said a day ago, Delun might have felt differently. He had sought the trust of Chao for weeks now, and it looked like he had finally earned it.

Delun just wasn't sure how much he wanted it anymore.

27

Lei sat in the skywell of the Heron, sipping at tea and wondering at the events of the past few weeks. The princess was missing, the wraiths were active, and he and Yang's students seemed caught in the middle of events they didn't understand.

As the sun rose in the sky, Lei's thoughts turned in a familiar direction. Today was another day he had with Daiyu, a gift he needed to treasure.

Even if it allowed the empire to burn.

Bai slept until the sun was high in the sky. Given her ragged appearance the night before, Lei assumed she had driven herself to the edge of her abilities. She would catch up on rest, knowing Lei would protect her.

He smiled at the memory of their argument with the innkeeper last night. He hadn't been pleased to have so many uninvited guests arriving late in the night, but some persuasion from Daiyu was all that was needed. The innkeeper had eventually relented.

It was just another reminder of what he would lose when Daiyu passed on. She had always been better with people than him. She knew how they worked and what motivated them. With a few words she could often accomplish more than he could with all his strength.

His dark thoughts ended when he felt Bai up and moving in her room. Before long, she came out and joined him in the skywell. She still looked tired, but much better than the night before. She needed a few days to recover completely.

Lei hoped she found the time.

Bai practically crashed into the chair across from him. She eyed his plate the same way a predator eyes helpless prey.

Lei chuckled and pushed his plate towards her. Bai gave him a quick bow of thanks and then dug in with surprising hunger. While she ate, Lei reported the most recent news from the attacks the night before. Most of it had been provided to him by the harried innkeeper. "Word of the attacks last night has spread. The city is frightened but no one is quite sure what to do. The watch is in disarray. Apparently, no small number were members of the Order. Citizens aren't sure if the worst has passed or if last night was only a prelude to something worse. The most disturbing new rumor, though, is that an army is on the march toward Jihan." He shrugged. "I cannot tell truth from rumor anymore."

Bai couldn't either. He could see the confusion on her face, the questions she wanted to ask. He suspected the only problem that held her back was the knowledge he didn't have any of the answers.

His next question almost caused her to fall out of her seat. It would have been funny had the news not been so serious. "Have you heard that the princess was kidnapped?"

She had not heard, and Lei had to spend the next several

minutes telling her about his summons and what he'd discovered. Lei decided he felt sorry for whoever took the princess. Bai finished her meal and appeared outwardly calm, but Lei could see she had found a new purpose. The wraiths who took the princess would end up regretting their decision, he figured.

As Bai finished her meal, the two of them traded information. They each knew parts of a larger story, but neither of them had any idea where any of it led.

"If the wraiths were responsible for the princess's disappearance and last night's attacks," she mused, "it stands to reason that this is all part of a larger plan."

"I agree. I wish I knew what that plan was, though, and how the princess ties into it all."

Bai nodded. "I can see why they attacked the Order. That's no stretch, and if so many were gathered last night, it stands to reason they were about to make a move themselves. But why kidnap the princess? Most of them wouldn't even recognize her as gifted, and if they did, wouldn't they want her on the throne?"

These were the same questions running through Lei's mind.

Just then, they were joined by Daiyu. She preferred to sleep in late these days, and from her disheveled look, she had just woken up. She also collapsed into her seat. Lei sighed. The table had only been set for one. He passed his teacup over to her and she took a grateful sip. He no longer had any part of his breakfast.

Bai asked Daiyu a few polite questions, but then turned back to Lei. "How are we going to find her?

Lei shrugged. "I had hoped that perhaps Shu's gift would work for you. She sensed me as I entered Kulat. Given a little bit of time, she could probably find the princess."

Bai shook her head. "I have reservations about Shu. She froze during the ambush, which is one thing. Worse, though, is that she didn't sense the ambush coming any earlier than I did. I'm not sure that I would trust her gift to something so vital."

Lei stared off into the distance. "I'm not sure what else to do. With so many people in this city, anyone else would practically have to be on top of her before they sensed her."

"There has to be another way," Bai said. "With only the handful of us, it would take us forever to comb the streets of Jihan. We don't have time for that, and it leaves the possibility of the wraiths moving her while we search. We'd have to rely on luck."

The silence stretched between them. Lei agreed with Bai's assessment, but he had no other ideas.

Daiyu spoke up. "There is another possibility neither of you are considering." They both looked at her. Lei's wife held the teacup tightly in her hands, warming herself around the liquid. She returned their gaze as though they were fools.

"You say that the princess is gifted, so anyone else who is gifted should be able to help you. It seems to me that there is one considerable group of men that you are ignoring."

Lei figured it out first. "The monastery."

Bai backed away from the table. "No, no, no."

Lei laughed at Bai's discomfort. He was no fan of most monasteries, either, but Bai's reaction amused him. After all this time, she still felt so strongly about the monks.

Bai almost stood up, but appeared to restrain herself through a tremendous force of will. "You want me to work with the monks to find the princess? As soon as they see me, half of them will want my head."

Daiyu answered Bai's objections. "I don't think so. The

wraiths may want your head, but don't make the mistake of considering all monks to be wraiths. The monastery may be more moderate than you think." She turned to Lei. "Didn't we hear a rumor that the monks in the monastery hadn't really left since the attack?"

Lei nodded.

Daiyu glanced back to Bai. "It could be that the wraiths aren't even in the monastery. If that's the case, your odds seem much better."

Bai still didn't seem convinced.

Lei gave her a nudge. "After all, if there's anyone in the world who doesn't have much to fear from monks, it's you."

Bai's face fell. "I think that's less true than I once thought it was." She looked the two of them. "Do you think they'll say yes?"

Daiyu gave Bai one of her encouraging smiles. "The only way to know is to ask."

28

———

Bai ran through her thoughts, placing them in some order she could recall later. In the other room, Rong had gathered Yang's students. They waited for her now, and she wasn't sure what to say to them. A higher ideal drove Yang's students, a certainty they could create a better world. Bai found such certainty hard to accept. She didn't want to make the world better, she just wanted to punish those who thought their crimes would never see justice.

Through the strange knotting of fate and coincidence, they gathered to listen to her. Yes, she had saved them from an ambush, and Yang had been telling them stories of her for years, but they barely knew her.

She'd considered Daiyu's suggestion long after their meal ended. She wanted to find fault with the idea, but could not. If the princess was gifted and in the city, other gifted could find her. Walls might block sight, but not one's power. The more people who sought the princess, the likelier they found her before harm came to her.

She didn't want this task, but no one else stepped

forward. Bai preferred following the guidance of another. Lei should have been the obvious choice, but his refusal was immovable.

She had once been a seamstress, the only daughter of a widowed mother. Her mother had done what she could, but they had grown up powerless. Bai had learned how to hide, how to be unobtrusive even in the middle of a crowd. When she had discovered her power, she learned to stand up for herself. But she still shunned the light, preferring shadows and darkness.

Who was she to ask Yang's students to take this risk with her?

Bai clenched her fists. Any alternative was worse. She'd spent much of the early afternoon trying to find one.

She stepped into the room before she could think more about her lack of qualifications. A sudden silence greeted her. Every eye turned on her, expectant. They already believed her and she had yet to say a thing.

Bai had practiced a speech, but it fled her memory as she looked at those faces. Her voice came out quieter than she had practiced, but everyone in the tiny room heard her.

She could feel them, her sensitive gift picking up different patterns within each of them. These were all people passed over by most monks, their gifts unique and strange to the established order.

She wasn't alone.

That mattered.

She took a deep breath, then began. She spoke of the kidnapping of the princess. Being Yang's students, they all knew how important the princess was, not just for the continuation of the empire's rule, but for their own futures. Then Bai spoke of her plan to find her.

At the mention of the monks in Jihan, they all leaned back, as though her idea was a plague they didn't want to catch.

Shu answered quickly, almost before Bai finished. "None of us dare set foot in that monastery. They will hunt us."

And that was the crux of the problem. Bai believed the same. But the chance of them helping seemed greater than the chance of the five of them finding the princess in a place as large as Jihan.

They needed the monks, even if that help risked everything.

"Maybe. But we have the backing of an abbot. It's also why we must go as a group. One of us they might ignore. But all of us prove that the world is changing. The gift is changing."

"Never," Shu replied.

Bai clenched her fist, angry at the woman's flat-out refusals. "Do you have a better idea?"

Shu nodded. "I will find the princess. My gift will be sufficient."

Bai grimaced. She hadn't wanted the argument to come to this. This might be enough for her to lose the group. She didn't dare voice her concerns about Shu's gift, not in front of the students she was supposed to lead. "Even if you can find her, we still need the monks. What if she's being guarded by a lot of wraiths?"

The group seemed to hesitate, torn between Shu's easier path and Bai's riskier one.

"Look," Bai said. "At some point, all of you are going to have to come to the monks. You're not living the way I have lived since I discovered my powers. You're growing in strength and numbers, and you're recruiting. They will know about you sooner or later. Why not make it now, when your revelations could get us the help we need?"

Bai gauged the reactions of the small group. She saw some almost imperceptible nods. They wanted to believe, but a lifetime of hard-earned experience argued against her words. All she could offer was her promise.

"I will lead the way. The monastery in Jihan has been weakened by betrayals within their ranks. I believe they will not resort to violence, but if they do, I will protect you all with my life."

The promise felt like a noose around her neck. But they needed the princess, and this was how it was done.

Bai let the room remain silent. She had promised, and anything more felt like empty words, noise that meant nothing.

When Rong stepped forward and bowed to her, leading the others, she knew there was no turning back.

THEY WORE NO ROBES, carried no weapons, and rode no warhorses. Still, as they walked through Jihan, people moved aside for them. They walked down the middle of the street, their feet aimed for the monastery.

Bai walked in the front, Rong taking the rear. Bai sensed no trouble, but she still felt as though she was walking through a battlefield. Few people were outside today. Colder weather and news of last night's chaos kept most home. This wasn't the Jihan she had visited regularly over the past ten years.

Bai didn't sense another gifted until they reached the monastery. Even there, she was surprised by how few she felt. No more than two dozen monks remained in the empire's largest monastery. Why were there so few?

Either way, fewer monks meant less danger. That was something, at least.

Bai considered ignoring the gate and making for the hole in the wall created by the explosion several weeks ago. It felt like the wrong message, though. They wouldn't make their entrance through the holes in the monastery created by violence. The would enter through the front gates, like any other monk.

As they approached, Bai studied the monastery's wall. If her history was correct, this was the second time in two generations the monastery's walls had fallen. Like the monastic system itself, the monastery in Jihan came under regular assault. The scars in the wall testified to that.

She calmed her heart as she stepped up to the gate. The monks standing guard looked confused, glancing uncertainly to one another.

"We are here to see the abbot," Bai announced.

One of the monks replied, but with a question of his own. "You're gifted?"

Bai bit her tongue. Anyone in the vicinity could tell as much. "Yes."

The other monk scurried into the monastery. He looked dazed, frightened even. Bai worried they wouldn't even be allowed in the gates.

He returned a few tense minutes later. "The abbot will see you."

Bai turned around and gave what she hoped was a reassuring nod. The group walked through the gates into the monastery.

The gate opened up into a large courtyard. Evidence of decades of hard training were everywhere, and Bai felt the history in this place. Despite the fact she had never been here, it still felt like a home.

She noticed the monks lined up on the walls surrounding the courtyard. None of them had signed anything yet, but they were clearly prepared for a disaster. The man who she assumed was the abbot stood in front of them. He was at least a decade older than her, but her first impression was of a deep-rooted tree. This was a man she could trust.

She hoped her impression was correct.

Bai gave the man a short bow. The movement pained her, but she swallowed her pride for the sake of something larger. The bow was still more shallow than the abbot would have expected from a young monk.

For a long moment no one spoke. When the abbot stepped forward, Bai saw that his steps were strong and graceful. He approached until he stood only a few paces away. He looked them all over like a shepherd examining a lost flock. "You're all gifted."

She heard the wonder in his voice, the final stripping away of disbelief. The abbot continued, "Yang told us that the gift was changing. That he had found many with different skills. I didn't believe." His eyes met Bai's. "Is this everyone?"

Bai didn't know, but Rong answered. "No. Many more are in Kulat."

The abbot nodded. "For decades now, there has been a sense among the abbots that we don't understand this gift of ours nearly as well as we think. It has been hard, letting go of what we believed to be true."

He turned around and returned to his original position, a section of the courtyard slightly raised above the others. "I assume you come with purpose."

Bai stepped forward, feeling the hopeful eyes of the gifted behind her and the questioning eyes of the abbot in front. "We've come to ask your aid. We believe the wraiths have taken the princess. We plan to search for her, but your help would be invaluable."

She spoke for the next few minutes, telling the abbot what she knew and what she planned. Then she took a slight step back to await the answer with the others. Already the meeting had gone far better than she expected.

The abbot stood in silent contemplation, and Bai finally broke, her curiosity getting the better of her. "Where is everyone? We expected far more of you."

The abbot's eyes traveled to his feet. "Those who have aligned with the wraiths have finally broken from the rest of the monasteries. The man who leads them, Chao, was a monk here. He had a greater influence than I ever believed. Those you see are all that remain. Almost half left when Chao called for the wraiths to gather."

Bai didn't believe. "How can he have such authority?"

The abbot let out a long sigh. "I do not know. I believe he has connections to the emperor, but he has built his following one monk at a time for years. His vision has attracted far more monks than any of us realized."

Bai supposed the sword cut both ways. On one hand, it was terrifying to realize so many followed Chao. But it meant the monks most predisposed to violence weren't here. No wonder their audience had gone so smoothly. The monastery had already been rocked. It searched for any anchor it could.

Eventually he looked up, his eyes meeting Bai's once again. "And what is it you desire? When we became monks, we swore to protect the empire. If your story is true, our duty is clear. But you have taken no such oaths."

"But we live within the same lands, shoulder to shoulder with you and everyone else. Right now, there is little safety for us. Most of this group has been in hiding since coming within sight of Jihan. Abbot Yang began a new path. The rule of the princess gives us a way to continue it."

The abbot nodded, his decision made. "We will help you in this. Our interests align."

The abbot gestured, and the monks along the walls visibly relaxed. They came down from their perches. For the first time outside of Kulat, monks and other gifted began to freely mingle. Bai stood apart from it, watching as greetings were exchanged and some of her group began demonstrating their unique abilities. She wished Yang was here to see his vision beginning to take root in new ground.

The abbot came up beside her. "You are Bai, are you not?"

She nodded.

"Some abbots would have killed you on sight. Yet you led this group here, risking them all."

There was a question there, but Bai wasn't quite sure what it was.

"Are you bold, or just a fool?"

She smiled a little at that. "Probably a bit of both."

His eyes were fixed on her, studying her reactions. "You believed you could beat the remaining monks, didn't you?"

The question wasn't threatening, but curious. She could tell this abbot was uniquely suited for his position. In her experience, as people aged they closed themselves off to new opinions and experiences. They preferred the comfort of the familiar. But in front of her stood a man still driven by curiosity. He was exactly the type of leader the monks needed.

"I hoped so. But I also hoped it wouldn't come to that." She looked at the group of gifted that had followed her here, trusted her with their lives. She realized she thought of them as hers now.

"You are not what I expected," the abbot confessed.

"People rarely are," Bai replied. "Let's hope that our alliance is just as surprising to the monks who have the princess."

29

Delun's doubts faded. They didn't disappear, but he could safely ignore them. It was difficult to maintain doubt when surrounded by so much certainty. By the time he woke from a nap on the afternoon after the attack, his attitude had shifted. His heart felt lighter as he looked upon his celebrating companions.

Delun grabbed some breakfast. After the long night and the celebrations that followed, most wraiths didn't awaken until the afternoon. Breakfast had been prepared to welcome the wraiths back to the waking world. Delun ate slowly while stretching sore limbs.

Delun wandered among the monks. Last night meant more than he had guessed. Not only had the Order been destroyed, but the fellowship of wraiths had vanquished an enemy together. Delun felt the heady mix of pride, freedom, and community. He didn't feel like an outsider any longer. Everywhere he turned, men invited him into their circles and shared their food and drink with him. They all knew he had been the one to kill the captain.

He told the story time and time again, never forgetting to highlight Ping's honor.

A warm glow surrounded him. This warehouse reminded him of the monastery above Two Bridges many years ago. Here he was welcomed and made whole.

Eventually, he found Chao by his side. The monk waited patiently as Delun recounted the story one last time, then pulled the favored warrior aside. "How are you?"

"I am doing well." Delun realized he meant it, too. How long had it been since he'd been able to honestly answer that question with a positive response?

"Will you come with me?"

At that moment, Delun would have followed Chao through a wall of fire. He nodded and trailed Chao through the warehouse to the rooms near the rear of the building. Chao stepped into one and asked Delun to close the door behind them.

The door shut out the growing chorus of sounds coming from the main area. If not for the enormous power Delun felt pressing against his senses, he might have thought the warehouse empty.

Delun ran his eyes around the room. A glance told him this was where Chao planned his operation. A large table dominated the center of the room. Delun stepped up to it and saw a map of the empire rested on it, with another detailed map of Jihan off to one side. The map was covered in small flags.

Chao noticed Delun's interest. "The Order of the Serpent was not just in Jihan. The map shows all their locations. Different flags represent our latest news. Last night we hoped to ambush the Order throughout the empire. Now I just wait for word."

Delun studied the map. The number of flags surprised him. The Order, it appeared, had spread further than he expected. The only area of the empire without a strong presence, it seemed, was near Kulat. Delun ignored that. It saddened him, though, to see in one map how far the discontent had spread.

But Chao's explanation only covered some of the flags. Delun guessed at some others. "There are wraiths in all these places?" He pointed.

The corner of Chao's lip turned up briefly. "That surprises you?"

"Yes."

"We've been working toward this moment since even before the Massacre of Kulat, Delun."

"How many do you have?"

"Over a hundred pledged. But I believe that when word of our deed last night spreads, nearly all the monks will join us."

Delun nodded. A hundred was less than he would have guessed. Chao had most of his force here in Jihan already.

Chao turned to the map of Jihan, as though answering the unasked question. "This is where our campaign begins and ends. The emperor has already sent us his congratulations. He is grateful that the traitorous order has been eliminated. Soon, we will be guaranteed seats on the council."

With that, Delun finally understood Chao's ultimate plan, the goal that had eluded his questioning. His ambition was breathtaking.

The emperor sat at the head of the empire, but his council stood right behind him. Currently limited to a half-dozen lords, a seat on the council gave one direct access to the emperor. Should the emperor die without an heir, or should an heir be found unsuitable, only members of the council could ascend to the throne.

Monasteries had never been given a seat on the council. Long tradition stood against them. The acquisition of a council seat could change everything. It also opened up the possibility of having a gifted emperor.

Chao planned to someday put a gifted monk on the throne. His vision was long.

Delun approved. The same objective had long appealed to him, but somehow Chao had found a path to the goal.

Chao's statements revealed one of his advantages. The man had connections at court. How else would he be in nearly direct communication with the emperor?

Chao looked up from the map and at Delun. "One large hurdle remains in our way, one that I think only you have a chance at resolving."

Delun could only think of one hindrance. He knew Chao's request before it was even spoken. "Bai and Lei," he said.

Lei's strength was unknown. He'd torn up no small part of Jihan thirty years ago. If he'd gotten stronger since, his threat couldn't be underestimated. Delun knew Lei was stronger than him. And Bai's gift made her the perfect warrior to fight against monks. Together, their threat couldn't be overstated.

Thoughts of them caused Delun's doubt to resurface. He didn't want to fight them.

"Yes. They need to be removed," Chao said. "We do not know how they will act, but we can assume they will respond. Bai, in particular, has never been a friend of the monasteries."

Delun chuckled softly at that. Chao had a gift for understatement.

Chao gazed earnestly at Delun. "Truthfully, I do not know how to handle them. They are strong and possess unnatural gifts. If anyone can figure them out, I believe it is you."

Delun didn't know how he would accomplish Chao's mission, but he understood the importance. They were so close to gaining everything they wanted. Lei and Bai wouldn't understand. This needed to be done, for the good of the monasteries.

He didn't know how he would solve the problem.

But he knew he would try.

"I will do it. Can you give me a few days?"

Chao looked down at his maps. "I think so. Our strike last night has given us some breathing room." He paused. "I have called all monks together for an assembly."

Delun couldn't hide his shock. Assemblies were only called on rare occasions, a summoning of every monk willing to make the journey. How many would respond to Chao's call? "Here?"

Chao nodded. "This will be where the emperor will make his announcement. I've given everyone a few weeks to get here. So long as Lei and Bai are taken care of by then, you should be fine."

Delun felt the importance of the moment, the excitement that rang in his bones. It was happening.

In his lifetime.

The monks would finally step out of the shadows and become the leaders of the empire they were meant to be.

The cost was high, but he was willing to pay it.

They stepped out of the room and walked back down the narrow hallway leading to the renewed festivities. Delun's mind already churned on the problem of Lei and

Bai. Still, he noticed the energy of a gifted warrior in another room.

The energy was unlike that of a normal monk. Delun barely recognized it as being gifted. He paused. "Who is that?"

Chao waved it away. "Another traitor we caught, one of those unnaturally gifted. She's nothing for you to worry about."

Delun took one last look at the door, then continued on his way. For the first time in ages, he felt as though he was actually making progress. Thanks to Chao and his connections to the emperor, the monks were only weeks away from obtaining the power they deserved.

Now he only needed to figure out how to get rid of two of the strongest warriors the world had ever seen.

30

———

Lei watched Daiyu sleep, the steady rise and fall of her chest belying the frail state of her body. She had barely finished lunch before asking Lei if he would mind lying down with her. They'd been resting for less than a minute when he heard her snoring softly.

Watching her tore at his heart. He loved her, and step by step, she was leaving this world. No matter how comfortable he was with risking his own life, he couldn't imagine his days without her.

He would soon have to, though.

Lei stood up and walked to the window that looked out on the street beyond. The Heron was in a nice neighborhood where the streets were rarely loud. Today, though, they looked deserted. Two days had passed since the wraiths had struck at the Order of the Serpent, but citizens only stepped out into the streets if they needed to. Most people probably considered their homes the safest places around, and Lei didn't blame them at all.

Bai and the others had decided to settle down at the monastery. Their alliance with the remaining monks provided them some protection from the wraiths. The abbot of Jihan had no interest in fighting other monks, but he would help Yang's students with their search.

Lei still found it difficult to believe the world had gone so sideways. Growing up in the monasteries, he never could have pictured monks fighting against monks. Yet day by day, the wraiths asserted their control over the direction of the monasteries. If the more moderate monks didn't fight, what would be left for them?

Lei pressed his forehead against the cool wall of their room, absorbing strength from the sturdy inn that had lasted for decades. He was losing everything he knew.

He sat back down by the bedside, his thoughts a jumbled mess. His reverie was interrupted by a soft knock at the door.

Lei opened it to find the innkeeper, nervously looking up at him. "Apologies, Master Lei, but there is a man here looking for you, and he is quite insistent."

Forced from his trance, Lei realized he could feel the presence of his visitor. How distracted had he been to miss such a power? "It is no problem. I will meet him in the skywell in just a moment."

The innkeeper scurried away. Lei took one last look at Daiyu. Delun would not threaten her. Despite their differences, he trusted the other man that much. Lei tied his sword to his hip and left the room, closing the door quietly behind him.

Lei stepped out into the skywell, ignoring Delun for a moment. The sky was cloudless and sunny above him, the barest whisper of a breeze rustling the few remaining leaves near the tree that grew in the center of the space. That same tree cast a large shadow during the summer, cooling the space nicely. Now that winter was near, the bare tree let the sun's light warm the area.

Lei sat down across from Delun. He hadn't seen the monk properly in years, not since the incident at Kulat over a decade ago. Although Delun's strength wasn't in question, Lei thought the monk looked more unwell than he had years ago. He carried too much of the weight of the world on his shoulders.

"Delun. Thank you for visiting."

The monk inclined his head, his only acknowledgment of Lei's words. He seemed distracted and unfocused. But the monk's question still cut like a dagger. "What was it like, fighting again within the walls of Jihan?"

"I had hoped never to return. Once I returned, I hoped never to fight. Now that I have fought, my greatest desire is to leave again. I do not wish to bring any more harm to those who live here."

"Then why do you remain?"

Lei nodded toward his room. "Daiyu is dying. She is not well enough to travel. She, more than anyone else, brought me here, and I expect she plans to die here."

Delun's emotions broke through his distraction. "I am sorry to hear that. I did not know."

Something about Delun's response set the hairs on Lei's arm to standing. The man hadn't come here without reason. "Why are you here?"

"I had hoped to convince you to leave."

"I am not the one you need to convince. I agreed to follow Daiyu here, but little would bring me more joy than to leave this all behind me." Delun looked surprised by the answer. Lei spoke before he could respond. "I am surprised you joined with the wraiths. Their methods seem too violent for you."

Delun shifted uncomfortably in his seat. "I have been convinced. Their goals are worthy. Some have gone too far, but that has always been true."

Lei leaned forward. "It's also not like you to equivocate."

Delun stiffened, power flooding through his body. Lei had struck a nerve there.

For a moment, Lei thought Delun might attack. Tension hung over the table. Delun was strong, but Lei had no doubts as to who would win a duel between them.

Delun visibly relaxed. "You should leave, Lei. Return home, where you belong."

"Once the princess is safe."

Delun's eyes focused on Lei. "What did you say?"

The monk's surprise had been genuine. Interesting. "The wraiths kidnapped the princess, the same night you fought Bai and left her for dead."

Lei saw the denial on Delun's lips. Then his eyes darted to the side. He was thinking.

Watching Delun was like looking straight into the man's soul. He searched, then found something that disturbed his calm. Finally, the storm passed. The monk believed him, but his course remained unchanged.

This wasn't the same Delun Lei had once known. This was a man worn down by time and tragedy, a man who saw hope in an insane chase.

Delun's gaze flickered to something happening behind Lei. He turned his head to see Daiyu enter the room.

Even ill, she seemed the ideal of beauty. He rose to greet her, offering her his arm as he guided her to the table.

Delun's behavior changed suddenly. He stood and bowed, showing her even more respect than she was due. Lei noted the behavior. The Delun he was familiar with still existed, but he had been buried by the sands of time.

For a moment, the three of them sat awkwardly, none quite sure what to say. Daiyu, as always, found the way forward. "Master Delun, it is a true pleasure to see you again. It has been so long since you visited our home."

Lei marveled at his wife. In a few short phrases, she reminded Delun of the alliance they had once shared, and had accorded him all the honor due his position.

Delun remained still, but Lei had the impression of a man squirming in his seat. "Lei was just telling me of your illness. I am truly sorry."

His regret was genuine.

Life was indeed a strange thing, to turn those who agreed on so much into enemies.

Daiyu shrugged away the sympathy. She had little time for it, as always. "It happens to us all, I suppose. Few of us are fortunate enough to see it coming."

Delun smiled at that. "You are indeed a remarkable woman. Lei is a lucky man."

"He is, but that's not why you're here, is it?"

"I was trying to convince your husband to leave the city."

"Why?"

Delun leaned back, clearly enjoying his verbal sparring with Daiyu. Although Lei wished she would stay in bed, he was grateful for her presence. Negotiations were her battlefield much more than his. He had never possessed her sharp wit or quick retorts.

Eventually, Delun answered. "Because I have been asked to kill you, and I have no wish to do so."

With that simple statement, Lei viewed the whole conversation in an entirely different light. Delun believed in the wraiths. Lei didn't doubt that. But the morals hadn't been driven out of the monk. Not completely.

Daiyu barely looked up from the menu, as though she

heard about shadowy organizations wanting to murder her husband every evening. "You want Lei out of the way."

Delun shrugged. "Personally, I do not understand the wraiths' strategy, but they wish your departure strongly."

Lei saw an opening. A chance for him to get everything that he wanted. He turned to Daiyu. "Perhaps we should leave."

She gave him a slim smile that let him know that he wouldn't be escaping that easily. She then caught the attention of the staff. "A reunion requires wine, does it not?"

Lei thought a drink sounded excellent, and to his surprise, Delun also agreed.

A few minutes later a carafe and cups arrived. Daiyu poured the rich liquid and served them all. Delun bowed to them as he accepted the cup.

Daiyu took a sip of her drink, then turned her attention fully on the monk. "You ask us to take a lot on faith. Lei might be exactly the deterrent the city needs."

"I agree. If this comes to a fight, there is no one I would rather have on my side than Lei. But Chao, the man who leads the wraiths, has sent birds throughout the empire, calling upon every wraith to gather here in Jihan."

Lei, mid-sip, started at that. "Every wraith?"

"Yes. He is poised to have more monks listening to him than anyone has before."

"Do you believe that is wise?" Daiyu asked. Lei realized she was genuinely curious. She trusted Delun and his judgment.

Delun seemed to understand the same. He pursed his lips. "I'm not sure. The situation in the monasteries is delicate. Chao has seized authority for himself during a time that many monks are willing to listen to him. His beliefs are persuasive." He turned and looked at Lei. "If you are here when the monks arrive, I tremble to think of the damage that Jihan will suffer."

Lei grimaced. As much as he hated feeling like he was being manipulated, Delun was right. Not only was there the question of whether or not he even had a chance against such a gathering, but the harm caused to the city could be irreparable. One pressing question remained. "What will you do?"

"I do not know. I only know this must be done."

Daiyu poured another cup for both her and Lei. "If Lei leaves, though, there is no one to check the wraiths' power."

"It's a risk I need to take. I can't have the lives of so many citizens at stake."

Lei looked between the two people. He noticed that Daiyu looked sleepy. She really needed more rest. Perhaps she would disagree, but Lei found that he agreed with Delun. Not just because he wanted to leave the town anyway, but because the man's argument made sense. "We'll do it, Delun. I'm not sure how far we'll be able to travel, but we'll leave today."

He turned to Daiyu, expecting to see her disapproving gaze. Instead, he saw that she was slumped over in her chair. For a moment, he feared the worst had happened. Then he saw her chest rise and fall and knew she was asleep. She really should have kept resting. Her condition was getting worse.

"I'm sorry, Delun. She's been so tired lately and..." Lei's voice trailed off as he, too, suddenly felt a wave of exhaustion crash over him.

He looked at Delun, who was studying him closely, regret on his face. Realization dawned, too late. Already, he felt his limbs getting heavy. He fought to keep his eyes open.

Delun turned and made a gesture. Through Lei's rapidly

closing eyelids, he saw the waiter approach. The man's bearing was completely different than it had been a few minutes ago when he brought the wine. He walked like a monk.

Delun leaned forward. "I am sorry, Lei. I truly am. I admire you, but I couldn't take the chance that you would turn me down."

Lei wanted to be angry.

He wanted to scream, to clench his fists and punch at the man who betrayed him.

But he couldn't find the anger inside him. His emotions were a murky blackness, calm and still.

He opened his eyes wide one last time, the effort taking everything he had. Delun still sat there, calmly watching.

Then Lei closed his eyes and couldn't find the strength to open them again.

31

As evening approached, the monastery became a hive of quiet, purposeful activity. Despite their promises of assistance, the monks refused to leave their walls after the sun set. The evenings now belonged solely to the wraiths. Bai didn't blame them, as much as she wished for a different situation. Ever since the attacks several nights ago the wraiths had become more bold. They stalked the streets with impunity. Rumors claimed the city watch had tried to enforce the curfew twice against the rebel monks.

Both times they'd been beaten aggressively.

The wraiths had decided to assert their control over the city. They held the dominant position.

The monks from the monastery went out in groups of four to walk the town, seeking the princess. During the day, the wraiths hadn't attacked the monks, although there had been several confrontations.

However, the night after the attacks, one nighttime encounter had ended the monks' evening searches. A pair of monks had come across a group of wraiths. When the wraiths discovered the monks refused to join them, they'd attacked. The poor monks from Jihan hadn't been prepared, and from their reports, they'd barely escaped with their lives.

A tenuous peace held, but Bai didn't think it could last much longer. For one, they were nearing the completion of their search for the princess. Thanks to the help of the monks within the monastery, they'd scoured the city several times over. They'd never sensed her.

That left only three possibilities. The princess had escaped the city, been killed, or was being held in the warehouse where monks from across the empire trickled in.

Bai didn't think it was either of the first two. Killing the princess now made no sense. The emperor had heard no demands, and why go to the trouble of kidnapping the princess if one wasn't going to demand concessions?

The questioners also insisted the princess hadn't left the city. Bai didn't trust the questioners. She didn't trust any information she hadn't acquired on her own. A questioner came every day to the monastery, always in a different guise. The questioner met privately with both Shu and the abbot, ostensibly the two leaders in the monastery. The visits made Bai uneasy. But the questioners hadn't led them astray yet, and the information mirrored what Bai felt in her own gut.

If the wraiths gathered in the warehouse, the princess would be there also. Why keep such a valuable prize anywhere but in your most secure stronghold?

Even now, halfway across the city, Bai could feel a hint of the power. More monks lived in that warehouse than Bai had ever seen in one location. The power radiating from the building intimidated even her, and if the princess was there, no one in the world would be able to pick her out.

All of which led to one question. If the princess was in

the warehouse, what should Bai and the others do? To that, they had no clear answers.

The abbot had called a meeting tonight to address that very question. For an hour Bai had wandered the grounds, hoping to find some solution she could present at the meeting. All she came up with was a dozen ways to get herself killed.

She was the last person to arrive, and from the commotion coming from the room, she figured the discussion had started without her. Several monks were present in the room, as well as Yang's students. From the way they'd positioned themselves, Bai could tell Rong and the abbot were arguing against everyone else.

The division of Yang's students didn't surprise her. Of them, Rong was the least influenced by the abbot's particular breed of enthusiasm and idealism. Rong saw the world how it was, not how she wanted it to be.

Bai was curious how Rong and Jihan's abbot ended up on the same side of what appeared to be a losing argument.

The commotion died down when Bai entered. Many in the room turned to her.

Shu spoke first, asserting her authority within the gathering. "Bai, I'm glad you could finally join us."

Bai chose to ignore the pointed remark. "What's the argument?"

Rong stepped in, pointing her finger at the other side. "They want to attack the warehouse."

Bai's gaze traveled over to Shu. The leader of Yang's students nodded. "It is absolutely vital that we attempt to rescue the princess. With our unique gifts I believe that a surprise attack will work."

For a moment, Bai found herself unable to respond. Did

Shu really believe that? The idea seemed outlandish, but she appeared to have no small degree of support.

Bai couldn't imagine the attack. She knew her own strength, and confident as she was, she also knew there was no chance she could break the princess out of that warehouse. "I believe that is unwise," she said.

"It can work," Shu asserted. "With my gift, if we can get close to the warehouse I should be able to locate the princess. You and Rong can break your way in while the others provide cover. Perhaps if we set some sort of distraction nearby that would also help." Shu spoke with absolute conviction. "I believe that we are the princess's last chance. Even if the odds are slim, we must take this opportunity. We can teach the wraiths the error of their ways."

Many of the monks nodded along in agreement. They were tired of being cooped up in the monastery. They saw Shu's plan as the path to freedom.

Bai shook her head. "Against such an overwhelming force, I do not see how such a rescue is possible. Not even Rong and I are that gifted."

Shu looked at them both, stubborn. She knew she had numbers on her side.

Bai turned to the abbot. "What do you think?"

The abbot spoke carefully. "I agree that we need to take action, but like you, I can't see any way that an assault, even a surprise one, could work."

The two sides seemed set in opposition to one another. If she didn't propose an alternative, Shu might simply lead an attack with everyone who was willing.

Bai wished Hien was here. Of all the people she knew, the sly warrior would be the one most likely to come up with a plan that had some odds of success.

Thoughts of Hien triggered another thought within her, a plan Hien would be proud of.

"I have a better idea. Let's turn the wraiths' strategy against them."

Shu swiped at the air as though she could bat away the idea. "What are you talking about?"

Bai warmed up to her idea the more she thought about it. "Consider this: Any attack on the warehouse poses tremendous risk. There are just too many wraiths. But the wraiths aren't just in control of the warehouse. They are trying to control the city. I think we can stop them."

"What do you mean?" one of the monks asked. He seemed interested. Bai realized the monks didn't care much what course of action they took, so long as they actually did something.

"We set ambushes throughout the city. If Rong and I have support, we can take out three, maybe four wraiths at a time. We interrogate them and search for weaknesses, but we make them react to us. They'll either need to commit more forces to the city to hold it, or they'll retreat back into the warehouse, giving us the city. Either way, we fight them back."

"But it will take too long," objected Shu. "Every day that passes is another the princess is in danger."

"And your idea is always there if we need it. But we can change the course of this fight without risking everything. And they haven't used the princess yet. Whatever Chao is planning, I think he still needs time. Let's make them react to us, and let's ruin these plans. If we can force them into a corner, we can get them to make a mistake."

Now it was Shu's turn to look around the room. She saw her supporters switching sides. As eager as they were to get out of the monastery, Bai's idea gave them a way forward that risked far less. Bai saw the play of emotions on Shu's face. The woman was disappointed, but more deeply than Bai expected. When Shu conceded the argument, Bai thought she looked like she was giving up on something much larger.

Bai didn't understand, but with Shu's concession, she'd created a much larger problem. Everyone in the room now looked to her, expecting her to tell them what to do. Even the abbot of Jihan waited for her to speak.

Despite her best efforts, she had taken over the leadership of the battered monastery and the survivors sheltered within.

32

Delun cursed Lei and the man's final words. Even safely out of the way, Lei caused him no end of trouble.

Delun detested doubt. He didn't consider himself a zealot, but he was a man rarely troubled by deep uncertainty. Over the course of his life he had seen hundreds, if not thousands, of selfless acts committed by his brothers. He believed that the strength and discipline forged in the crucible of monastic training was crucial to the attainment of excellent leadership.

Because of that, the violence he had engaged in to protect and promote the interests of his brothers had never bothered him. Pacifism was for idealists. The world responded to strength.

Lei's comment about the princess had watered the seed of doubt Delun had been ignoring.

His actions toward Lei didn't help. Strangely, though he had shown the old warrior mercy, he suspected he would have felt better had he fought Lei face to face. Poison was a dishonorable way to remove an opponent. But Delun was no fool. Had he fought Lei, he wouldn't be breathing today.

The justification didn't ease his conscience. He'd betrayed the man who had shown him nothing but respect, and he did it on behalf of a cause he didn't fully understand.

He'd heard nothing from Chao since. Delun wanted to challenge the man, to find out what his whole plan was, but he hadn't been around the warehouse lately. Ping was the most visible leader, and he only told Delun that Chao would return soon. Delun spent his days idling around the warehouse with nothing to do.

The lack of activity gave him time to think. Thinking led to doubt.

While Delun wandered the small space aimlessly, more wraiths continued to appear in response to Chao's summons. The warehouse was always warmed by the number of bodies moving around.

Despite his daily exposure to the rows of sleeping monks, Delun had expected a larger turnout. At the last census there had been over a thousand monks throughout the empire. For as many bunks as were filled, there were that many that lay unoccupied. One night, Delun had tried counting the wraiths. He suspected there were about a hundred total. An impressive force by all accounts, but not even close to a majority of the monks.

If he doubted, he was one of the only ones. The others didn't see the empty bunks. They saw only how many had gathered. Only Delun questioned why the turnout was so much less than Chao expected.

The first possibility was that there were far fewer monks than estimated. He didn't know how devastating the Order's attacks had been against the monasteries. Perhaps they'd killed more monks than Delun realized. If so, the monks here were a much larger part of the whole community.

The other possibility, which elicited less despair but more uncertainty, was that Chao overestimated how powerful his message would resonate with the other monks. The vast majority of the monks had remained away.

Delun suspected the latter. Certain trends were becoming obvious the more time he spent among the wraiths. The first was that he was among the oldest of the wraiths. The movement attracted the young monks far more than those of Delun's generation.

In his wandering he had listened in on dozens of conversations. Most of them were driven much more by hot emotion than cold reason. He enjoyed partaking in conversations he felt comfortable with. Unfortunately, that number was less than he would've liked.

Delun did not feel any particular fellowship with many of the other wraiths. His fame had worn off, and the differences between them reasserted themselves. Most of these young wraiths saw change as an inevitable process, not something that needed to be worked towards. Whenever Delun urged caution, he received condescending looks that made him feel twice as old as he was.

With all these new worries, one nagged at him more than any other: Lei's claim that his brothers had kidnapped the princess.

As much as he wanted to deny the charge, it simply made too much sense. If the princess possessed gifts similar to Bai's, the wraiths would find her very existence blasphemous. They would have no problem treating a member of royalty with such disrespect. Delun feared for her life, if the rumors were true.

That chain of thought was the one that caused him to

fidget endlessly and to keep glancing back at the rooms where he had felt another presence after his last meeting with Chao.

There was one way to know. No one had explicitly told him he couldn't go there, and as far as he could tell, no one paid him any special attention. Eventually, his curiosity overwhelmed caution. He had to know the truth.

He stood up from his bunk and walked toward the rooms. He had little difficulty locating the same place from where he had felt the power emanating.

Unsure of proper etiquette, he knocked softly on the door. He heard no answer, but now that he was close he could feel the faint energy from within. It felt a little like Bai's, but not quite. Whoever was inside was gifted, yet not in the traditional sense. Delun felt the energy moving around the room and so he took the risk and stepped inside. Delun had never seen the princess before, but he'd seen her likeness plenty, and it matched clearly what he saw in front of him.

But it wasn't just her face that identified her, it was her character, revealed both in the way she held herself and in her raised eyebrow at his uninvited entry. This was a woman used to deference.

Delun bowed, not wanting to offend unnecessarily. "Princess, I am sorry for the intrusion."

She didn't look like she believed him. "What do you want?"

The question was asked almost as a formality, as though she had asked it a dozen times before and never received a satisfactory response.

Delun wasn't sure. Coming here had been a whim, a flight of fancy. He hadn't actually expected the princess to be here. Now that she was, he had no idea what to do with that information. As always, when Delun encountered a problem he didn't understand, he reverted to naked honesty. "I heard a rumor that you had been taken hostage. I desired to see the truth of it for myself."

"And?"

"I'm disappointed to find that it is true."

That focused her attention. "You are not part of the leadership here?"

Delun shook his head. "My name is Delun, and I am not that trusted." He realized, as soon as he spoke, that was the heart of his discontent. After all he had done for the wraiths, Chao still hadn't trusted him enough to tell him this.

Her eyes widened at his name. "*The* Delun?"

"Yes."

"I'm surprised."

Delun imagined she would be. If she knew anything about him she would know about his attack on Kulat and possibly his role as a monk tracking down other monks. The fact that she had heard about him at all surprised him, though. It would make her quite well-informed.

Before he could speak more he felt a presence approaching. He'd spent enough time around the man to recognize him.

Ping.

Delun bowed one more time to the princess as the door opened and Ping stepped in. He looked between Delun and the princess, his expression unreadable. After a moment his gaze settled on Delun. "Chao has returned. He would like to speak with you." Delun nodded and followed Ping. Part of him worried that he had overstepped his bounds, but he suspected he was safe. Chao had a plan for him that wasn't completed yet.

Delun met the princess's eyes as he turned to leave. Her

curiosity was piqued, but she said nothing. Ping closed the door behind them, then the two of them completed the short walk down the hallway and turned into Chao's headquarters. Somehow, Delun suspected that Chao already knew he had visited the princess.

His guess was confirmed moments later. Chao skipped straight to the point. "Does her presence change your ideas about us?"

Delun shook his head. His mind raced. He didn't actually know how he felt about the princess being here. A suitable answer came to mind, though, a question that had troubled him when he had only suspected the princess's presence. "I am surprised. If we have the princess, why has there not been a greater effort to retrieve her?"

Chao focused his gaze on Delun, and Delun knew that once again he was being weighed and judged. Chao wasn't deciding whether or not he trusted Delun, he was deciding exactly what information to provide Delun. More than ever before, Delun felt like another piece under Chao's guidance. He would only be allowed to know so much at certain times. The information would manipulate his decisions.

Chao came to his conclusion. "There hasn't been any effort to find her because the emperor doesn't want her found. He wants her dead. We actually saved her life."

Delun's head spun. He couldn't keep track of this game any longer. "What?"

Chao waved Delun's confusion away. "For now, you will have to trust me. I am certain the emperor was about to kill his own daughter. We saved her and are protecting her. Her presence limits the emperor's options. But that isn't why I asked you here today." Chao dove straight to the point again. "You let Lei live."

"You asked me to remove him. I did so. I am certain that he will no longer interfere with your plans."

Chao clenched his fists. For the first time, Delun saw the anger inside the man. "Who are you to know what plans I had? I meant that he needed to be killed. Do you have any idea how much your mistake has cost us?"

Delun defended himself. "Then you should have been more clear. I do not think Lei will return. Whatever you have planned in Jihan will continue without his interference."

"You do not *think*?"

Delun stood his ground. "This has never been Lei's fight. He doesn't care what happens within the empire. He only wants to live in peace."

"You drugged him! If that was your plan, why didn't you just kill him?"

Delun sensed himself nearing the edge of a precipice. Chao doubted him; of that, Delun was certain. Between Lei and the princess, Delun suddenly wasn't sure how far he could push the man before Chao simply had him killed.

But the truth seemed his best way out.

"I don't want to kill Lei. He is a good man and a remarkable warrior."

Chao's eyes were cold. "You would put your friendship with the man over the lives of your brothers out there?" He gestured toward the rest of the warehouse.

"I would be honored if that man called me a friend, but I didn't think that I would have to choose. I want to build a new world, too, but I don't want to do it over the bodies of good men."

Chao stood up from his desk, rounded it, and stood right in Delun's face. "Sometimes, good men must die for a cause greater than themselves. I thought you understood that." He turned on his heel. "I thought you understood me."

Delun defaulted to obedience. He felt as though he walked on the edge of a knife. "I am sorry, Master. What would you have of me?"

Chao's fist clenched again as he turned to his maps. "I don't believe you are sorry."

"Not that I let Lei go. Had I known your exact desire, I might have done differently. But I am sorry that I have failed you. I thought with him out of the way, your objectives would be met."

Chao growled as he spun on his heel. "It is his life that matters, not his presence in the city. Where did you leave him?"

Indecision tore Delun in two. Chao only had one purpose. He would send people for Lei, people who didn't possess the mercy Delun had.

Delun saw the lack of trust in Chao's eyes. The wraith wouldn't allow Delun to make another mistake.

The choice wasn't as hard as Delun thought it would be. Lei was the strongest warrior Delun had ever met. No doubt, Delun's confession would put him in danger, but the man had faced far worse. Delun trusted him to stay alive.

"Do you have a map of the land to the west of Jihan?"

Chao gestured to an aide, and within a minute, Delun was pointing out the abandoned farmstead he'd left the couple at.

Chao looked up at Ping, who had observed the entire exchange in silence near the back of the room. "Summon the questioners. Have them kill Lei. They'll have a better chance of it than any wraith will."

Delun noted the command. Chao continued to work closely with the questioners. He was connected to someone close to the emperor, but who? How was he so well connected with the palace's secrets?

Chao turned his attention again to Delun. "Trust is more valuable than gold, Delun. As a gesture of my faith in you, I will say this: You are welcome to speak with the princess whenever you wish. She will confirm what I have told you."

Delun sensed more coming. He wasn't wrong.

"But if you fail me one more time, I will not be able to trust you. Do you understand?"

Delun heard the threat perfectly. He nodded.

Chao dismissed Delun, leaving him again with more questions than answers. Chao had a specific endgame in mind, but Delun couldn't unravel it. What was the wraith planning, and why did Lei need to die for it to happen?

33

———

Lei opened his eyes and stared at the unfamiliar ceiling. He blinked and a wave of memory washed over him.

The wine with Delun.

His first thought was for Daiyu.

He sat up, surprised not just that he was alive, but that he felt completely fine, as though he had slept long and hard through the night. His body was stiff, but that was hardly news anymore.

Lei didn't recognize the room, but Daiyu lay next to him, wearing the same clothes she had when they met with Delun. For the briefest of moments, Lei worried that she had died. Then he saw the subtle rise and fall of her chest.

Lei exhaled sharply and held his head in his hands. If Daiyu had suffered at Delun's command, no amount of understanding would ever lead to forgiveness.

Lei watched her for a few minutes to make certain that she was fine. Once he had convinced himself, Lei turned his attention to his surroundings. They looked to be in the bedroom of a small house. Lei's sword rested in a corner of the room.

Lei rolled out of bed, the aches and pains in his body familiar friends. He pulled the sword from the sheath, checking it carefully. The steel looked untouched.

Tying the sword at his hip, Lei glanced again around the room. It held no decoration and no furniture beyond the bed.

He was fairly certain they were alone. He hadn't heard any movement beside his own, and he didn't sense anyone gifted nearby.

Lei took one more look at Daiyu to ensure she slept well, then stepped through the bedroom door.

They were indeed in a small house. Lei found a low table and plenty of food. As another surprise, he found their chest of clothes that had come with them to Jihan. He opened it, finding it in much the same state as he last remembered.

Besides that, the house stood empty. Lei saw a folded paper on the table but ignored it for the moment. Following his curiosity, he stepped out the front door.

Endless plains greeted him. As far as his roving eye could see, they were alone. He turned back to the house. From the outside it looked well-maintained.

The geography provided few clues as to their location, though Lei was pretty certain he could guess well enough. Delun wouldn't have been able to move them very far, at least not easily. And Jihan itself was surrounded by plains. Delun had removed them from the fight, but little else.

He wanted to be angry with Delun. The man had drugged him and forced him to leave Jihan. Lei hated being told what to do at the best of times, and this was an order of magnitude beyond that.

He wasn't upset, though. If anything, he felt better, being out here in the middle of nowhere with his wife. Perhaps he should be thanking Delun for his efforts.

Lei returned to the house, checking on Daiyu once again. Satisfied that she slept well, he turned to the letter on the table. There were no surprises within. Delun apologized for his actions, again explaining the necessity. The house was theirs to remain in as long as they wished.

In all, Lei found himself impressed by Delun's thoughtfulness. Lei wasn't sure if the monk was friend or enemy, but he respected the man.

His stomach rumbled. He didn't know how long he had been drugged, but he figured it was no wonder he was hungry. He set about making some food with the supplies on hand.

Lei wasn't as versed in kitchen duties as Daiyu, but he was no fool, either. Within a few minutes he had a fire going and water heating for noodles.

He had almost finished his preparations when he heard Daiyu waking up in the next room. He went to her.

She smiled when she saw him enter. Despite the fact she had been drugged and carried to a location without her consent, she seemed remarkably at ease. "Delun?"

Lei nodded.

"He's one of the more interesting men you've ever met. I hope he survives this storm. You will need friends soon."

"Please don't talk like that."

"There's no hiding from this, love. I can feel it in my bones."

He walked over and then supported her as they made their way to the table in the next room. She felt as light as a bird in his arms. She needed food.

Lei finished cooking as she watched, smiling at his efforts. "I should have taught you how to cook better."

He gave her a warning look, but there was no intensity behind it. Was he nearing acceptance, finally?

He poured the noodles into two bowls and set them down on the table. Daiyu gave them each an exaggerated examination. Lei handed her a pair of chopsticks. "Your food is getting cold."

Daiyu took a tentative bite. "This isn't as bad as I was expecting."

"Thank you," replied Lei, sarcasm dripping from every word.

Like Lei, Daiyu was hungry enough to eat several bowls. Lei figured the food had been good but not great. Daiyu certainly would have done better, but she was kind enough not to remind him of that.

The meal complete, they both relaxed at the table. Since her waking, they hadn't spoken at all about their situation.

"Remember when we first came to Galan and that thief tried to steal your sword?"

Lei laughed at the memory. With a gesture, he'd blown the kid across the tavern. "I do."

"Life seemed simpler then, didn't it?"

"Complexity comes with age."

Daiyu's mood turned more serious at that. "I used to think so, but not anymore."

Lei turned to her. "How so?"

"I think there are only a few things that matter in life. Family. Duty." Daiyu met his gaze, her eyes still smoldering with intensity. "Love."

Lei leaned across the small table and kissed her. She returned the gesture, grabbing him by the back of the neck and pulling him close. Her eyes wandered toward the bedroom. Lei stood up, came around the table, then picked her up and carried her there.

The next few days challenged them both.

Daiyu took a turn for the worse. Lei didn't know if something in Delun's poison had harmed Daiyu or if the disease had simply advanced further. Daiyu struggled to do much more than walk around the house.

She didn't talk anymore about him returning to Jihan.

Their days were spent in quiet companionship. They made love when Daiyu felt up to it, and Lei felt the desperation in the act. His wife clung to life. He did most of the cooking under Daiyu's watchful gaze. The quality of their meals improved.

At night, they bundled up in their heavy clothes and watched the stars spin overhead.

As the days passed they ran out of words to say to one another.

Four days passed, and Lei wished they would never end.

That night, as evening fell, Lei sat on the edge of the bed while Daiyu sprawled across it. He could tell, as the moonlight cast soft shadows over her, how much weight she had lost. Her hunger had disappeared.

A coughing fit wracked her body, and as she bent over double, Lei thought he'd never seen anyone more frail.

Once the fit passed, she turned her head to meet his gaze. There were tears in her eyes, a deeper understanding within than he wanted to acknowledge. "I love you, Lei."

He reached out for her hand and lifted it to his lips. "I love you, too. I always have."

"Will you keep watch tonight?"

A knot formed in Lei's throat, catching his breath, choking the life from him. Somehow, she knew. Unable to speak, he nodded.

She smiled, then pulled him closer, her lips expressing truths deeper than words. Their kiss lingered, and when they separated, there was nothing left to say.

He held her hand as she fell asleep, sitting up on the bed while he watched her rest.

The night lengthened, and his thoughts wandered to matters of the soul. He knew the monastic teachings, the belief that some part continues past death. He knew it personally, too. He still felt the lingering effects from his brother's death.

The belief provided some slim comfort. It helped, knowing that something waited on the other side of the veil.

It wasn't death that caused him to mourn, but the absence of a presence in his life. Over three decades had passed and he still missed his brother. The loss of Daiyu would be worse.

Outside, the world spun. The stars turned overhead, pinpricks of cool, uncaring light.

Daiyu was at ease, her breath soft and slow. More than once he leaned over to ensure she still breathed. Her face was serene, painted by the silvery glow of the moon.

The moon reached its apex and started to fall. But Lei barely noticed, his eyes focused exclusively on Daiyu. There was no place he would rather be.

She breathed deeply, a sudden change in the steady tempo of her breath. A slight change, but with every sense turned on her, he couldn't miss it.

Then she breathed out, and didn't breathe in again.

34

———

Bai's plan, for the moment, seemed to be working. Every night, Bai and Rong led teams of monks through the streets of Jihan. When they encountered wraiths, they attacked, delivering vicious beatings.

Their interrogations hadn't revealed anything of note, but Bai hadn't expected them to. The wraiths hid in the warehouse. They followed orders. Unless they came upon someone high up in the group, there was little to be learned.

After the first night, the wraiths changed their patterns. Instead of wandering in pairs, they wandered in groups of four.

The additional help didn't save them.

After three nights, the wraiths stopped wandering the streets altogether. Bai and Rong estimated they had crippled over twenty men in the last three nights.

The city watch returned to the evening streets.

For the moment, order held within Jihan. A few buildings suffered damage, but it was a shadow war, conducted at night between two small groups of warriors. The citizens obeyed curfew.

It couldn't hold. The wraiths would respond.

Their progress, encouraging as it was, wasn't enough. The wraiths still outnumbered them, and by all accounts, they still had the princess. Bai worried that if they wanted the princess, they were eventually going to have to attack the warehouse.

She didn't know how to do so.

During the day, when she wasn't sleeping, Bai studied the warehouse from a distance. The building took up an entire block, and was surrounded by large streets. Wraiths patrolled the buildings across the street, forming a perimeter around the warehouse. Bai would barely be able to get close before being spotted. As soon as the first blast came at her, she'd have dozens of monks attacking.

Bai had thought of plenty of plans, but all of them ended with her dead on a warehouse floor. She couldn't get the numbers to work.

She needed a distraction, but she couldn't think of any. The best idea she'd come up with was to have Rong try to lead a group of monks away, but she didn't think the diversion would be big enough. At least half the wraiths needed to be removed from the building before she had a chance.

Bai walked into the monastery through the front gate. She felt the pressure of time building on her shoulders. They needed a break.

Shu found her as soon as she was through the gate.

Bai had less patience for the woman than ever before. Since her plan to attack the warehouse had been overruled, she'd been prowling the monastery grounds silently. She barely spoke, and when she did, the results were less than pleasant. Today, however, she looked eager. "Bai, the questioners might have just the information we need."

What Bai wanted was to go to bed and hide under a pile of warm blankets. Exhaustion gripped her tightly, but Shu's news didn't look like it would wait. She followed the other woman.

Shu led her to Rong. She didn't look any happier to be there than Bai.

Shu kneeled down in front of them, acting more like a child with exciting news than the woman entrusted with guiding Yang's students. "The questioners have discovered where the wraiths' leadership is going to be this afternoon. It's outside of the warehouse."

Bai perked up at that. "They're certain."

Shu nodded. "The wraiths have been meeting quietly with some nobles, it seems. They are meeting later today."

That explained why there hadn't been a greater outcry over the kidnapping of the princess. The wraiths had learned from Kulat. They didn't seek a violent coup, but one coordinated by nobles and wraiths alike.

Still, Bai didn't like trusting information she hadn't found herself. The questioners hadn't led them wrong yet, but it was hard to trust those who traded information for a living.

She didn't see how she had much choice, though. If there was a chance to drive a stake through the heart of the wraiths, she needed to take it.

Rong looked as uneasy as Bai felt, but they both nodded. They would do it. After their long night on the streets, they needed rest. Shu promised to wake them when the time neared.

Bai and Rong walked together toward the dormitories where their beds were. Rong spoke softly. "Do you trust her?"

"No."

"Do we go through with it?"

Bai nodded. "We need the break. It's worth the risk. We'll keep our eyes open, though."

The two women crashed in their respective bunks, not waking until Shu shook them each awake.

After a few minutes to stretch and wake up, the women were off.

The streets of Jihan recovered slowly from the excitement of the last few evenings. More people were on the streets than before, but the mood was still subdued.

Shu led the two warriors directly to a house near the outer wall of Jihan. Bai kept glancing behind her, looking for signs they were followed. She saw none.

Shu pointed out the house from a few blocks away, as soon as it came into view. Rong and Bai nodded, then took to the roofs on an unspoken signal. It didn't take them long to find a vantage point above the building.

The house was nicer than most in the area. It was two stories tall and the walls were kept well. Bai saw the windows were all boarded up, but beyond that, saw little to remark on.

Rong whispered next to her. "What do you think?"

Bai shook her head. "It's an excellent location for an ambush."

Rong agreed. "What should we do?"

"Don't go in, no matter what. If they are there, they'll have to leave eventually. Do you want to work your way around the back? If you see anyone, give me a wave."

Rong nodded and took off across the rooftops.

Bai didn't like the look of the house. With the windows boarded up there was no way to see inside. With two stories and multiple rooms, there were plenty of places for warriors to ambush them. She wanted to trust Shu, but she wouldn't go into that house without a very compelling reason.

A minute later she heard Shu climbing up the roof to join her. The older warrior looked around. "Where's Rong?"

"Watching the rear."

"Why? The meeting is already happening. We need to attack."

Bai kept her face carefully neutral. Either Shu was a warrior with a single strategy or she was up to something. "There's no need for us to attack. The streets are better for Rong and me. We wait until we see them come out."

Shu grabbed Bai's shoulder and turned her so they were facing each other. "Bai, we can't risk any of them getting away. We need to attack."

Shu sounded determined, but there was something else in her voice.

A hint of fear.

She was lying.

Bai's eyes narrowed. "We won't let them escape. Trust me. But Rong and I aren't going in there. It's too dangerous."

Shu snarled and turned away. Bai kept one of her eyes on the woman. She didn't trust her.

Bai didn't sense anyone in the building, but that definitely didn't mean it was empty.

They waited, a bright sun warming them on the chilly afternoon.

They continued to wait. Hours passed with no sign of anyone. If there was a meeting, it was one of the longest Bai had ever heard of. She gestured at Rong, who came across the rooftops and rejoined them. The sun was beginning to set. Shu sat sulking on another corner of the roof.

"Let's flush them."

Rong nodded. "How?"

"Let's burn it."

Rong smiled. "I'll get some oil. I saw some a few blocks back."

Bai began a small fire while she waited. A few minutes later, Rong returned with a jug of oil. She began dousing the walls of the house. Bai dropped down with the fire and set the house ablaze.

A few minutes later Shu came down from the roof, looking dazed. She approached them. "What are you doing?"

Rong looked over at the woman she'd once considered her mentor. "I was cold."

Shu stuttered but said nothing. She knew Bai and Rong didn't believe her. Bai was surprised she didn't try to run.

A few minutes later, five men in black robes came through the front door, coughing and choking.

Bai and Rong set on them the moment they stepped out of the house. Knees and elbows dropped the men to the ground. Bai considered killing them, but hated the idea of killing without need. The danger had passed, and Shu was caught in the act.

The battle done, the two warriors turned on Shu. She didn't run or fight. She just held up her hands in a gesture of surrender.

"Who are they?" Rong's voice rang with the hurt of betrayal.

"Questioners," Shu confessed.

Bai looked back at the downed enemies. Weren't the questioners helping them fight the wraiths?

"I don't know their game. But I do not think they are your allies."

Bai wasn't surprised, but Rong was still hurt. "Why?"

Shu looked at her young friend. "They took my family

and threatened them. I had left them behind to spare them the consequences of my life, but the questioners still found them. They leaned on me and I couldn't resist. My daughter is too young to come to harm."

Rong turned to Bai. Bai saw the hope in her eyes, the desire for a new leader. "What should we do?"

Bai glanced between the two women. "She was your master. She has done no harm to me. The punishment is yours to assign."

Part of Bai regretted trusting Rong with that responsibility. Rong was a sharp blade, but she could cut a friend just as easily as an enemy. She didn't seem as though she'd suffer betrayal well.

The struggle flickered across her face. "You were the one who let them know exactly when we were leaving Kulat, weren't you?"

Shu nodded.

Rong shook her head. "Run from here, Shu. Find your family. And never show your face to us again."

Shu nodded, a tear in her eye. She bowed deeply to Rong, then gave a nod to Bai. Then she turned and was gone, leaving Bai to wonder who in this city she could still trust.

35

————

Armed with permission to visit the princess, Delun arranged an official meeting with her. Instead of just knocking on the door, he did his best to mimic the etiquette he'd been taught in the monastery. He sent a written request, which was replied to within a few minutes.

She had smiled a little at his attempts when she hand-delivered her reply, as though it was a kind but useless gesture, but Delun did not believe that. It was true that he could visit the princess at any time. But his attempt at etiquette wasn't just about permission, it was about preparedness. This way the princess was prepared for his visit, ready to discuss her captivity and future. There was no point springing such a conversation on her when she wasn't ready.

At the appointed time, Delun arrived, knocking softly on the princess's door. This time, she welcomed him in. He bowed deeply and offered a gift. She looked down at it in surprise. "Tea from one of the finest local shops," Delun explained.

That brought a genuine smile to her face. Delun

imagined that she had been eating the same food as him since her arrival. The food in the warehouse could have been worse, but it was basic fare that only filled the body. It didn't touch the soul. Besides that, the tea would provide an excuse for each of them to delay their answers.

The princess began to heat water. From her practiced motions Delun noticed two facts. The first was the evidence of her martial training. She moved well, maintaining balance and poise at all times. Delun suspected her training was deeper than anyone in the warehouse suspected.

The second fact he noticed was that her hand didn't shake one bit. Though she was a captive here, fear had yet to seize her heart. Her motions were calm and controlled, not the movements of a woman who feared for her life.

Delun revised his opinion of the princess. He'd first judged her as a spoiled young woman. Yet, the person he saw in front of him was anything but. She'd grown up in luxury, but she had still developed an enviable character.

She sat down across from him as the water began to heat. "What do you want?"

The question wasn't asked with the same dismissive attitude as last time. Now, she was genuinely curious. Delun considered his response carefully. "Answers."

"A difficult demand."

Delun detected no trace of sarcasm in her voice. He pushed forward. "What is the extent of your powers?"

She shook her head. "I might be a captive, but information is power, and I would be a fool to give it away freely. What would you offer me in return?"

"What do you desire?"

"Answers."

Delun smiled at that. His respect for her grew. Being as

he was the captor, he offered a token of his trust. "The first question is yours."

"What goal do you seek?" Delun couldn't help but notice the emphasis on "you."

He considered the question. He suspected that the rote answer wouldn't get him very far with the princess. If he wanted her knowledge, he would need to part with some of his own. A thorough examination of his heart revealed an answer that he hadn't expected. "I seek an end to the fighting within the empire. I wish to live in peace."

The princess looked skeptical. "If that was true, all you would need to do is move out into the country and begin farming. Peace is not so hard to find."

He shook his head. "That would be too selfish. It is not just for me, but for my brothers as well, and the citizens of the empire."

"But mostly for you."

"Mostly for me," he echoed.

She considered for a moment, then spoke. "Attack me."

Delun was confused for a moment, then realized what was being asked. He nodded and formed the first attack with his right hand. When she nodded, he released it at her.

Her reaction was almost too quick for him to follow. Out of nowhere, a blade of energy formed around the edge of her arm. She swiped across his attack and watched with pleasure as it unraveled in front of her. The attack hadn't been strong enough to do anything but blow her hair back, but she had sliced through it as though it were nothing at all.

Delun's jaw dropped. In all his years he had never encountered such an odd gift. The power of it immediately occurred to him. Many monks liked to compare absolute strength, but absolute strength was not the ideal marker of martial prowess. Focus was just as important, if not more so. That was the reason why those who used bladed weapons were so dangerous. It allowed them to focus energy into a very tight space. A weak monk who could use a weapon was more dangerous than a strong monk who couldn't. The princess had gained the ability without the use of a weapon. If she could project that power, she might be one of the most dangerous people in the empire.

And she sat in captivity.

Delun shook his head to clear it. "How strong are you?"

"I have unraveled attacks through the fourth sign. I have not trained with anyone stronger. Although, I do believe the fourth might be near my limit."

If that was true, it was an incredible feat. The princess wasn't nearly as strong as Delun, but he did not wish to encounter her in a fight. Her ability virtually negated his. It would be like fighting Bai, but worse.

"What does Chao plan?" the princess asked.

Delun shrugged at that. "I wish I knew. I have the sense he is a man who has plans within plans, and contingencies for all possibilities. He will see either a gifted on the throne or members of the wraiths on the emperor's council. How he gets there is beyond my knowledge. I suspect that he will follow one course of action while preparing another." Delun paused, uncertain if he should continue. "He claims your father wants you killed."

Her response was immediate, as though she'd already suspected. "Possible, although unlikely."

Her calm acceptance floored him. "You are his daughter."

She smiled and took the water from the fire, pouring it over the tea leaves with a practiced motion. "He is my father, but he is driven far more by duty than by any sense of affection. He will not allow a gifted to sit on the throne. Although I doubt he would resort to such dramatic actions."

"Chao says he saved you from assassins."

"I suspect that is more for fools to believe than the truth."

Delun drank his tea. The fragrant beverage warmed his throat and helped stop his head from spinning. "How did you end up here?"

The princess sipped at her own cup, her smile evidence enough that Delun had made the right choice in bringing the tea. "There is little to tell. One night I went to sleep, the next morning I woke up here."

"You were drugged?"

"I believe so."

"How did the wraiths manage that?"

"Chao has many connections in the palace. No doubt one of them assisted him."

"Who is Chao?"

The princess eyed him. "You really don't know?"

Delun felt self-conscious. He didn't.

"He is Lord Xun's younger brother. And Lord Xun is the emperor's closest adviser and most likely successor."

That was the resemblance Delun had noticed. Now that the princess made mention of it, he couldn't help but see the similarities. That was how Chao had access to so many resources and so much knowledge.

"How did Chao first come in touch with the emperor? It seems unlikely a wraith would do so."

"That I also know. It was just a year ago. Chao had built up his following, and he used that influence. I believe my father, Lord Xun, and Chao formed an alliance of sorts. My father traded the promise of a council seat for Chao's promise of an obedient monastic system."

Delun didn't understand. Politics had never been something he knew how to manipulate. "Why would the emperor believe the wraiths would be more obedient?"

She frowned at him. "You don't?"

"Of course not. The wraiths want more authority. They won't accept the yoke of another."

The princess took another sip of her tea. "How many wraiths demanded evidence of wrongdoing the night you attacked the Order?"

Delun felt his stomach twist.

"You took Chao at his word. Who is to say every house you attacked held members of the Order? Perhaps some held activists, or other men the questioners wanted killed. The wraiths killed dozens, if not hundreds, on that night, based only on the word of Chao."

The princess paused for a moment. "Wraiths don't want authority, and the responsibility that comes with it. What they really want is to flex their power. My father and Chao understand that. Chao promises to direct that desire, and in return my father will provide what the wraiths ostensibly desire."

Delun hurt. His beliefs had been quietly decimated as he sipped his tea. He wanted to shout at the princess, to tell her she was wrong. But such action would be a lie. "A risky gamble."

"Perhaps, but my father is no fool. The two systems of monasteries and government can no longer exist as they have in the past. He saw an opportunity for both sides to win. Chao will get his seat on the council and an eventual path to the throne. My father gained the monasteries."

"If Chao can deliver on his promise."

They each returned to their tea. Delun tore through the

new information, trying to make sense of it. His head was still muddled.

The princess took her question. "So, why did Chao abduct me?"

Delun considered that. Chao wouldn't want to see the princess on the throne either. If he believed her claims, the emperor and Chao would agree on that much. So why take her from the palace? His own last words came back to him. Chao needed to deliver the monasteries to the emperor to gain his seat on the council. "You're bait."

She looked up from her tea, surprised. "For who?"

"The monks who don't agree with Chao. They'll find out you're gifted and will want to rescue you." Delun's thoughts raced. "Chao's enemies will come to him. They'll come here." Delun looked around the room, but his thoughts were about the building. The whole place was a trap. Delun focused back on her. "What will you do?"

"I'm undecided. For now, I must remain here."

"Why?"

"Chao is threatening violence against vulnerable targets if I attempt to escape. At some point, the benefits of escaping may outweigh the potential risk, but that moment has not yet arrived. For now, I am content to bide my time."

Delun's respect for the woman increased yet again. He realized that for the first time in his life, he had found a noble worth following.

36

———

When morning came, Lei left Daiyu's body in bed while he visited a small grove of trees not far behind the house. He selected an appropriate tree and went to work, chopping the old birch down with the help of an axe he had found behind the house.

He could have cut through the tree with one swing, using his gift. But he craved the labor. He wanted to honor Daiyu's life with his sweat. He worked his way through the trunk of the tree, cutting out a larger wedge from the base, one swing after another.

In time, the repetitive nature of the work calmed him. His world narrowed until there was nothing left but the swing of the axe and the sound of the sharp blade slicing deeper into the heart of the tree.

When the tree fell, the sun was already well into the sky. His work had just begun. Lei started cutting the tree into more manageable logs.

Now and then he looked over his shoulder, feeling as though someone stood behind him, watching him. But the fields surrounding the house were empty. He hadn't seen anyone come this way since they'd first woken up here. Delun had stashed them well off the beaten path.

He believed Daiyu's spirit remained close, observing the preparations for her last rites.

Lei worked at the tree with a practiced ease. Back home, he often used chopping wood as a way to distract himself. The work demanded focus, emptying the mind of the meaningless thoughts that tended to crowd in day after day.

The axe head rose and fell again, cleanly splitting a log in two.

Lei thought of the years he and Daiyu had spent together, the meals she had made for him, the nights they had spent on the balcony of their little house watching the stars come out and dance above the mountain peaks.

He focused on the wood and drove the axe into it once again, hands sliding smoothly along the shaft as it picked up speed.

More memories, older memories, of a time when they hadn't been together. When he had treated her poorly and almost lost her for good. Bitter memories of the pain he had caused, softened only by the knowledge of the married life that had come to pass as a result.

The sound of the axe, sharp as it bit into the tree.

Daiyu's insistence that he do something to help Bai and her friends, to be involved in the affairs of the world after spending so much time divorced from it.

When he looked up, the tree was done, chopped into pieces suitable for carrying, suitable for building a small pyre.

Lei carried the logs and pieces of the tree closer to the house for the rest of the late morning and early afternoon. He took a short break to eat, the food tasteless in his mouth.

Then he returned to the work, grateful for the mental oblivion the physical labor created.

By late afternoon the pyre was finished. The wood sat nicely stacked, with plenty of kindling prepared to light it. Lei had cleared the grass away from the structure to ensure the fire wouldn't spread.

He dreaded the next part.

Lei walked back into the bedroom and prepared Daiyu's body for the pyre. There was blissfully little to do. He dressed her in her favorite robes, then wrapped her in cloth. He picked her up, amazed at how light the body was, no longer burdened with the weight of life.

Lei carried the body and placed it gently on the pyre. Then he took a few steps back to ensure everything was as it should be. He didn't want anything out of place for tonight.

Finally, he rested for a while.

At rest, his grief finally caught up to him. He knew she was gone, had known this moment was coming for some time. But his mind refused to believe. Every time a breeze came up and caused the house to creak, he looked around, expecting to see her there, smiling at him as though nothing was wrong.

Sorrow seized him then, crushing him, making it difficult for him to breathe. He had lost too many of the people he loved. His parents were only the faintest of memories, dead now for more years than he cared to count. Jian, his estranged brother, also gone. And now Daiyu, the woman his world had centered around for most of his adult life.

On the plains outside of Jihan, Lei had never felt more alone.

As the sun dipped toward the horizon, Lei started the fire that would consume his beloved. The kindling caught without problem, the wood mostly dry from the afternoon out in the sun. Lei patiently tended the fire, feeding it larger and larger pieces until the logs that formed the pyre had caught.

After that, it was simply a matter of waiting.

He thought of the monastery up above Two Bridges, the thick walls he had called home growing up. That was where he had last seen a pyre, the flames consuming his brother, some fragment of his brother's soul coming to rest with his own.

Part of him wondered and dared to hope that something similar would happen with Daiyu. She had only been gone a day, but already he wanted to hear her voice, to hear her advise him on what to do next. The pyre invited him. They could travel beyond the veil together.

Such thoughts would have disappointed her.

If she had been standing right next to him, he had no doubt what she would say. She'd made her final wishes clear enough. "Return to Jihan. Finish the fight."

A certain part of him wanted to. Diving into the conflict would distract him, keep him from thinking about these moments and the losses he'd suffered.

But what was the point? As he watched the fire, it all seemed so meaningless. What was the point of people fighting and dying for control of the empire? Lei had spent his life with Daiyu, and he didn't regret those years one bit. Life was far too precious to waste on what didn't matter.

The flames rose higher and began to consume Daiyu's body. Lei forced himself to watch, wishing that he had at least one companion here to share his grief.

He took a deep, shuddering breath and was suddenly calm, as if someone had come behind him and given him a firm embrace. He closed his eyes, sinking into the sensation.

His breath came easily now, his lungs filling deeply with every inhalation. He'd felt this before, at Jian's pyre.

Lei wasn't alone.

He carried the memories and the souls of those he'd lost. He spread out his arms and welcomed them.

A strange mix of emotions ran through him. He felt deep sorrow, not so much at Daiyu's passing, but at the awareness that he had survived and would have to go on without her. But she gifted him a deep determination, the desire to see his life through.

He would go on through the days. Jian and Daiyu wanted no less from him. If he carried a part of them with him, he wanted them to be proud of their vessel.

By the time the flames burned down, leaving nothing but ashes and memories, Lei was decided. He looked up at the stars above, amazed by the mysteries of the universe.

Then, Lei heard them. A cough in the darkness, well behind him.

Anger swept over him, aggression he hadn't felt since he was a young man kicked out of the monasteries and bitter at life. How dare they interrupt Daiyu's final rites? He turned around, opening himself up to the power that surrounded him.

The power came easier than it ever had, filling every pore of his body. His senses sharpened and his vision shifted. Though it was dark, he saw as though the sun shone overhead. There were five men creeping toward his position, hiding in the tall grasses of the endless prairie.

The men deserved no mercy.

Lei's hands moved through the signs he'd learned as a young man, signs that still came naturally to him after all these years. Each hand was a mirror of the other, two one-handed signs preparing for an attack.

He shifted as he saw a man bring a bow up. In the dark, Lei saw better than they did and the arrow missed wide.

Lei finished his signs. In each hand he held a Dragon's Fang, the sixth one-handed sign, a focused attack that was virtually unstoppable. Most monks couldn't even form one.

It was the same attack that had killed his brother.

Lei aimed the first attack at the archer, the blast opening a hole in his chest.

A second man stood up, becoming the victim of the other attack.

His attacks spent, Lei cast a shield over himself. He saw no point in worrying about being attacked. Then he drew his sword, letting just a trickle of power flow into it. Two more cuts ended two more lives.

Whoever had sent these men was a fool. They had no chance against him.

When the final man tried to run, Lei swiped an energy attack across his legs, slicing through muscle and bone as though they were butter. The man collapsed to the ground, crying out in pain as he attempted to crawl away, pulling himself with his hands.

Lei stopped him. "Did Delun send you?"

The man's face was ashen from blood loss. He shook his head. "Lord Xun."

Lei frowned, not understanding. But the man wouldn't either. He was just a soldier, bleeding out in these empty wastelands. Lei pushed a bit more energy into the sword and sliced again, taking the man's head off and ending his pain.

He looked back at the pyre. He still held onto the power, his vision altered. The veil between his reality and the power seemed thinner than ever, a gossamer weave separating him from an eternal mystery.

Lei swore he saw Daiyu then.

Not real, but not a ghost, either. He stepped toward her and felt a pressure push against him. He heard nothing, but the message was clear.

Lei collapsed down to his knees. He wanted to go with her.

But it seemed his road led only to Jihan.

37

Bai was half-asleep when Lei arrived at Jihan's monastery. As honed as her own senses were, her drowsiness almost caused her to miss his entrance completely. He stirred up quite a panic, though, and gongs rang throughout the monastery, ensuring Bai wouldn't fall asleep anytime soon.

"Someone is coming!" a young monk shouted, eyes wide with alarm. "Someone strong."

Monks flocked to the walls to defend their home. Bai stumbled after them, rubbing sleep from her eyes. Once she stood on the walls of the monastery, though, she knew who their guest was. She made a calming gesture with her hands. "There's nothing to fear. It's just Lei."

A few moments later Lei came into view from the wall, many blocks away. He walked with his head held high, but Bai could almost see the sorrow radiating from him. His steps were slow, as though he pulled a great weight. Only one event could burden him so.

Bai's heart broke for Lei. She had never known him

without Daiyu. The two of them had always been as one in her mind. Now they had been cut in half.

Bai rushed down the stairs and ran toward him, meeting Lei just outside the gates. She had never embraced him before, but she did so now.

He wrapped his strong arms around her. She could feel his deep pool of energy trickling into her, a subconscious ability she had no control over. This close, she could feel how near the edge of despair he stood. He was connected to the power still. It was unlike him, but it was also how the monks had sensed him so far away.

Bai rooted herself like a tree, shifting her feet and lowering her weight. She held on tightly to him, keeping him steady as he grieved.

When his tears slowed, they separated. Bai looked up at Lei, not sure what to say. "I'm sorry."

The words seemed small, a tiny drop of water in an empty well.

Lei nodded, tears forming again near the edges of his eyes. "She passed away in her sleep. Peacefully."

Lei wavered, his balance slightly off. Bai almost reached out to him to steady him again, but her instincts told her Lei didn't want her help. He wanted to plow forward, to keep pushing ahead so he didn't have to look back.

"Come in," she said. "You're just in time for the excitement."

Lei gave a small nod, took a few steps forward, then stopped. He looked up at the walls, an unreadable expression on his face.

Bai gave him a moment, but he still didn't follow her. Had grief completely broken him? As gently as she could, she asked, "What is it?"

He gestured toward the walls. "I was thinking about how the past seems to hold us all in its grip." He paused for a moment as his gaze took in the walls and the pile of rubble that was all that was left of a section of the defenses. "The last time I was here, there was also a hole in the wall, caused by the Dragon's Fang. When I was last inside these walls, the monks wanted me to remain forever, to study me for the rest of my days. Daiyu and I ran from a broken monastery; now I return to one alone."

Bai couldn't think of a single response. She stepped closer to him, lending him support with her presence.

Lei took a deep breath, then stepped through the wall. Bai performed introductions.

She enjoyed watching the reactions to his arrival. Some knew of him, but many did not. Many had no idea such a power existed in the empire. They left with their mouths hanging open.

Once introductions were complete, Bai took Lei aside so they could each tell their stories. Bai couldn't believe what had happened to Lei. She hadn't even known he and Daiyu had been abducted.

Bai recognized the desire in his eyes, though. He wanted to move forward. She told him about the warehouse, about how the monks had gathered there and taken the princess. When she finished, Lei leaned back and scratched his head. "Where is this warehouse?"

Bai described the area. Lei paled.

"What's wrong?"

"I believe that is the same place where I once fought Fang. I destroyed the warehouse thirty years ago, but it doesn't surprise me that they have rebuilt it. Chao is very much a student of history, I think."

Lei continued to look thoughtful, but he didn't provide a clue to his thoughts until Bai pressed him on it.

"This doesn't add up. None of it. The emperor tells me he wants his daughter found, but the questioners, who report to the emperor, want you dead. Chao and his wraiths abduct the princess, but no effort has been made by the emperor to save her. There's more going on here than we know, Bai."

Bai agreed. The same thought had been troubling her. Her only solution had been to keep thinking of ways to free the princess.

Lei glanced over at her. "You're too tired. Get some sleep, and then we will leave."

"Where are we going?"

Lei smiled, but it seemed empty. "To have a talk with the wraiths, of course."

BAI SLEPT WELL through the morning and into the afternoon. Lei's presence calmed her, made her feel like it was safe to surrender to sleep.

When she woke, Lei was still on the same bench he'd sat on when they had spoken. He didn't look like he'd moved since she left. She sat down next to him. "How do you plan on doing this?"

Lei looked around the monastery. "Bring Rong. Her gifts may come in useful if our conversation doesn't go well. Otherwise, we'll leave the rest."

Bai wouldn't have minded more protection, but fewer people were easier to manage. She found Rong, then told the abbot where they would be. He looked apprehensive, but even he had started to defer to her.

The trip passed in silence until they neared the warehouse. Lei turned to them. "I will cast a shield and speak to them, but be prepared for anything. If you see an opening in their defenses, take it. I don't know all that is happening, but I believe the princess is safer with us."

The warehouse came into view a minute later. Bai and Rong stepped closer to Lei. Bai could sense the wraiths within. They filled the warehouse with their power. Several stood on nearby roofs, keeping watch over the approaches. No doubt, word of their arrival had already reached Chao's ears.

Lei kept a steady pace, and Bai wondered what it must be like to be so strong that he didn't need to fear so many wraiths gathered together. If she'd been gifted with such a strength, she would have charged in days ago.

No one attacked them as they approached, but Bai could sense the activity surrounding them. Wraiths were leaving the warehouse through side doors, taking to the buildings surrounding it. Less than a dozen wraiths remained inside. Lei stopped two dozen feet away from the main door of the warehouse.

Bai felt the gazes of the wraiths upon her. Where they stood, the three of them were surrounded. If there was going to be a battle, it was clear they intended to fight it outside the walls of their new home.

The main doors opened. Of the three men who stepped out, Bai only recognized Delun. The other two gazed straight ahead, but Delun looked at his feet. Bai noticed he carried a staff and a bag of stones at his hip.

He had come prepared to fight, then.

The man who stood in front of Delun spoke first. Bai guessed he was Chao.

"So, you are Lei," he said.

"I am," Lei replied.

"Did you come to join us?"

"We came for the princess, and to put an end to this

madness."

Chao opened his arms wide. "What madness? Monks, taking their rightful place as rulers of the empire?"

Shouts from the rooftops answered the boast. Chao knew his audience well.

Lei shook his head. "You are no rulers. You are crammed into a warehouse near the edge of Jihan while the emperor rests in an enormous palace."

The words cut deep. Chao gritted his teeth. "You are as shortsighted as the rest of them. Change takes time, but we are well on our way. You don't see what is possible."

Lei opened his arms. "When the gifted fight, no one wins. Please, Chao, surrender the princess. We can find a better solution."

Chao swept Lei's idea away with a wave of his hand. "I propose a more interesting test. The training of the monasteries against this disease that has spread since the Battle of Jihan. Delun against Bai. If Bai wins, I'll let you leave here alive. If Delun wins, you surrender yourselves."

Bai had little doubt what surrender entailed.

"No thanks," Lei answered.

Chao's grin dripped with malicious intent. "It wasn't an offer." He gestured toward the surrounding rooftops. Nearly a hundred attacks were signed. The air crackled with energy.

Bai met Lei's gaze. She didn't mind the offer.

Bai knew Lei believed he could hold off the attacks. The power he touched was immense. But the damage to the city would be as well. She knew he did not want to destroy the city again. That would not be his legacy.

He capitulated, nodding toward Bai. She stepped forward, and Bai prepared herself for the battle that came next.

38

Delun's heart sank like a stone thrown into a river. Chao, in one simple move, had pushed Delun straight into a corner. A corner from which there was no escape.

Delun felt the energy thrumming around the intersection. Dozens of monks stood at attention, ready to fight. Lei, Bai, and the other woman stood in the middle of a killing ground.

The amount of power gathered within these few square blocks was absurd. They could level most of the city and still have power left over.

Chao uttered his pronouncement.

Delun wavered.

He thought of the princess and her warning, the way she had wrenched his eyes open to see a truth he would rather not acknowledge.

But what could he do?

If he joined with Lei and Bai, perhaps they would have enough strength to mount a rescue of the princess. There was no telling. But that way lay chaos. Did he believe it was for the best?

In the end, Bai forced his hand. She leaped forward, hatred in her eyes. Before he could react, she had knocked the staff from his unsuspecting grip. His greatest advantage over her vanished.

Delun weaved backward, sliding around her punches, hoping none of them struck. Most days, Bai was more controlled than this. She snarled as she swung at him. When her fist didn't connect, she slipped off balance and he kicked her away.

She believed he had betrayed her, that he still intended to kill her.

Strangely, it was that belief that finalized his decision. He wouldn't disappoint her.

But he didn't know how to convince her before she killed him.

Delun dodged, then dodged again. Bai's strikes weren't as focused as usual, as though her heart couldn't quite convince her body of what it believed. That, at least, was something.

Bai flew past him and he landed a fist to her torso. He felt the energy flowing through her, preventing him from truly hurting her.

He hadn't hit as strongly as he might.

When she turned to look at him, he saw that she knew it, too. Her eyes narrowed, doubt flickering within.

How could he convince her, without words, with the whole world watching, that he was on her side?

He laughed when he knew.

Both of his hands danced an intricate pattern, forming a powerful attack. Bai's eyes widened with surprise, a gesture soon masked.

Delun waited for one of the monks to yell, to understand Delun's deception.

But the intersection was silent.

Expectant.

None of the monks understood Bai's powers. They didn't know how foolish a mistake Delun was making.

She was one of their greatest threats, and they didn't take the time to understand her.

Delun detested their willful ignorance, their absolute belief in their superiority.

Bai shifted, acting as though preparing to attack. She put herself directly between Delun and a group of the rebel monks.

She understood.

Delun held onto his attack for another moment, doubt warring against action. His only chance was here.

He took it.

With a roar, Delun thrust out his arms and released the attack.

Bai, expecting it, leaped high into the air, higher than any human should.

Delun's attack passed underneath, launched straight at the group of monks.

Caught by surprise and their own sense of superiority, the monks never had time to react. Delun grimaced as his attack struck true.

The blast of energy caved in ribs, slammed heads and bodies back against walls. Three monks dropped without a fight.

For the second time in his life, Delun had turned against his brothers.

He had no time for regrets.

Before his brothers could react, he readied two more

attacks, one in each hand. He searched for Chao, but the man had already melted into shadows. Delun settled for two random monks, the first in his sights.

The monks fell easily, but they would be the last. Surprise had worn off, leaving only the anger of betrayal.

Delun formed a shield and released it as several attacks were launched at him. His shield held, but barely.

Beside him, Bai paused for a moment, giving him a glance that thanked him for all that he had done.

To be understood by her was gift enough for him.

She passed him, heading for the warehouse. He yelled after her. "She's in the back!"

Bai nodded and disappeared into the building.

Delun turned to his own battle. He focused more power into his shield while forming another attack with his other hand. His shield took another two hits, but Delun knocked a monk from a nearby building in response.

Then any advantage his betrayal gave him completely vanished. Half a dozen attacks struck in quick succession. He poured all his energy into his shield. There was nothing else he could do. The strength of the attacks brought him to his knees, a heartbeat or two away from crushing him beneath their combined power.

In that moment he finally found peace, elusive after all this time. Perhaps he had done well, or perhaps not. But he had remained true to his beliefs, and that was enough for him. It wasn't pride, exactly, but a contentment at his actions.

Just as his shield began to fail, another power blossomed beside him.

In all his years as a monk, Delun had never felt anything like it. The power of an individual always had a flavor to it, a hint of personality that a sensitive warrior could identify.

It was missing here.

This power felt pure, like a clear mountain stream high above any civilization. Like the trickles of water that formed every summer near his home monastery of Two Bridges.

The power expanded, swallowing all sense and reason. The giant hemisphere grew, immune to every attack launched at it, and steadily approaching Delun.

He closed his eyes. One way or the other, his end was here.

Then the shield was above him, a trick of control he didn't understand. The crushing blows he had resisted simply vanished, unraveling and dispersing like dust on the wind.

Instead, Delun felt a tremendous lightness, a pleasant tingling over his skin.

Delun opened his eyes, expecting the darkness of his final moments.

Instead, he was inside a dome of energy, crouched in the intersection, the world calm and peaceful.

Lei stood in the center of the dome. His eyes glowed as he stepped toward Delun. When he neared, he reached out his hand.

What was happening? Delun could only figure Lei was at the heart of this, but how?

He looked up, and he sensed the battle happening outside the dome. Over a dozen attacks lashed at them, but Lei stood calmly.

It was a shield.

But it made no sense.

No monk, no matter how strong, could last against the blasts Lei's shield now easily stopped. Delun was one of the strongest monks alive, and he had almost collapsed in just a few moments under the onslaught.

He took a deep breath, focusing himself. He took Lei's outstretched hand and was pulled gently to his feet.

As he held Lei's hand, he felt the power flowing within.

Once his senses opened, he learned more. The power wasn't within Lei, but passing through him.

"You begin to understand," Lei said.

Delun wasn't sure that was true, but he took a few moments to take in everything, to understand what he was feeling. When he did, he noticed the attacks against Lei's shield weren't being blocked so much as they were being absorbed.

"Amazing."

Then he remembered it was Lei standing next to him. The man he had drugged and sent away. The man whose location he had given to Chao without a second thought.

"Lei, I'm..."

Lei held up a hand. "None is necessary, Delun. I understand."

Lei understood him, as did Bai. To be understood, to have the respect of warriors like this, eased the burdens Delun had carried. He had never been alone. He saw that now.

The gesture seemed foolish, standing underneath as many attacks as they were, but Delun didn't feel afraid anymore. He bowed, deeply, to Lei. "Thank you."

Lei answered with a smile. "It is we who should thank you. Your path has not been an easy one." He glanced to the warehouse. "And it is not ended yet."

Delun's strength slowly returned to him. He followed Lei's glance. "The princess must be saved."

"And Chao must be stopped."

Delun brushed off his robes. "You should go in. I'll hold them off as long as I can."

"You know you won't last more than a few seconds. I will stay here. I can give you time and space."

Lei was right, of course. Delun prepared to leave, finally finding the courage to ask. "How have you done all of this?"

Lei only answered with another smile. "Someday you will know."

Delun shook his head at the cryptic response, and he walked with Lei back toward the entrance of the warehouse. Lei provided cover almost all the way to the door.

The attacks against Lei were coming more sporadically now, but still often enough to destroy even a strong monk. Delun looked at the mysterious man one more time. There was so much he wanted to say, so much he wanted to ask.

But it would have to wait. He had a greater task in front of him.

For now, they had an understanding. It was enough.

Delun gave Lei a short bow and sprinted from the shield.

He left a place of peace and stepped directly into the realm of chaos.

The warehouse looked like a storm had passed through. Bodies of several monks littered the ground. Beds were thrown everywhere, and what furniture had been inside was shattered.

For a moment, Delun gaped at the scene before him. Bai was swinging a chair, launching it at a monk standing a dozen paces away from her. The monk only had an attack prepared, so he launched it at the chair.

The effect was not desirable. The wood shattered, sending splinters and debris raining down on the monk. He protected himself from the shards.

Bai took full advantage of the opportunity. She launched herself through the air, her foot connecting squarely with the monk's jaw. None of the hesitation she had shown against Delun was present.

Bai was joined by the other woman, who, from a glance, seemed to have Bai's powers as well. She danced around a wraith, stabbing him repeatedly with a dagger until he fell, covered in wounds.

Delun's gaze wandered from Bai's fight to the back of the warehouse. If the princess was here, she'd be back there. Delun saw a group of monks, led by a familiar figure, heading that way.

"Ping!" he yelled.

The other monk turned at the sound of his name. With a small wave, he turned and ran into the spaces near the rear of the warehouse.

Delun ignored the rest of the fight. Bai and the other woman could take care of themselves. The princess was the key to everything.

"Delun!" Bai called out. There was a warning in her voice, but Delun ignored it.

He shouldn't have.

As he neared the individual rooms, a sudden blast of energy exploded outward, sending a wall of rock toward him. Delun covered himself with his hands, but the wave of stone and force knocked him back.

Once his vision cleared, Delun got a glance of Ping, leaving the room he had just destroyed.

Delun extricated himself from the rubble, grateful he hadn't been seriously injured. He formed the signs for a shield but held it. This had the feeling of a trap. He ran to a corner that opened up to the hallway the rooms were connected to.

Three monks waited for him. With Lei's energy so bright behind him, Delun hadn't even noticed.

Their attacks came fast. If Delun hadn't already had a shield prepared, he would have had no chance. He released it, blocking the three strikes.

The monks wasted no time moving in, forming signs with one hand even as they lashed out at him with their feet.

Delun stepped into the fight, the only safety being among the group.

One monk tried to kick his chest. Delun caught the kick and spun as a second monk launched a one-handed attack at him. The attack missed by inches, blasting into the wall behind Delun.

Still holding onto the first monk's leg, Delun used his momentum to toss the monk into the second one, sending them both crashing against the wall behind them.

Before he could take advantage of the downed monks, he was attacked by the third. Delun blocked a punch but couldn't avoid a pushing kick to the chest. Delun bounced against the wall behind him, his head cracking against the stone.

Stars swam in his vision, but he still felt the third monk make the first two signs for the attack with his hand. The monk was fast. Delun couldn't focus enough to create a shield. Instead, he slapped the hand aside.

The monk released the attack a moment too late. He hit one of his comrades instead of Delun.

Blinking away the stars, Delun stepped forward and kneed the man hard in the stomach. The monk's eyes rolled in his head, and Delun caught the man's head in his hand, slamming it hard against the stone wall.

The first two monks only took him a few moments more. One was disoriented from being attacked by his friend, and the other was still getting up.

Delun walked toward the princess's room at the end of the hall.

He stopped before he got there, feeling Ping in the room next to him. Chao's office.

Delun only hesitated for a moment. Sounds of the battle in the main hall were dying down, and Delun assumed that meant Bai was simply cleaning up. Delun had time. Perhaps there would be information there they could use, information that would reveal Chao's plan.

Delun stepped into the room, ready to fight Ping.

But the room was empty.

He shook his head, trying to make sense of what he saw. He'd been certain Ping was in here. He'd felt the man's energy, as clear as day. Delun closed his eyes, shunting away the myriad distractions.

There.

Underneath him, moving away.

Somewhere in this room there must be a trapdoor, a secret entrance.

Nothing came immediately to mind. However they'd hidden the door, they'd done a good job. Ping could wait.

Before he left the room, Delun looked around, searching for any clue that Chao might have left. Papers lay scattered about, but a map drew his eye. Delun approached it, recognizing it as a map of Jihan instantly. There were red lines and markings scribbled all over it. It looked like lines of escape from the warehouse.

Had Chao planned for a defeat here? Delun wished he possessed a window into that man's mind.

Another flash of color caught his eye. A sealed letter, opened and on the table. Delun picked it up and glanced at the seal. It was from Lord Xun. Delun pocketed it. He could read the missive after the fight ended. For now, he needed to get the princess to safety. He could explore this room and its treasures in more detail later. He left Chao's headquarters, then walked to the end of the hallway.

The princess's room was locked from the outside. Delun unlocked it and threw open the door, finding the princess sitting composed within.

"Princess, we must leave."

She nodded, as though she'd been waiting for him.

Delun checked the hallway. It was as empty as it had been a moment ago. They ran down the hallway, coming out into the main room a few moments later.

As Delun had predicted, Bai was just finishing her fight against the monks in the room. Delun looked around, wondering if Chao could be found. He didn't see the leader of the wraiths among Bai's defeated.

Delun stepped toward Bai, eager to be out of this building. He saw Bai's eyes widen even as she dove to the side.

Acting on instinct, Delun formed the sign for a shield. He made to release it, but was too late.

He felt two punches to his lower back.

When he looked down he saw two arrowheads extruding from his stomach. In surprise, he turned around, seeing movement in the hallway he'd just come from.

Delun managed to make the second sign for the shield, casting it around him and the princess just as another wave of arrows thunked off it. Beside him, the princess bled from a wound in her thigh. It didn't look deep, fortunately.

Beyond him, Bai had an arrow through her arm. She was running to hide behind his shield as cover.

Delun took a breath, feeling the piercing agony spread through his body. He would need to get his injuries looked at soon. "Come on," he said to the princess, stumbling toward the exit.

Streaks of flame shot over his head, arcing toward barrels placed in the corners of the building. Delun stared dumbly at the sight for a moment. Behind him, he heard the slamming of a heavy door.

Then Bai was beside them. "Sign a shield!"

Her shout brought him out of his daze. His fingers slid through the signs, acting on a level below conscious thought. Bai wrapped an arm around him and one around the princess.

Delun felt another stabbing wound. The arrow in Bai's arm dug into his back. The pain blended in with that he already felt, causing him to grind his teeth together as he focused on his hand moving through the sign.

This close to Bai, he could feel the enormous amount of energy she was drawing, unsure of what she had planned. Then he was in the air, higher than he had ever been before. The ground flew beneath him as he arced toward the enormous ceiling and then back down to solid ground.

"Release your shield!" Bai yelled.

He did, just as there was a flash from below.

It all became chaos then.

Delun's world became filled with fire and stone. Waves of pressure buffeted his shield, and then the ground came up to meet them.

The impact was softer than he expected. Bai had landed first, had taken most of it. But she couldn't take it all. They fell, Delun and the princess crashing on top of Bai.

The stone caved in around them, and still Delun held onto his shield.

When Delun breathed, he felt as though he was coating the inside of his lungs with dust. All was dark and gray.

Beside him, he could sense movement, another gathering of power.

Bai had kept her senses about her. She shouted and a stone crumbled to dust, broken under the power of her enhanced fists. Another shout and another stone cracked into pieces.

Daylight shone through now, the dust settling around them.

Delun couldn't hear, could only make out the dull vibrations of shouted words near him. His torso burned with agony, worsening with every breath he took.

Hands reached through the hole and the princess was pulled through. Delun breathed a sigh of relief. She, at least, would be safe.

Bai turned to him next. She said something he couldn't make out. She reached behind him and suddenly his insides were vibrating as though they were trying to escape. When she was done, she looked at him with concern in her eyes. He felt different.

As she helped him up, he saw that she had broken the shafts that stuck out of his back.

Hands reached in again. Groaning, Delun grabbed onto them, his own hands slick with blood. They pulled. He could feel his torso tearing as the arrowheads and shafts still protruding caught on pieces of stone.

Then he was out in the light, surrounded by concerned faces. The princess was there, as was Lei.

Sometime later, Bai joined them. Delun saw that she had broken the arrow in her own arm. She was pale with pain, but on her feet.

Delun tried to stand but couldn't.

He saw the concern in their eyes.

The sorrow.

And that was when he finally realized he wasn't going to stand again.

He took a deep, shuddering breath, trying to keep a lid on his emotions. He had trained for this. But he had always imagined it would be quick and relatively painless.

Not like this.

A hand grabbed his own. Smaller, but strong, with calloused palms. His eyes followed the hand up the arm to Bai's face. "Thank you," she said.

He wanted to tell her there was no need for thanks. That he had always done his duty. But he found his jaw didn't work anymore.

On his other side, another hand clasped his, this one larger and softer.

Lei bowed to the monk, saying nothing.

As he held onto their hands, Delun felt... everything. He felt the tremendous powers they drew on, the connection they had made to an energy far deeper and more mysterious than the monasteries could ever imagine.

He tried to bow, inclining his head just the slightest amount. Passing through in the presence of these warriors would be an honor.

And at his end, he wasn't alone.

39

Lei felt the life slip away from the man who lay at his feet. The body, once so full of energy and life, became nothing more than a hollow reminder of who the man had been.

Lei stood up, his own recollection throwing him back to a past that was thirty years dead. Delun had been a believer, and Lei had watched him die. It reminded him uncomfortably of Fang, another devout believer who had died on the streets of Jihan. The beliefs of the two men could not have been more different, but they had both held onto those beliefs through the end of their lives.

Lei respected them both.

There was no time for mourning. As in the past, the warehouse had been destroyed by tremendous energies, and once again, there was no safety nearby. Lei had held back the wraiths, but they still hovered around the rubble, surrounding Lei, the princess, Rong, and Bai.

Dust from the rubble still settled, choking the air and reducing visibility. The monks had used black powder, the same substance that had brought so much pain to their own ranks.

He suspected they were not out of the ambush yet. Barrels had been placed around the intersection, and Lei had a sneaking suspicion he knew what they contained. With a little bit of flame, this entire intersection would blow.

For now, his shield held. The attacks against it had ceased, and Lei thought he felt the wraiths moving away. He couldn't guess what they planned next.

A few steps away, the princess waited, remarkably calm for the events she had just undergone. Lei wondered at that, but he couldn't ask her now. Right now, his only real concern was their survival. His strength was immense, but even his body could only take so much.

"We have to go," Lei said.

Bai stood up. "We should take Delun with us."

Lei opened his mouth to argue. The body would only slow them down, and Delun himself wouldn't have cared. When he saw the look in Bai's eyes, though, he knew it was an argument he would not win. Instead, he asked, "Can you carry him?"

Bai nodded.

Lei wondered at that. Bai's arm was bloody and she looked pale from blood loss, but there was little point arguing with the determination in her eyes.

"Everybody! Gather near me!" Lei's voice boomed in the intersection beyond the rubble.

The small group of warriors pressed close around Lei, forming a loose circle around him. The princess took her place as well.

As soon as they gathered, Lei saw an arrow fly overhead, lit by flame. He cursed, throwing more energy into his shield. The arrow embedded deep in a barrel, depositing the deadly fire. A moment later the world exploded, the first barrel leading others in a continuous roar of fire. Waves of pressure rocked the buildings surrounding the intersection and the ground trembled beneath their feet.

The pressure strained against his shield, but he held.

The world shifted around him, his vision dancing, voices ringing in his ears. He had one foot in this world and the other somewhere he couldn't describe.

He waited for the flame to die down before he released his shield. His vision mostly returned to normal, only a few ghostly outlines wandering through his gaze.

All the buildings which had stood in front of the warehouse were nothing but smoking ruins. The powder had leveled the entire area. The people within Lei's circle survived without injury, though.

He looked at Bai. "We need to go, now."

Rong led the way. As the woman moved, Lei couldn't help but think of a younger Bai. The two moved as though they were of one mind.

The princess followed and Lei took the rear. They stayed tight together, and Lei had a shield ready to go at any sign of danger.

Before they even cleared the ruins, they ran into another ambush. Archers stood on nearby buildings and in windows, launching waves of arrows.

Lei cast a shield, calmly surveying the situation.

They hadn't anticipated this, but Chao had. The monk had prepared barrels, archers, and his own warriors for an assault on the warehouse. From the degree of preparation, it seemed as though he had expected far more than the three of them.

But they were the ones trapped now. Lei couldn't shield them forever.

They needed transport. Rong could move quickly, but Bai carried Delun's body and was already looking pale. The princess was gifted, but Lei didn't know her powers. If they tried to escape on foot they would continue to be harried until they cracked.

Lei grabbed Rong by the shoulder. "We need horses."

Rong looked uncertain for a moment, then nodded. Lei pointed down the street he planned on taking. "We'll start that direction. Hurry."

With that, Rong was off. She darted away before the archers or the monks could take her down. She cut an impressive sight.

Lei looked at the other two women. "Let's get going."

Before long, the wraiths resumed their attacks. Blasts of energy crashed against Lei's shield. He didn't worry about them breaking through; his worry was how much longer his body could sustain this effort. Whatever he was tapping into, he became more certain it wasn't something he was supposed to. It wasn't a power meant for living beings.

He saw ghosts, more spirits than he could count, flowing into and out of buildings, pressing against his shield with expressions of rapt curiosity.

Had he pierced the veil, or was his mind losing its grip on reality?

He didn't know. He just kept putting one foot in front of the other. Beside him, Bai didn't seem to be moving any faster. Her steps faltered, and she left a trail of blood behind her.

Only the princess seemed relatively unharmed, but there was little for her to do. She walked a few paces in front of them. Lei felt the focused energy running along her limbs. In other circumstances it could be a useful skill. But against the ranged attacks of archers and wraiths, she could do little but hide behind Lei's shield.

They made it two blocks under withering fire before they had to pause. Lei could feel the muscles spasm as he took each step. He couldn't last much longer.

The sound of thundering hooves lifted his spirits. Lei looked up to find Rong on a horse, another pulled behind. Gathering more strength, his reality fading as he did, Lei launched attacks at the surrounding buildings.

The attacks weren't strong enough to kill. They weren't enough to bring down buildings. But they forced the monks and archers back, if only for a moment.

Lei dropped the shield so Rong and the horses could enter. Then he cast it again, collapsing to his knees with the effort.

Blasts ringing against the shield told him he hadn't gotten the protection up a moment too soon. Rong looked to him, and he gestured to the princess and Bai. "Get them mounted first."

The princess took the reins of the first horse. Lei was grateful to see she seemed comfortable with the beast. Bai climbed up as well, then helped position Delun's body behind them.

Once that was done, Rong helped Lei onto the other horse. He felt the power coursing through her arms, giving her the strength to lift everyone up.

If they survived, all of them would suffer through a very unpleasant tomorrow.

They rode. They couldn't move too quickly. The princess's horse carried an unwieldy load, and galloping through the streets of Jihan risked other disasters.

But they moved faster than they could on foot, and Lei could focus on maintaining his shield. The horses plowed through the streets close together, Lei's shield clearing a path for them.

After a minute, the attacks had lessened. Their assailants couldn't keep up with the increased pace.

Another few minutes passed and the last attack faded. They were close to the monastery now.

Lei didn't think he'd ever been so happy to see the walls of a monastery in his life.

He didn't last through the whole ride. His world went to black as he slumped against Rong before they even passed through the walls.

40

———

Bai leaned against the cold stone walls of the monastery. Her body had found a place beyond exhaustion. Blackness nibbled at the edges of her vision, but sleep wouldn't come. Her mind raced in circles. They had saved the princess. And Delun had died for them.

A dozen tasks demanded her attention, but for now she needed space. She needed time, sleep, and a healer.

The healer found her after attending to the princess.

He looked at her arm, most of an arrow still through it.

"How is she?" Bai asked.

"She'll be fine. The arrow cut fairly deep, but the wound is clean and stitched shut now. Your arm will be worse."

"Just get it over with."

The healer nodded. He examined the arrow, then looked up to her. "Ready?"

Before she could reply, he pulled the arrow out. Red hot fire burned over her arm. For a moment, the blackness swallowed her whole.

Her awareness returned with blinding suddenness as

the healer cleaned the wound. She wished the blackness had lasted for much longer.

After another few minutes of unending agony, the healer was done, clean white bandages wrapped around her arm. He stood up. "Try not to use it, if you can." With that, he walked away, leaving Bai to her thoughts.

They had done it. The princess was safe, at least for the moment.

She could feel the eyes of Rong and the other students on her. Even the other monks inside the monastery kept glancing at her, looking to her for some direction.

But she had nothing to say. She had no idea what came next, and she needed rest. But there were things to do first. She wouldn't sleep until they had taken care of Delun's body.

She sensed a presence next to her. A gifted, but not a monk. Bai cracked open her eyes to see the princess standing next to her, staring at the body lying in the center of the courtyard. There was a hint of tears in the princess's eyes. "He and I spoke, a few times, before he died."

Despite herself, curiosity won Bai over. She stood and joined the princess in looking at Delun's body.

The princess continued. "He always seemed torn between what he knew was right and his own desires."

Bai thought about that. The princess was on to something. She replied, her voice soft. "Our paths only crossed twice, but both times he was forced to turn against the brothers he spent his entire life trying to protect."

The princess nodded. "I would have liked to know him better."

"I think he would have felt the same." Bai wasn't sure what led her to say that. She'd just met the princess, but the woman impressed her. Throughout the escape the princess had remained calm, and Bai had felt her gift as well. She was a force not to be dismissed. Bai could see Delun enjoying her company.

The princess seemed lost in thought for a minute, then turned her attention back to Bai. "What comes next?"

Bai bit her tongue to prevent her retort. Why did everyone assume she had a plan?

It wasn't the answer the princess was looking for, but Bai did know what needed to happen now. "We need to light a burial pyre for Delun."

"May I help?"

Bai nodded, touched by the gesture. They set to work.

There was much to be done. Bai spoke with the monks, asking for enough wood for a pyre. They not only showed her where they stored their firewood, they helped carry it to a corner of the courtyard. The blackened stone told Bai it wasn't the first pyre lit within these walls.

Everyone began to pitch in. Bai watched the monks and Yang's students work side by side. She could do little but direct the process. Her one good arm prevented her from being useful. While they worked, she went over to Delun and tried to straighten out his robes. She was grateful he had died in them, at least. He had died as he had lived, honoring the monastic traditions.

As her hand wandered over the folds of his robe, she felt and heard the crinkle of paper underneath. She reached into his pockets, wondering what he had died with.

When she saw the seal, she knew it was important. Her eyes ran over the letter once, then once again to make sure. Mysteries unraveled in front of her. Even in death, Delun had aided them. She bowed to his corpse, thanking him.

There would be time to discuss the letter later. For now, it was time to honor Delun.

They finished building the pyre not long before the sun was to set, the symbolic time when monks said goodbye to their brothers.

Every monk in the monastery gathered in the courtyard. There were more than Bai realized. Yang's students joined them.

Only Lei was absent, but he had seen enough death lately, and she wasn't sure she could wake him even if she wanted to. He needed rest.

Again, everyone looked to her. This time, she didn't mind. She had fought by Delun's side twice, and she wanted to speak for him.

She approached the pyre, then turned to address the gathering. What could she say about Delun that did his life justice? She didn't want to lie about his failings. He had committed horrible crimes in the course of his life, but he had done great deeds as well. Both sides were a part of the man she had known.

"Delun's life is both an inspiration and a caution to us all," she began. "He was a man of tremendous strength, discipline, and loyalty. If he called you a friend, or fought by your side, you couldn't ask for a better ally.

"But those same strengths were also his weaknesses. He didn't understand the consequences of his actions until it was too late. His belief made him a killer. He took fathers away from their families. He tortured enemies."

Bai paused. "He also stopped the monks of Kulat before they could harm even more innocents. He saved a princess and gave his life. I do not know if Delun is a hero or a villain, but I am grateful that I have known him.

"Let us remember Delun as we walk our own paths. Belief can give us strength. Taken too far, it can also destroy us and those we love."

The wood, dry from being sheltered for months, caught without problem, the flames eagerly jumping over Delun's corpse. Bai wanted to cry for the man she dared call a friend, but she couldn't bring herself to do it. He had her sympathy, but little else.

The flames licked at the sky, sending the remainder of Delun's soul on to whatever existed past death.

41

Lei ran the edge of his sword across the whetstone, the distinctive sound of the blade against the stone soothing his frayed nerves. The routine, so long embedded in his life, brought him a measure of ease that he couldn't find any other way.

After the death of his parents and the murder of his brother, Lei thought that he had learned all of life's lessons concerning grief. The loss of Daiyu was teaching him otherwise.

He supposed it stood to reason. He lost his parents when he was young, and after their death he had never been alone. His brother had stood by his side, a rock to brace himself against whatever grief washed over him.

His brother's death had been a complicated affair. The two of them had not been on speaking terms when Jian died, and the grief from that death had trickled in through Lei's defenses one drip at a time, like a leaking roof under a constant drizzle.

Daiyu's loss was like nothing else. Despite the company and warmth of Bai and her friends, Lei bore his grief alone.

He was part of this world and yet not. When he closed his eyes, he thought he heard her voice.

She had been the tree that he built his life around, and that tree had suddenly been uprooted. Even though he had known the storm was coming, he had not been prepared.

His grief was like the tides of the ocean. For hours, he would be fine. He went through life the same way he did every day before. Then his whole outlook would change, and a giant wave would rise up and swallow him whole, consuming every thought and action. When those waves crested he felt truly helpless, alone and abandoned against a force he could not fight.

And yet he could not bring himself to surrender. Not yet.

He didn't understand the changes afflicting his body and mind. After the energy he'd used outside the warehouse, he should be on death's door. But after his sleep, his body felt as light as a feather. Bai had brought him food that he had only nibbled at. He wasn't hungry.

Bai couldn't hide the concern from her eyes, but she'd deferred to him in the end.

Since then he remained alone in his room, his thoughts his only company.

His silence was interrupted by a knock at his door. He glanced up, extending his sense and feeling the power on the other side. "Come in."

The door opened slowly, revealing the hesitation of the person on the other side.

Although Lei had known who his guest was, he still found himself slightly surprised when the princess poked her head around the edge of the door. She took in his posture and his blade in one sweeping glance. "Is this a bad time?"

Lei made a few final polishing strokes. The truth of the

matter was, he had already been done for quite some time. "No. I was just finishing up."

The princess gave a smile, clearly not believing him. But she stepped in all the same.

"I'm sorry to bother you like this," she began. "But I have some questions, and I was hoping you could help me."

"I would be honored. Please, come in and make yourself comfortable."

The princess followed the first instruction, but the second seemed beyond her ability. She sat in the lone chair in the corner of the room, but she kept fidgeting. Lei maintained his silence, wondering what help she thought he could give.

"I don't understand your power," the princess said, her eyes focusing on Lei's sword. "How do you do it?"

He heard the curiosity in her voice, the concern.

He was a weapon she didn't understand. Her first reaction was to learn more.

Combined with her composure outside the warehouse, Lei painted a picture of this woman. She was strong, and ready to rule.

"I have a connection to the source of energy that gives all gifted their strength," he began.

The princess shook her head. "I'm sorry, that wasn't the right question. What I mean to ask is, the power that you possess is incredible. Doesn't it frighten you?"

Lei leaned back. "All the time."

The princess's eyes widened, genuinely surprised by his answer. She leaned forward. "Then how do you decide to act? How do you fight with that knowledge of what you are capable of?"

Lei sheathed his sword, for no other reason than to give him something to do while he considered his answer. He took a deep breath. "Training and experience is one part of your answer. You see only the results, but I have spent over thirty years of my life training for most of the hours of the day. I mostly know what I can do. That knowledge is deep within me, and I am not sure I would fight without that certainty. I did when I was younger, and the cost was too great."

The princess leaned her head on her hands, considering his answer carefully. She was silent as she turned his words over in her head. Then her eyes came up. "With the power you possess, why haven't you done more? I am well aware of the events in my father's land. Why have you avoided action for so long?"

Lei gave a small shrug. "Though I can control my own power, the results of my decisions echo far beyond the action itself."

The princess wasn't satisfied. "But how do you decide when to act?"

It was Lei's turn to pause. It was a good question, and a hard one. He had often relied on Daiyu to help him make those decisions. She had always had a clarity around what she wanted and the wisdom to know how to pursue those goals.

And like that, he knew his answer. He met the princess's gaze. "I had it easy. I was married to a woman who helped me make those decisions, and make them well. If there is one thing I can say, it would be this: don't rely solely on yourself. That is a path towards eventual ruin. Surround yourself with advisers you can trust, who will want what is both best for you and for the empire. Finding such people may be difficult, but having other viewpoints from trusted individuals is a precious gift.

"I would also suggest this: have a vision for where you

want this empire to go. Without a goal, you are only making random decisions, or the decisions that seem best at the time. Know what you are striving toward and let that be your guide. Once you know that, when difficult decisions present themselves, listen to your advisors and listen to your instincts. You will probably make mistakes along the way, but in the grand arc of your life, I believe you will be satisfied."

"Are you?"

"Am I what?"

"Satisfied."

Lei shook his head. "I was. But no longer."

"You need a new vision, then."

Lei grinned at his words being turned on him. "Visions are for the young. I need peace."

"Then fight for it."

Lei met her eyes. He'd never spent any time around nobility. He'd briefly interacted with Lord Xun's father many, many years ago, but that was the extent of it. He'd never met a leader like her before. If anyone could straighten out the problems facing the empire, it would be her. "You want my oath?"

The princess shook her head. "I'd settle for your sword for now. We haven't seen the last of the wraiths."

Lei imagined Daiyu, grinning in the afterlife. Her hopes for him had been fulfilled after all.

He'd never regretted following Daiyu's suggestions while she lived. He might as well try following them after her death.

He gave the princess a short bow. "My sword is yours."

42

———

Bai looked out over Jihan from the walls of the monastery. She felt Lei's presence behind her as he joined her high above the surrounding buildings. The soft glow of lights in the distance cast warm shadows everywhere she looked.

The city slept, though Bai knew she would get none tonight. While most citizens slept, hoping that the disasters they had heard about were over, she worried about her future, and the future of the empire. The message that rustled in her pocket confirmed her worst fears.

Their battle had just begun. They had rescued the princess, but accomplished little else. The wraiths still had the upper hand, and Delun was dead.

She glanced over at Lei as he also took in the sight of Jihan below them. She almost thought she could see through him. The power emanating from him set her teeth on edge, but he seemed lesser, somehow, as though one of the strong breezes coming up the wall would blow him away.

Lei interrupted her melancholy thoughts. "The view

from the monastery above Two Bridges is much better." His voice was strong, despite his appearance. She couldn't believe he could even stand after all he had done.

Bai gave a wry smile. "I'll have to add it to my list of destinations to visit."

Lei laughed. "One day, monasteries across the empire will welcome you, and then you will have no more excuses."

"I doubt that I will ever see that day."

"Don't be so sure. The last time I visited this monastery, I had to escape through a hole in the wall because I feared they were going to imprison me forever. Now they treat me as a revered guest. Time changes people and institutions."

Bai conceded the point. She didn't believe, but the hope was pleasant. "Very well, someday I will visit. But on one condition: you must visit with me and show me the sights."

Lei smiled at that. "Few journeys would bring me greater joy."

They looked out on the city together. "It's too quiet," said Bai.

"Quiet is good."

"Unless your enemy is right behind you."

Lei nodded and they leaned against the wall. Bai fished the letter out of her pocket and handed it to Lei. He held it up to a nearby torch and read. He sighed. "That explains much."

"The entire empire has turned against us."

"It is not so bad as all that."

"Lord Xun makes it pretty clear that all resistance to the wraiths must be eliminated. That's as good as saying the emperor wants all monks who don't agree with Chao to be killed. It includes the princess, as well."

"Which means the emperor and his advisers have been

plotting with Chao. It doesn't mean the whole empire is with them."

"It might as well."

They stood in silence, each trying to solve the problem. Bai didn't have the slightest idea where to begin. "What should we do?"

A hint of a smile appeared on Lei's face. "All I know is that we must leave Jihan. The warehouse was a trap. If they attack the monastery, more innocents will suffer." Lei's hand swept across the sight of the nearby buildings. "Beyond that, we must ask the others. Perhaps they will have better ideas."

Though the night was late, it didn't take long for Bai to summon most everyone together. It appeared few people were getting the sleep they needed tonight. Bai wondered if Delun's death hung over them all.

Bai began by sharing the letter with everyone. The look on the faces of the monks broke her heart. She couldn't imagine what they must feel, the betrayal of the very empire they had all sworn to serve.

"Why?" asked one of the monks.

The princess answered. "My father has struggled with the monasteries for years. The abbots are indecisive, and most prefer being locked up behind their walls instead of patrolling the empire as they once did." She shot a withering glare at the abbot, who shrank from the accusation. "I believe Chao has promised him the obedience of the wraiths, a gift my father can't refuse."

Rong challenged the letter. "Chao has been one step ahead of us the entire time. What's to say this isn't another trap?"

Lei shook his head. "It's possible, but the whole warehouse had been set to blow. I don't think this was meant to be found."

Bai interrupted the argument. "We need to decide on a course of action. If this letter is true, Chao will certainly attack us soon."

"We must leave the city," Lei added. "I will not fight again within the walls of the capital."

There was silence around the table. The abbot spoke first. "I will send word to all other abbots. They will know of this betrayal."

It was the princess who stepped forward and solved the problem. "There is an abandoned fort, about a week's journey north of here. We can use it as a gathering place, where we can decide how to react."

The abbot nodded. "If you will let me know the location, I can let the abbots know where we can be found. Some will prefer to stay within their walls, but some will come."

"And some, with their backs to the wall, will join with the wraiths." Rong spoke the fear no one else had the courage to voice.

The princess stood tall. "Alliances will fall where they will." She turned to the abbot. "If I may, there are some who I would like to contact as well. The true monasteries are not without friends."

Bai wanted to believe the princess, but it was hard to from where she stood. The city was quiet. No one had come to their aid.

The preparations happened quickly. Monks hurried to and fro, packing food and supplies in barrels and crates. Carts were loaded, axles groaning under the weight. Bai stood apart from it all, nearly useless thanks to her injured arm.

The gates were open, and two or three monks left without a word to their brothers. Bai knew that by sunrise, they would be numbered among the wraiths. No one tried to stop them. No one had the heart to fight a brother.

Not yet.

The streets were still quiet when they evacuated the city before dawn.

For the first time in hundreds of years, the monastery of Jihan stood empty.

43

Lei meandered the plains that surrounded the abandoned fort they all now called home. The fort was situated on a small rise that was the only elevation for miles in any direction. According to the princess, the fort had once served as an outpost. Though it had been empty for years, the walls stood strong. The building meant little against the forces that might be brought against it, but the comfort of thick stone walls couldn't be understated.

Despite the number of years behind him, Lei had never been to this part of the empire. Travel throughout the land wasn't difficult. The roads were well-maintained and for the most part were safe. In recent years, especially, he could have traveled as fewer people paid attention to his exile. But he'd always been content in the quiet mountain valley he called his home.

Now that Daiyu was gone, Lei found himself revisiting many of the decisions they had made together. Maybe they should have traveled more, seen more of the empire. Both of them enjoyed the pursuit of novelty and of unknown vistas.

It was too late now.

He heard hooves behind him, and he turned to see the princess ride up to him. She slowed her horse with an expert hand, stopping less than five feet from him. "You look thoughtful," she said.

Lei shook his head. "If only any of it was useful."

"What troubles you?"

Lei struggled to put his thoughts into words. "For years, I have felt—something—growing." He grasped at the air, trying to capture the vague feeling. "Tell me, do you believe in fate?"

The princess shook her head. "We find our own way through life."

"I used to believe the same."

"And now?"

"Now I'm not sure. I've felt a change in the air now for years, the shifting of forces I thought I understood. Here, I feel it stronger than ever. This is where the old dies and the new is born."

"A good omen, then."

Lei shrugged. He didn't know what change was coming. All he knew was that he belonged here.

The princess turned to the business at hand. "Scouts have returned with news of an approaching army."

"Lord Xun's?"

"Yes."

Lei sensed them, a presence on the fabric of reality miles away. "They come with the wraiths."

"Yes." The princess couldn't hide the worry in her voice.

"So your father does intend to wipe us all out."

"It looks that way."

Lei stared out in the direction of Jihan, where the army came for them. A tremendous weariness settled over his bones. He did not want to be a part of an empire where fathers plotted against their daughters for power. With Daiyu gone, he wasn't sure how much he wanted to be a part of anything. She had anchored him.

The princess gestured to her horse. "Climb on. We are gathering to discuss our options. Your presence is needed."

Lei took one last look at the endless stretch of grass in front of him. Then he accepted her hand and climbed up into the saddle.

He PAID little attention to the content of the meeting. His eyes were only for Bai, watching his one-time student with undisguised amusement. He didn't think she noticed what had happened.

Everyone in the room, from the abbot of Jihan's monastery to the princess of the empire, looked to her. Bai didn't speak the loudest, or the most, but when she chimed in, every eye and ear was attentive. The meeting was purportedly for the group to come to a consensus about their position. In reality, it was a chance for Bai to listen to the others and make the decisions the rest would follow.

Lei could guess the outcome. They would sue for peace, but if it wasn't accepted, this land would be the site of a battle of unimaginable energies. Lord Xun's army and the wraiths were already stretched out beyond the walls. Lei could feel their collected power pulling at the fabric of the world.

He watched Bai, so clearly uncomfortable in her new role. Ten years ago, when he had first trained her, he hadn't imagined this future. She had always cared deeply. Though she tried to hide the depth of her feelings, she had always cared for others. In that way, she was a far better person than Lei. He had never cared much beyond his own happiness.

Others were drawn to that concern like moths to flame. Combined with the strength of her gift, she made a natural choice for others to look to. But it was more than that, Lei knew.

She made decisions.

Simple enough to say, but hard in reality. The princess possessed the same quality, but as the new arrival to the group, she deferred to Bai. Most people preferred to wait, to be convinced, to react to the world around them.

Not Bai. She listened, then made her decision. A small quality, but one that had landed her the leadership of this group.

Eventually, the group broke apart. Lei focused his attention as Bai came to him. "Can you fight?"

He wondered how he appeared to her, that she even had to ask the question. He was still connected to the currents of energy flowing around them. He worried that if he severed the connection his heart would cease its constant beat. "If I must."

Bai offered him her hand. "We're sending out a delegation. I'd like you to be there."

He let her help him up. Like the princess, Bai was a woman worth following.

A few minutes later the gates of the fort opened and Lei saw their enemy for the first time. He had never seen so many people at once. Lord Xun's army stretched across the field, lined up and ready for battle. Lei identified the cavalry and the infantry, impressed by the sheer force that had been collected to destroy them. They came with siege engines, ready to make war. All in all, they had brought far more than seemed strictly necessary.

Lei knew little of Xun's army. To his knowledge they had a stellar reputation as disciplined fighters, but beyond that, he had never bothered to learn much of them.

They certainly looked fearsome enough from a distance.

A small contingent broke from the main ranks with a white flag in the air. Lei watched them advance until they were a few hundred paces away from the fort. They might be traveling under a white flag, but that didn't mean they would put themselves in bow shot of the walls.

The abbot had brought a looking glass, and Lei heard him gasp. "The emperor is there!"

That, more than the letter, proved the emperor's betrayal. Lei felt no anger, though. He only felt disappointment. He had hoped for more from the man who led the empire. But he couldn't summon the hate he might have felt as a younger man.

"What kind of man would plot the death of his own flesh and blood?"

Lei heard the fire in Bai's voice. She was upset enough for both of them.

Their own little group gathered just outside the walls of the fort. The abbot signed a shield but held it.

Bai looked around and issued orders. She might claim she wanted no part of command, yet it fit her like a fine robe. She would figure that out for herself soon enough, Lei decided.

Before long, he, Bai, the abbot, and the princess approached the emperor's party. As they neared, Lei could make out the emperor, Lord Xun, Lord Xun's questioner, and Chao. They stood as close as conspirators. Lei saw now they had all been manipulated from the beginning. A flickering fire lit in his gut as he saw them all together.

They stopped ten feet from the emperor. Lei paid

particular attention to the dynamics between father and daughter.

The emperor seemed an entirely different man than Lei had met earlier in his palace. This one was even colder, made of unbreakable stone. Lei saw the true nature of the man who ruled the empire.

The emperor spoke first. "There can be no quarter given. By the time the sun sets on this day your fort will be overrun. Those of you who have completed the rites of passage through the monastery may surrender and pledge yourself to Chao. If you do not, your fate will be the same as the rest. Those are your choices."

Lei's side looked to the princess. This was her negotiation. If she was intimidated by the cold glare of her father, she didn't show it. "And what about those of us who haven't completed the monastic rites, Father?"

"Your lives are forfeit, princess. The empire has no place for you."

Even though he had expected the answer, the proclamation caused Lei to take a step back. The emperor and Chao wanted nothing less than complete control over the gifted, over the power itself.

Lei saw the error right away. Yang had told him that more unusual gifts were being discovered every day. The emperor and Chao were trying to seal a box that had already been shattered. No matter how they tried, the gift wouldn't be contained. Even if the emperor won this battle, his war was already lost.

"You are wrong, Father," the princess said, her voice steady and strong. "There is a place for us here, and I do not think you can stop us. Is there no way we can avoid bloodshed? Many will die on both sides."

There was a moment of silence. For a few heartbeats, Lei

thought the princess might have gotten through to the emperor.

He shook his head. "There is no other way. This must be done."

The princess looked like she had taken a beating, but she kept her chin high. "Goodbye, then, Father. Thank you for teaching me what lessons you could."

The emperor turned without saying another word.

44

———

Bai hated the fortress.

In her mind, the thick stone walls of the structure served as little more than another form of prison. She watched Chao and the emperor assemble their forces, far away from any harm she could cause them. Her gift gave her strength, but on a battlefield of this scope, she was worth little more than a foot soldier. She could do little but watch as the enemy prepared.

Their enemies came for them not long after Bai and the others returned to the fort.

Against such a force, Bai didn't know how much of a chance they had. The wraiths had been weakened by Bai's earlier attack, but they still vastly outnumbered the monks sheltering behind the walls of the abandoned fort.

The princess's defenders had the benefit of a simple strategy. They would rely on Lei's strength as much as possible. If the wraiths approached closer, Bai and Rong would leave the walls to cause as much disruption as they could. Outnumbered and cornered, though, Bai and the others could do little but react to their enemies' movements.

Rong and Wu stood next to her on the wall. Bai caught their glances in her direction, could see the worry they carried.

She spoke, just loudly enough for them to hear her. "The only mistake we can make today is to give in to fear."

The students leaned in, as though they were vines growing around the trunk of her courage. She felt like a fraud as she looked at each of them in turn. She hadn't been this frightened for a long time. It was one thing to go into a fight when you controlled the surroundings and were confident in your victory. It was entirely another experience when you didn't think you would see the next sunset. "Before I met you, I believed that I was alone, that I was the only one who possessed such gifts. The thought itself isolated me."

Off in the distance, there was movement among the emperor's troops. She looked back to her friends. "I'm not sure what will happen. In many ways, the final outcome of this all is beyond our control. There is only what I can do. I will stand firm. I will not abandon you, no matter what happens. If you will do the same, it is all I can ask."

She received determined nods in answer.

It would be enough. She felt her heart settle. The simple fact of their presence eased her worry. She returned to looking out over the wall. She meant every word. Yang's students were new additions to her life, but she would never leave them behind. They were closer to her heart than even her own life.

If she could give her life to save them, she considered that a worthy trade.

Xun's army stepped forward as one. Bai tensed. The time had come.

The advance was as orderly as anything Bai had ever

seen. The line of soldiers was as straight as a ruler. Bai fought the urge to summon her power. They were still too far away for her gifts to be useful.

The march of the army stopped well beyond the reach of even the strongest archer. A line of white-robed figures emerged from the ranks, stepping in front of the emperor's troops.

After about a minute, the monks began marching toward the fort. The rest of the soldiers remained behind. Bai watched, curious. It appeared the monks planned on taking this fort on their own.

Her eyes ran over the collection of monks quickly. Sixty monks, at least, remained after the fight in Jihan. An impressive number by any count. More monks than had ever been assembled for combat.

She gripped the walls of the fort tightly beneath her hands. She couldn't think of anything to do.

As one, the monks stopped about two hundred feet from the walls of the fort. They all began signing at once, their energy growing as it focused.

Bai swore. All of them attacking at once?

The power swelled, making her head pound with the gathering energy.

From further down the wall, standing next to the princess, Lei answered. He drew in power, building to an intensity that matched that of the monks against him.

The powers were beyond Bai's comprehension. Her sense, finely honed after years of searching for traitorous monks, was blinded, the entire world more vivid than it should be. She felt like the blind man from the parable, trying to identify the elephant from what little she could understand. Judging which power was greater was an impossible task, the magnitude of each beyond compare.

Her body absorbed the latent power in the air, filling her with strength she didn't ask for.

Bai stepped back and looked over at Lei, surprised to find he was looking at her. He nodded toward the line of monks, and it took her a moment to realize what he meant.

Of course.

If all the monks planned to attack at once, there would be an opening for one with her gifts.

She nodded her acknowledgement, then turned to Rong. "Be ready. Once those powers collide, we'll have an opportunity."

The response made perfect sense. Bai expected the monks planned on keeping their distance, pummeling the fort until it was nothing but rubble and bones. Lei could defend, and they could disrupt.

Rong looked downright eager. Bai wondered if the younger woman had any sense of fear.

Drawing in power was no problem in the charged environment they stood in. If anything, Bai had to be careful not to draw too much. The temptation pulled at her, but experience helped her resist.

The wraiths attacked. A wave of energy rolled over the grass that separated the two forces. Bai saw the air bend, distorting the view of the enemy. Never in her life had she *seen* an attack. For a moment, she just watched as that confluence of strengths barreled toward her. Nothing could stand in the way of such a force. Even the stone of the fort would tear as paper.

Nothing except Lei.

With a yell that originated deep in his stomach, Lei released his shield. Bai glanced at Rong and nodded. This was their chance.

The opposing energies came into contact, and the

distortion of the air became severe. Bai could barely make out the army just hundreds of feet in front of her.

Bai and Rong dropped from the wall and sprinted toward the collision of energies.

Soon, Bai realized something was wrong. The competing powers wrestled against one another, but the magnitude of the powers was such that reality itself seemed to tear like thin fabric. Bai held out a hand, halting their advance. Her body could absorb an impressive amount of power, but no one could be near the meeting of those energies and hope to live.

A sudden wind picked up, pulling them toward the line where Lei's power and that of the wraiths met. Bai scrambled for purchase, her feet kicking up the dirt under the grass, now fighting to stay away from the powers.

She heard footsteps behind her and turned just in time to see Wu running behind them. She'd never seen the eager young man run so fast. His face was a mask of fear, and he leaped, tackling both her and Rong.

They slammed into the dirt and Bai felt Wu throw a shield over them, his unique talent allowing him to do so without the need for a sign. The chaos they had been running through abruptly disappeared.

Wu's shield saved their lives.

The world boomed and shook, the energy releasing with an anger that put a thunderclap to shame. Bai saw the wave of energy wash toward them, grass and dirt thrown up hundreds of feet in the air. It smashed against Wu's shield and he grunted with the effort of holding it. He wasn't even fighting against an attack, but the after-effects of an attack. It still took all he had.

Fortunately, he held.

The wave passed and dirt trickled down against his

shield. He dropped it, exhausted, and dirt drifted down over them.

Bai looked over at Wu. The young man was sweating buckets and breathing hard. He didn't have the deep wells of strength other monks had, and protecting the two of them had taken everything he had.

"Get back to the fort," she ordered.

Wu nodded. "That sounds great."

With that, Bai got to her feet and charged the wraiths.

As she passed through the dirt she realized the fight had been taken completely out of Chao's followers. They had challenged Lei with everything, and it looked like Lei had won. Most of the monks seemed like Wu, exhausted on hands and knees.

Bai smashed into them with a fury, delivering kicks and blows strong enough to shatter bone. Half a dozen fell before even one managed to find their feet.

Unfortunately, it didn't take long for the monks to find their second wind in the face of the assault. Attacks threaded their way toward her, the wraiths responding as they had been trained.

Bai absorbed the attacks, then launched herself at anyone who stood.

Around her, she heard the sounds of steel being drawn. Many of the monks had armed themselves with swords and long knives.

So, they had come prepared for today's fight.

Rong crashed into the lines beside her, her own fists and feet flying among the rebellious monks.

To Bai's surprise, she heard calls for a retreat.

The wraiths turned and ran, and Bai chased after them, unwilling to let any escape.

She felt a restraining hand on her shoulder. "Let them go!" Rong yelled.

Bai wrested her shoulder away. "They're running! We'll never have a better chance."

Rong pointed to the fields beyond the monks. Lord Xun's army was marching forward in lockstep. "They'll be in bow range soon, and even you aren't good enough to dodge a thousand arrows."

Bai cursed. Rong was right.

Turning her back on the retreating monks pained her. To have her enemy so close, and to let them escape, hurt. They caught up to Wu just as he made it to the walls of the fort.

FOR SOME TIME AFTER THAT, the field was quiet. The wraiths blended back in with Lord Xun's army, and Bai wondered if they might be fighting off a joint assault in the near future. The monks had been given an opportunity and they had failed.

They won the first engagement, but the victory meant little. Bai and Rong compared experiences and figured that between the two of them they had killed perhaps a dozen monks. It dented the forces facing them, but little else. They were still outnumbered, and the victory hadn't come without cost.

Lei looked like he was wasting away. He still glowed against her senses, but his physical body looked weaker than ever. He claimed he could still fight, but no one in the fort was sure of that. He looked even older than he was, resting on a bench with his head in his hands.

She'd always considered him invincible, and she had to remind herself that he was just another man, gifted with extraordinary abilities. When people approached him he didn't even reply most of the time. They couldn't depend on him anymore, but they had little choice.

Bai sat next to him, but there was little to say. His feat had gone beyond words, beyond description. Such powers had never been assembled before. The monks from Jihan now avoided him, his full power beyond their comprehension. His once strong arms looked flabby. However he was connecting with the energies he used, it was killing him.

The princess came up to where they sat. She kneeled down in front of Lei. "How are you?"

Lei continued staring at the ground, not reacting to the presence of the princess at all.

The princess looked to Bai, worry in her eyes.

Bai answered the question as well as she could. "He says he is fine, but I do not know. This is unexplored territory for us all."

"Can we rely on him?"

Bai shrugged. "He's never let me down before."

Bai stood up and stretched. She'd come through the first sortie remarkably unharmed. She didn't think the same could be said of the second time she would leave the walls. "How bad is it?"

The princess stood up, too. By unspoken agreement, they wandered the courtyard. "I can't imagine it could get much worse."

"Your allies?"

The princess shook her head. "Most would accept my rule, if it came to that. But peace has made us complacent. Most lords will wait to see who emerges victorious, then offer their support. I'm afraid we can't rely on outside aid."

The last small hope flickering inside Bai died. Even if

the abbot's letters had reached other abbots, a monk approaching the area would quickly turn away from the gathered forces.

She hated thinking that Chao's plotting and betrayal was going to succeed. She considered leaving the walls in the middle of night and making a last attempt at his life. Stopping the force against them was beyond her abilities, but perhaps she could make sure Chao didn't get to enjoy his victory.

"How are you?" Bai asked.

The princess came to a stop, looking up at the walls and the monks who kept watch. Bai followed her gaze. There were so few of them.

"As well as can be, I suppose. My father has always been an emperor first and a father second. Maybe it's strange, but I can see his fingerprints over everything that's happened, and I'm in awe. The monasteries have been a problem for years, and he's finally found a way to bring them to heel and harness their power. He's committed horrible crimes, but still."

"He has?"

The princess gave Bai a sorrowful smile. "He's always played both sides. I'm sure of it. He must have aided the Order of the Serpent with their attacks. How else could so much black powder have gone missing, and been transported throughout the empire? Not only did he ally with Chao, he gave Chao the perfect method for recruiting more members."

As soon as Bai heard the princess's explanation she found herself agreeing. "Do you think Chao knows?"

"I doubt it. He hated the Order, and for good reason. I'm sure my father gave Chao the information needed to destroy the Order."

Bai nodded, her mind fitting everything together. The emperor supported the Order to give Chao an event to rally support from. Then he used the wraiths to destroy the Order and any evidence of his involvement. She understood the princess's point. It was brilliant, if horrible.

And there was nothing she could do about any of it. For all her strength, she was as good as useless.

But she would fight and die by her new allies.

Perhaps that was enough.

A shout from up on the wall interrupted her reverie. "Movement!"

Bai stood and climbed the stairs to the wall, wondering what fate held in store for them next. She expected a joint attack, with the wraiths supporting the army.

Her guess was wrong.

The wraiths had stepped forward again, separating from the main force.

Bai frowned. She supposed if the monks hadn't trained with the army, they might be almost as much of a danger as a help. The two forces had trained apart, so they would fight that way as well. Or perhaps it was pride. Chao insisted that the wraiths be the one to crush those who opposed them.

Whatever the reason, the monks marched forward alone, and again Bai felt the energy gathering. Their numbers had been lessened, but not by enough to matter. The joint strength of so many monks was still enough to destroy the fort and everyone inside.

Bai wondered at their strategy. Were they just going to keep attacking and regrouping? Could they sense Lei getting weaker? She couldn't understand why they would resort to a tactic that had already failed.

Bai looked back at Lei. He remained sitting on the bench, his posture unchanged since she had stood up to walk with the princess, but she felt him summoning more energy. But it felt lethargic compared to his earlier attempt. Could he possibly stand against the forces arrayed against them?

It was too much to hope.

She returned her gaze to the field beyond. It truly was hopeless, then. With the amount of energy being focused, the walls of the fort would collapse like paper. She looked around for a place where she might survive the onslaught and fight against the wraiths. She didn't want to die without fighting to the end.

As one, the wraiths released their attacks. Still sitting on the bench, Lei formed his shield around the fort.

Bai knew, right away, that it wasn't enough. Lei had protected them one time too many.

The energies clashed, and Bai could do nothing but watch. Lei's shield shrank as a greater force battered against it. There was nothing left.

Just then, Bai watched as a dark cloud rose up from the army behind the wraiths. It took her a moment to realize what the cloud was, and a moment more to realize their target.

The emperor had turned on the wraiths, and at a perfect time. A wave of arrows sliced down, a second cloud flying into the air even as the first fell, aimed for the hearts of the wraiths.

The wraiths were completely blindsided. They were focused entirely on attacking Lei, confident in their allies behind them. None of them had even considered preparing a shield. The arrows fell with deadly precision, the attacks of the wraiths winking out just as Lei's shield fell.

Some of the attacks reached the walls, but the stone endured for the few seconds that remained in the attack.

Bai couldn't believe what she had seen.

With one attack, the emperor had destroyed the wraiths.

45

A silence fell over the battlefield as the final cries of agony faded away. Behind the killing ground, Lord Xun's army stood motionless, as though they waited for the battle to begin.

Bai realized her mouth was open. She closed it, still not believing what she had just seen.

Betrayal on top of betrayal.

Why?

No one on the wall spoke. The wraiths had been enemies, but they had been brothers to most who stood on the wall. Brothers may argue and fight, but no one wanted to see another monk killed by an arrow to the back.

Bai kicked her foot against the stone wall, just hard enough to make her big toe throb. The pain focused her, brought her to the present moment.

What should they do?

Lord Xun's army had just murdered the men best capable of defending them. It opened a window of possibility. Bai and the others could attack. Without the gifted to stop them, the vast difference in numbers seemed more like a challenge instead of an impossibility. Bai had seen monks take on an army before. It could be done.

Before she could summon the others, an officer with a white flag rode out from the ranks.

Bai searched for the princess. She stood on the wall with everyone else, her eyes unfocused. Bai put her hand on the princess's shoulder. The woman gave a small shudder and turned to look at Bai.

"We should attack."

Bai didn't care what Lord Xun and the emperor had to say. They had left themselves open.

The princess shook her head, her eyes focusing on Bai. "No. If my father was willing to lose the wraiths, it means he had a plan in place. He would assume an attack and be prepared. We should listen to what he has to say."

Bai clenched her fist. Talking wouldn't solve this. But her desires didn't overrule the princess's orders. "We'll protect you, then."

"Thank you."

It only took Bai a few moments to round up Wu and Rong. Both seemed in a bit of a daze. Bai told them they would escort the princess to the parley. They both bowed in acceptance.

She glanced over at Lei, who remained as still as a carving on the bench. He didn't look to be in any shape to join them. She let him be.

The princess joined them at the gate a minute later. The heavy wooden gate creaked open and they walked through. The princess took the lead, the other three following about ten feet behind her.

Bai saw the emperor and Lord Xun astride their horses. If the situation deteriorated, she had little doubt they would turn and run in a moment. A dozen soldiers stood in a loose semicircle behind them.

The hairs on the back of Bai's neck rose. She spoke softly enough that the princess wouldn't hear. "I don't trust them, even under a white flag. Stay close, and be ready. Especially you, Wu. We might need a shield with little warning. If anything happens, we need to keep the princess safe."

They nodded. Bai saw the determination on their faces. They wouldn't fail her, nor she them.

They stopped across from the emperor. For the first time since she had met the princess, Bai thought she saw the woman come close to cracking. "Why, Father?"

The emperor shook his head. If he had any trace of regret, his face didn't show it. "The monasteries cannot go on. The power cannot be controlled, so it must be eliminated. Every disaster that has befallen the empire in the past thirty years has been due to the monks and their inability to understand and harness their gifts. I saw a chance to eliminate the problem for good."

"And so you will kill them all?"

The emperor's silence was answer enough.

Bai saw the princess pass through grief. She stood up straighter. "Why have you called us here?"

"To offer you a clean death one last time. We have come prepared for this, princess. Even with Lei, you cannot last. Save us all the trouble, and save the lives of my loyal servants who would otherwise have to fight."

For a bare moment, Bai thought the princess might accept. She hesitated for a heartbeat, then shook her head. "I cannot surrender, Father."

"Then this is goodbye."

The princess nodded. "It is."

She turned on her heel and approached Bai and the

others. The princess never saw the emperor's gesture, but Bai did. The man would even break the truce the white flag represented. Bai was already moving when she yelled, "Wu!"

She felt the shield cover them all. Less than a second later, small darts thudded against the invisible protection. The soldiers were armed with some small wrist-mounted device Bai had never seen before. She suspected the darts were poisoned.

Bai broke through the shield, letting Wu form it again behind her. She leaped into the line of soldiers, her fists smashing helms. She spun behind one soldier as another fired. The dart stuck in his fellow soldier's armor.

Bai only fought alone for a moment. Soon, Rong was in the midst of the soldiers, wreaking havoc. Wu stayed close to her, knocking soldiers off balance and throwing up shields between the soldiers and the princess.

As Bai expected, the emperor and Lord Xun turned and galloped away the moment the fighting broke out. Bai thought to go after them, but her priority had to be the safety of the princess.

A princess who wasn't making that task simple.

Bai saw her fighting the soldiers as well, her gift devastating. With the razor-sharp focus she achieved, her arms and legs were like blades. She saw the princess chop at a man's neck, but her hand went straight through. The princess didn't hesitate as she moved on to the next man.

The soldiers, lacking the element of surprise, had no chance. Bai and her group were almost clear when a flash of motion caught her eye in the distance. She looked over and saw a huge sphere flying up through the air and dropping straight toward them.

Bai pulled all the power she could summon into her body. Time slowed, and Bai saw that Rong had already seen the projectile. The princess, however, was oblivious. Bai ran toward the woman, grabbed her by the waist and physically pulled her away from the fight. She ran toward Wu, their only hope.

She saw the shadow grow around her. She dove, twisting so she would land on her back and the princess would remain uninjured. Wu's shield appeared over her just as the sphere plowed into the ground less than a dozen paces away.

Fire exploded from the projectile, spraying over Wu's shield and covering it in flame. The princess looked up, surprised to be covered by fire.

They couldn't stay here.

Bai urged them to their feet, still under Wu's shield. Wu gritted his teeth. "I can't hold out much longer."

"Then move!" Bai ordered.

They ran, the flame sliding off Wu's shield. A moment later, he dropped it. Bai directed them toward the inviting gate of the fort. "Run!"

She glanced back as they did, just in time to see a handful of arrows arc from Lord Xun's lines and fall toward them.

Bai cursed and made the first sign of the attack. She was next to useless when it came to projecting her energy, but perhaps she was strong enough to blow arrows off course. She stopped and turned, thrusting her hands out. She filled her body with as much energy as she could take, then released the attack.

The blow was probably enough to send a large man tumbling to the ground. The wave hit the arrows, sending them cartwheeling through the air. Bai didn't admire her handiwork. She turned and caught up to her companions, seeing their grateful nods.

They were about two dozen feet away from the gate when a lone figure stepped out. He walked calmly toward them, and the four of them slowed down as he neared.

Somehow, Bai understood.

Bai pushed gently on her friends' backs. "Go. Protect the princess. I'll be right behind you."

Rong turned to face her, and Bai saw the lack of belief. Bai nodded. "I promise."

Rong stared at her for a moment, then relented. She led Wu and the princess back to the fort.

Bai turned to Lei. Again, she had the impression of a man stuck between worlds, not fully in either. He gave her a short bow, and Bai had a sickening feeling it would be the last bow she ever saw Lei make.

46

Lei sat on the bench inside the fort, waves of sensation washing over him. His skin vibrated, his teeth ground together, a thin defense against feeling *everything*. He held his head in his hands as he sat, seeking his sanity. He heard waves of grass whispering in the wind a mile away. Snow fell softly, far to the north, far out of sight.

He didn't know how he knew such things, but they were as real to him as the tiny ridges on his fingers.

This had to be madness.

He had stepped into another world with his last defense. For all the training he'd done, all the preparation he had put his body and mind through, he had never dared use as much power as he just had.

He should be exhausted, searching for a bed to rest on for the remainder of the day. His body had acted as a conduit for energies even he didn't comprehend.

But he felt like he could skip down a road for miles without tiring. His body weighed nothing, as light as a paper lantern in the wind.

He knew well the danger of pushing his body too hard. He'd had to teach the same danger to Bai so many years ago.

This was something else. This was a problem of mind, a problem of spirit. He had no answers.

Light stabbed at his eyes, the real reason he hid his head in his hands. Sounds pierced his skull, as sharp as nails. The world was paper and the seams were ripping, an unbearable brightness hiding behind the veil of an early winter's day.

It occurred to him that the power had addled his mind. He focused on a blade of grass standing as still as a statue in front of him. He bent down and grasped it between thumb and forefinger, gasping as exquisite sensations rolled across his body.

Perhaps it wasn't that the world was paper, but that he was. Perhaps he had burned himself out from the inside with that last shield.

A part of him knew the wraiths prepared another attack off in the distance. The problem was, his sense of that attack blended in with everything else. The wraiths created the signs for an attack, but all Lei could hear was the cry of a newborn. Focus was impossible to find, but he had to search. Instinct took over, a primal response to danger guiding his actions. Lei grasped for the power he'd become so familiar with and it responded like an old friend, wrapping him in a warm embrace.

The ease of it terrified him, and he held back.

What was this strength? It couldn't be so easy. Everything he knew told him his body should be a withered husk standing in the middle of the fort. He defended again.

Lei felt the wraiths perish as one, their lives wiped from the planet the way Daiyu used to wipe crumbs from their table after eating. He felt Chao's dying breath, echoing in his ear as though Lei had bent over to catch his last words.

There had been none. The emperor's betrayal barely had time to register in the mastermind's consciousness before he passed through the veil.

Lei's heart broke at the loss of life. So much violence, and to what end? Perhaps it was his lifetime of isolation, but he saw it all so clearly. These games of power, these efforts to control the lives of others, all of them were meaningless. He loved Bai like a rebellious daughter, but she didn't anchor him here. He didn't care to take part in this world anymore. A deeper truth called to him.

Off in the distance, well beyond the attacking army, there were other monks who had responded to the abbot's call. For now, they remained at distance, silent observers to the events of the day. Lei was grateful the story would spread, no matter what happened.

Lei felt his sword in his hands. He didn't even remember drawing it from its sheath. He'd come across the sword as a young man and it had been the only item he'd kept through his journeys through the empire. Once, he had relied on it to help him focus his energy.

Such abilities seemed crude now.

He stood up and walked toward the gate. It was open. Some part of him realized that Bai was on the other side. He stepped through, looking up.

Seeing Bai brought him a few moments of clarity, of the singular focus he was used to. He saw Bai, and he saw the bonds she had built with Yang's students, and the princess. They would die for her, if it came to that.

An unwilling leader, but one all the same.

She urged them on, stopping to speak to him. She saw into him, and he knew that she knew. He gave her a short bow.

"You said that we would visit Two Bridges together," she said.

How could he tell her that he wouldn't break his promise? That though she may not recognize it, he would be there. That he would always be there. That it wouldn't be a hollow phrase?

The sword hung at his hip. He pulled it from his belt and handed it to her.

"We will."

She bowed to him, and he saw how she fought to keep her emotions in check. She struggled for words, but he understood.

"Thank you," was all she managed.

There had been one other teaching he wanted to pass on to her. But what was it?

Ahh. He looked back to where the others now sheltered in the fort. "Take good care of them. They love you, too."

She nodded, but her feet were rooted to the spot. He gently encouraged her. "Go now. All is as it should be."

Lei knew his course, and he knew the cost. To him, the cost was easy to pay. Hopefully Bai would understand. He thought she would. She had never been as close as Daiyu, but they had shared a connection over the past decade.

Bai passed him, and the brief clarity he'd experienced faded. Sensations attacked him with renewed vigor. He couldn't see the army, at least not the way he was used to. He knew they were there, but it was a knowing that went beyond sight, as though he looked into their souls. They were scared, as soldiers always were on the eve of battle.

Lei felt sorrow for what was to come. He still hoped it could be another way. "Surrender now," he said. Though he spoke softly, he knew his voice carried to every ear for miles. The power continued to course through him.

Lei stepped around the bodies of the wraiths that had fallen, arrows lodged in their backs. "Let us discuss your terms for peace. It is not too late."

He felt a wave of arrows being released, heard the hiss of thousands of them in the air. Lei wiped his hand across the sky and swept them off into the distance.

Surely they would turn, would retreat from their own destruction.

The army sounded the charge, causing Lei to halt. He felt the rumble of horses in front of him, the creatures charging with their riders into battle.

There would be no compromise, then. Before, he would have felt some sorrow at what he was about to do. Now, he didn't feel the same. Death wasn't an ending, but a door.

Death was only hard on the living.

Lei could feel the currents of power running throughout the land. Most days, he would have allowed some trickle of it to enter his body, but no longer.

This time he dove in, embracing the power and opening himself completely. He retained only the barest hint of control, shaping the force in the direction it needed to travel.

Lei thought he felt a hand guiding him. He opened his eyes, but he did not see the army charging him. He saw Jian, his brother, dead for thirty long years, showing him the way. His brother even had that slight grin on his face that had driven Lei mad with anger as a child. Today he gently pulled his younger brother further into the light.

The paper that was the world tore as the energy funneled through his body. It made even the power he had summoned before pale in comparison. This was the sun compared to the moon.

Lei focused the energy, but that process happened in the

back of his mind. His real focus lay on the thin membrane that existed between the reality he had always known and the world beyond.

Jian had disappeared, and he swore he felt Daiyu brush past his arm, the way she often had before sneaking into the bedroom. He smiled and took another step. The blinding light hiding behind reality no longer seemed so bright.

And then they were both there, Daiyu standing just in front of Jian. She held out her arms wide, welcoming him.

Tears ran down Lei's face as he stepped forward.

47

Inside the monastery, Bai just had time to run to the walls. When she got to the top, she looked out on the field to see Lei walking toward the army. A wave of arrows rushed at him, and Bai turned around to call for a shield, but she knew it was pointless. Lei was too far away for them to protect.

She needn't have worried. Lei swiped his hand across the sky and the arrows were thrown hundreds of feet to the north.

Bai had never seen an attack like that. It didn't even feel like an attack. It felt like a bending of reality.

The army charged.

Lei gathered his power, and then there was a bright flash, a cone of light that began with Lei and ended beyond Bai's sight. For a fraction of a second, it was only light. Bai thought she saw shadows dancing within the light, but she couldn't be sure.

Then the force of Lei's attack hit.

Stone cracked underneath her feet, and a wave of pressure slammed her onto her back. The earth trembled and the clouds fled as though chased.

Then it was over. Bai stumbled to her feet. Her jaw dropped, and she didn't bother to close it. Wherever the light had touched, only devastation remained. The grass, and at least a foot of the earth below, was simply gone. Off in the distance, she saw dust and debris in the air, but here, close to the fort, the air was clear.

What humans had been present were gone. No evidence remained of their existence.

The same was true of Lei. She could clearly see the place he stood when he released the light. The cone ended sharply just before it. But Lei was gone.

LATER, Bai, Rong, and Wu escorted the princess through what remained of the battlefield. Though Lei's attack hadn't been aimed at the fort, the power of it had almost been enough to bring the walls down. Many were injured, and their care had come first.

Then other monks began to trickle in. Not many, but a handful had traveled toward the fort in response to the abbot's summons. They had seen it all, and they bent their backs to aid those within the fort.

Once everyone was taken care of, the princess had stated her intention to examine the damage Lei had caused. Bai and the others had joined without asking permission.

The silence over the plains seemed deeper than before, nearly sacred. When anyone spoke, it was in a whisper. Bai stood where the cone of destruction began. Lei had stood right there, she was sure of it.

The princess approached and stood next to Bai. "Do you understand what happened?"

Bai slowly shook her head. "Lei always had a deeper

connection with the power that we all use. He never told me how he formed that connection."

"What happened to him?"

"I think he's gone."

"But how?" Bai had a glimpse of the princess's weakness. She didn't accept what she didn't understand. She knew her question had no answer and it dug under her skin.

Bai had no such problems. She remembered Lei's final words, and the warmth that had been within. Whatever happened to him, he had welcomed it. That was enough for her.

"Did any survive?" Bai asked.

"Not many." The princess's voice was flat.

"I'm sorry."

The princess shook her head. "Don't be. He was an emperor first and a father second."

Bai didn't believe that was the full story, but decided not to press. "What comes next?"

"My real work. The empire must learn what happened."

"What will you tell them?"

"The truth. My father and a rebellious sect of monks fought in the far north. It cost the emperor his life."

"People will rise up against the monasteries."

"No. Yang and I have been talking for a while, our plans mostly dreams, but now we have an opportunity. I'll announce a new deal with the monasteries. Perhaps I'll call it a surrender. But my father was right about one thing: the monasteries can't continue as they have. The new treaty will demand that they open their doors, just as Yang has done in Kulat. It will be a long journey, but one worth taking."

Bai understood the princess had learned the emperor's strengths well. She would lead the empire forward through whatever came next.

"What of you?" asked the princess.

Bai looked to where Wu and Rong stood together, giving Bai and the princess some privacy. "I'm not sure yet. But I suspect I'll have company."

The next few months passed in the blink of an eye. That winter saw the princess's ascension to the throne.

The transition wasn't painless. Several small revolts cropped up throughout the empire, but the empress put her resources to good use. She used diplomacy, military strength, and the monks to quell the unrest.

Yang became an adviser to the empress, with a seat on the council. In private moments, Bai would chuckle at the irony of it all. After all of Chao's efforts, his goals had been achieved. A gifted sat on the throne, advised by other gifted. It just wasn't the world the man had planned for.

That spring seemed particularly poignant. The turning of the seasons represented a new beginning for the empire. Bai felt it everywhere she traveled. She, Rong, and Wu had completed several errands both for the princess and for Yang. In every town they felt the energy of rebirth.

Bai could feel her friends getting impatient as well. In a way, their lives had been filled with uncertainty the past several months. Bai hadn't made any decisions; she'd only followed orders. It had given her the space to grieve while remaining active.

But it was past time to move forward. They all needed to.

One night she broached the subject while they ate supper. She decided the direct approach was best. "I think I know what I want to do next."

Wu and Rong shared a glance Bai couldn't read. The two of them had been spending more time together lately. Bai found the combination of Rong's cynicism and Wu's enthusiasm fascinating, but they made it work.

Bai continued. "If you would like, I would be honored to have you join me."

She spoke true. Over the past few months she had gotten even closer to them. The idea of striking out on the road again on her own held a new fear. But she didn't want to order them about. If they wanted to join her, it had to be their choice.

"Yang continues to believe that those with more unusual gifts are being born every day. I would like to wander the empire and find them, guiding them to the monasteries."

It was the best Bai had been able to come up with. She wasn't ready to settle in one place like Lei and Daiyu had, but she had little interest in seeking out fights. This way she could still travel throughout the empire and help however she could.

The two younger warriors didn't answer immediately. Bai waited a second, but couldn't contain her impatience. "Well?"

Rong and Wu shared another look, then burst out laughing, enormous smiles on their faces.

Bai didn't think her heart had ever been lighter.

EPILOGUE

E ven in summer, the wind that blew across the top of the mountains above Two Bridges knifed through Bai's robes.

The monastery above Two Bridges was empty except for her. As part of Yang's reorganization, several of the more remote monasteries had been shuttered, at least for a time. Once, monks had sought isolation for their training. Now, Yang demanded they be involved in the lives of the communities they served.

After the loss of the wraiths and the attacks from the Order of the Serpent, there hadn't been enough monks to man the monasteries anyway.

If Bai's work was any indication, that wouldn't be a problem for long. More gifts were being discovered every day. Wonder had become almost commonplace in Bai's travels.

It was a whole new world.

She held Lei's sword in her hands. She'd kept it sharp and polished over the months, but she'd never had to use it, thankfully. She had finally gotten used to the weight at her hip, though, and she'd taken enough lessons to be at least somewhat dangerous with it.

The sword reminded her of the past, but it promised a better future.

She figured Lei had wanted to leave the world. She could understand, even if she couldn't quite put herself in his frame of mind. He'd lost the person closest to him in the world, and at the end, he'd made a discovery Bai still couldn't puzzle out.

He had wanted to go, but she still missed him desperately. They hadn't seen each other often, but he'd been a pillar she could rely on.

She felt foolish, but speaking out loud to the rugged mountains beyond somehow felt right.

"You were right. The view is better here."

She paused, taking a deep breath.

"I think you would like what's happening now. I think you'd be proud of me. You'd be proud of all of us."

A lump formed in her throat.

"I miss you, Lei."

Despite her efforts, a tear welled up in her right eye. She ignored it.

The wind picked up again, but this time, Bai barely felt it.

She didn't believe in ghosts, but she could have sworn she heard his laugh, the same one she'd heard so often when they had trained together.

Bai spun around, looking for the source of the sound. It had come from just over her left shoulder, but no one was near.

Her heavy heart suddenly soared. There was no reason, just the change.

And then she *knew*.

Somehow, he was with her.

Not in any way she could measure or observe. But she was sure, all the same. He was there, watching over her. For just a moment, her vision shifted and she saw the world in a new way, her senses developed past human limits. She saw connections, everywhere.

Then her vision returned to normal, and she shook her head, not sure what had just happened.

Her tears dried, and she stared out on the mountains for a good long time. This had been Delun's monastery, too, she knew. She wondered if he had also enjoyed this view.

The sun was going down when she came down off the wall. Beyond the gate, Wu and Rong had set out a bedroll and were sunning themselves against the rocks.

"I thought you were going to look through local reports of gifted."

"You were up there a long time," Rong drawled.

"So where are we going?"

"Just down the mountain to Two Bridges." Wu tried and failed to contain a smile.

"What?" Bai knew they were saving a punchline for her.

"It's a child who loves playing catch," Wu said.

"Don't most children like playing catch?"

"They don't usually knock down their parents when they throw," Wu replied.

Bai endured their laughter as they watched her reaction. She shook her head. It wasn't the strangest manifestation of the gift they'd seen. Together, they began their way down the mountain.

Their work was just beginning.

WANT MORE FANTASY?

As always, thank you so much for reading this story. There's an amazing number of great fantasy stories today, and it means so much to me that you picked this book up.

If you enjoyed this story, I also have two other fantasy series, filled with memorable characters. My first fantasy series is called *Nightblade*.

Links to all of my books can be found at www. waterstonemedia.net

THANK YOU

Before you take off, I really wanted to say thank you for taking the time to read my work. Being able to write stories for a living is one of the greatest gifts I've been given, and it wouldn't be possible without readers.

So thank you.

Also, it's almost impossible to overstate how important reviews are for authors in this age of internet bookstores. If you enjoyed this book, it would mean the world to me if you could take the time to leave a review wherever you purchased this book.

And finally, if you really enjoyed this book and want to hear more from me, I'd encourage you to sign up for my emails. I don't send them too often - usually only once or twice a month at most, but they are the best place to learn about free giveaways, contests, sales, and more.

I sometimes also send out surprise short stories, absolutely free, that expand the fantasy worlds I've built. If you're interested, please go to https://www.waterstonemedia.net/newsletter/.

With gratitude,

Ryan

ALSO BY RYAN KIRK

The Nightblade Series

Nightblade

World's Edge

The Wind and the Void

Blades of the Fallen

Nightblade's Vengeance

Nightblade's Honor

Nightblade's End

Relentless

Relentless Souls

Heart of Defiance

The Primal Series

Primal Dawn

Primal Darkness

Primal Destiny

Primal Trilogy

The Code Series

Code of Vengeance

Code of Pride

Code of Justice

ABOUT THE AUTHOR

Ryan Kirk is the bestselling author of the *Nightblade* series of books. When he isn't writing, you can probably find him playing disc golf or hiking through the woods.

www.waterstonemedia.net
contact@waterstonemedia.net

facebook.com/waterstonemedia

twitter.com/waterstonebooks

instagram.com/waterstonebooks

www.ingramcontent.com/pod-product-compliance
Lightning Source LLC
Chambersburg PA
CBHW030833110726
47900CB00006B/1865